Dinosaur Blitz

Tales of Science Fiction,
Mystery, & Romance

by Gregory Urbach

Dinosaur Blitz

Dedicated to Mrs. Streeter
5th grade, Riverside Drive Elementary School
Who made me a writer

Cover painting by Doug Stambaugh
Dinosaur cover art courtesy of Keith Shaw
Cover design by Grayson Bowling
Tara VanTimmeren, editor
Matthew Bernstein, story consultant

Gregory Urbach
© 2023 All Rights Reserved

This book is a work of fiction. Names, characters, places, and events are products of the author's imagination or placed in a fictional setting. Any resemblance to actual persons living or dead is coincidental. No part of this book may be reproduced or transmitted by any means without permission of the author.

Table of Contents

Chapter 1	Dinosaur Blitz A pair of cloned dinosaurs play football		1
Chapter 2	The Last President A comet threatens to end all life on Earth		21
Chapter 3	That Which We Are Mankind faces its final days		25
Chapter 4	The Adventures of Snailwoman		39
Chapter 5	Evacuation A crisis forces the evacuation of the moon		49
Chapter 6	Veeleens Venture Creatures from another planet visit Earth		71
Chapter 7	Dispatch from the Alamo A reporter witnesses a desperate battle		85
Chapter 8	The Black Bird A Dashiell Hammett mystery		109
Chapter 9	The Further Adventures of Snailwoman		122
Chapter 10	Burning Flags Entrepreneurs seek to make money		130
Chapter 11	Cowboys & Indians A lunar orphan battles his computer masters		136
Chapter 12	The Actress & the Hermit A former child star struggles to save her career		187

Dinosaur Blitz

Gregory Urbach

DINOSAUR BLITZ
When Dinos Play Football

"Those creatures of yours are consuming our bank account!" Tom complained, storming into my office without an invitation.

I knew the licensing fees were bringing us a small fortune, and with the unending popularity of Dino-Mania, the fees were growing faster than the dinosaurs. What my younger brother really wanted was permission to put our cloned dinosaurs on public display again, boosting their market value.

"Save the crocodile tears, Tom," I said. "After what happened last time, I'm pulling in the reins. Aren't the video games and T-shirts enough? For God's sake, you even put them in comic books!"

"Hey, Dinos #1 is a collector's item," Tom smiled.

"I said no! Latitude and Longitude are sensitive young animals, learning and adapting just like children do. I won't have their development disturbed by another media circus."

"Damn it all, Herrick, everybody loves The Dinos. And The Dinos love the attention. The only one who doesn't like the publicity is you."

Twenty-five years old and fresh from Harvard Business School, my lovable scamp of a brother was anxious to make his mark on the world. I did not want him doing it at the expense of my dinosaurs.

Because Tom had ventured down from the accounting offices to ambush me as I entered our new Malibu compound, I was tempted to deny him clearance into the research wing. But getting rid of him was never that easy. Even though I was president of the Prehistoric DNA Reclamation Project, Tom was still the chief financial officer. And he had better relations with our shareholders.

Tom jumped the security desk to corral my chief of staff. "Where

Dinosaur Blitz

are they?" he asked.

Dr. Kimura glanced at her watch, barely acknowledging Tom's presence. She was short and petite where Tom was tall and broad-shouldered, so he expected her to be intimidated. But nothing ever intimidated Michiko Kimura.

"Three o'clock," Kimura said.

"Three o'clock? What the hell does that mean?" Tom asked, irritated by her condescending attitude—an attitude I occasionally shared. But Kimura was the best chief of staff I ever had, so I couldn't afford to let Tom insult her.

"Come on, they're in the dayroom," I said, taking Tom by the arm.

Our new research center was perched on a graceful sandstone bluff above the blue Pacific Ocean, much better than the rundown brick laboratory in Van Nuys we'd been in just a year before. The three-story white stucco administration building sat on fifteen acres of lush green grass and palm trees. Behind us loomed the beautiful Santa Monica Mountains.

We entered the spacious living quarters and found the dinosaurs stretched out in front of the wide screen television. Latitude and Longitude had just turned two years old, and for such young animals, were amazingly bright. Both were long, lean, and well-muscled, though still below the full strength they would eventually attain. They lounged like great ten-foot-long lizards, but they were far from reptilian in nature. Latitude, the female, was always prim and well-composed. Longitude was just beginning to display a tentative male assurance that made for moments of amusement. As warm-blooded members of the Ornithomimidae family, they had more in common with birds than reptiles.

"You're letting them watch television? In the middle of the day?" Tom asked.

The dinosaurs turned toward Tom with expressions of disapproval, twisting their oval heads around on long slender necks and frowning before turning back to the television. Their tails, which comprised nearly half their body length, lashed with pleasure.

"Talk shows. It's their latest phase," Kimura said. "First it was cartoons, then cowboy movies. Now they're watching afternoon talk shows. We don't know if they understand the principle of verbal communication or if it's something in the rhythm of the proceedings, but they've watched it every day for two weeks."

"Is this how you're raising sensitive young animals?" Tom asked. "Letting them watch trash TV? At least have them watch something educational!"

Tom picked up the remote control and switched the channel, much to the consternation of the dinosaurs. As the image of the host and her guest was replaced by a replay of the USC football game, Latitude leaped up on her heavy hindquarters and turned toward Tom, her muscles rippling under a tough, leathery mottled brown hide as her long tail swished back and forth for balance. At two meters in height, she could look Tom directly in the eye, but she didn't threaten to attack him. It wasn't in her personality to hurt anyone on purpose.

"Here, take the damn thing!" Tom said, handing me the remote control.

Latitude glared at me, impatience boiling in her big black eyes, but Longitude directed her attention back to the television screen. USC was third and goal in the fourth quarter, the linebackers packed tightly. The quarterback took the snap, rolled right, and handed the ball off to the halfback, who sprinted for the goal line while the linemen pounded away on each other. When the halfback was tackled at the 1-yard line, Latitude and Longitude twittered in pleased, high-pitched chirps.

"See! They love it!" Tom said with an irritating smirk.

He was right. They did.

For the next fifteen minutes, through the end of the fourth quarter and an overtime shortened by a spectacular eighty-yard run, Tom sat on the floor between the dinosaurs, avidly describing each aspect of the game. They hung on his every word, and when the game ended, they dashed out into the enclosed exercise yard to practice broken field running.

"This is great!" Tom said, watching them twist and dance past each other.

"There's no way they understood a word you said, Tom," I insisted. "They respond to simple commands, not expository sentences."

I turned to seek help, seeing Professor Wyatt in the back of the room, holding her ever-present clipboard. As a graduate of Stanford University and our resident expert on animal behavior, she would certainly back me up.

"Isn't that right, Christine? Isn't Tom just wasting his time?" I asked.

"Hard to say," Professor Wyatt said, sharing her notes with two young assistants. I gave her the frown she deserved.

"Can we take them down to the stadium for a game?" Tom asked.

"Absolutely not!" I replied. "They aren't leaving the compound again for at least a year. Maybe two years!"

As far as I was concerned, the subject was closed. I could not have been more wrong.

When I arrived at the research center the next morning, Tom had already smuggled a football into the complex. I was also surprised to find the yard occupied by half a dozen burly athletic types from nearby Pepperdine University. Though tall, leafy trees and an artificial waterfall occupied most of the enclosure, there was just enough open space to form a small playing field.

"What the hell's going on here?" I yelled, going out the back door and marching through the short winter grass.

Tom glanced up from a huddle and trotted over with an annoying air of confidence. "Just a little exercise. Don't want the Dinos getting flabby," he said.

"What are those kids doing here?" I asked. "If this is one of your schemes to exploit the dinosaurs ..."

"Hey, take a chill," Tom protested. "I just wanted to see how they'd respond to a little bump and run. No big deal."

I glanced to the area where Latitude and Longitude were standing at the edge of the trees, Longitude tightly clutching the football and gently chewing on it. Tom's young associates seemed perplexed. Kimura sat nearby typing notes on her laptop.

"It's hard to play when one side won't give up the ball," Tom said, reading my thoughts.

"According to Professor Wyatt, they're capable of playing games on certain basic levels," I said, "but you may be asking too much of them."

"Could be right," Tom reluctantly conceded. "We've been at it for an hour, and they still treat the ball like some kind of egg. Hey, Doc, can you make it give the ball back?"

"*It* has a name, Mr. Lawrence. Longitude. Longy to his friends," Kimura replied.

"Whatever," Tom said.

Kimura scrunched her thin black eyebrows and walked away in a huff.

"Maybe we'll try some more tomorrow," Tom said.

"Maybe not," I answered.

Tom waved in his players, and I told Kimura to keep the yard clear the rest of the day, feeling the dinosaurs needed more time alone. I didn't know it then, but Kimura later informed me that Latitude and Longitude started kicking the football around right after Tom left.

Once Latitude and Longitude discovered that the sports channels were inundated with football, they refused to follow any recreational program that didn't involve either watching the games or playing with their ball. Tom rarely came downstairs except to demand publicity photos, so I didn't tell him the dinosaurs had already worn out several footballs since the one he had given them, and I didn't mention that

Dinosaur Blitz

their gridiron fascination was enough for Professor Wyatt to begin a special study. She originally suspected their behavior had something to do with herd mentality and a desire for migration, but later she included theories about group defense against predators. The student interns, being young and naive, romanticized that the dinosaurs actually understood the game.

As the January playoff games concluded, I decided to refuse Tom's latest publicity stunt. I had already rejected his efforts to march them in the Macy's Thanksgiving Day Parade and vetoed a Christmas TV special. Now Tom had a new scheme.

"Darn it, Herrick, you're being stubborn for no reason," Tom protested. "This is a five-minute event, almost no traveling, and they're going to *pay* us a million dollars. It will be a media blitz like you've never seen!"

"No way, Tom, forget it. I'm not letting you parade them around a stupid football stadium while a bunch of drunks scream at them."

"It's not a stupid football game, for God's sake. It's the Super Bowl! The game's at the Rose Bowl this year. There'll be a hundred thousand people there and media from all over the world. A billion bucks in publicity, and they're going to pay us for showing up."

Tom was turning rabid, licking his youthful chops and foaming at the mouth. I had warned Mom this would happen when she insisted on me bringing him into the business. As much as I loved my brother, he could get awful greedy, and this seemed to be pushing him over the edge.

"Kimura, will you please give me a hand?" I pleaded, drawing her from the rumpus room where the dinosaurs were watching ESPN Sports Update. She appeared with that mysterious look of hers, a mischievous twinkle in her black eyes.

"Thomas is right," she said in a dry, calm voice. "A day trip would be good for them. I think Latty and Longy would love to see a football game."

Damn her eyes, she knew better than anyone what would happen next. Before I could blink, Longitude rushed into the room and interrupted our conversation, his long tail whipping back and forth in excitement. Latitude wasn't more than a step behind him, their latest football tucked neatly under her arm. I grabbed a lamp just before her tail swatted it across the room.

"See, they want to go!" Tom said with a grin so big I felt like punching him in the face.

"They don't even know what we're talking about," I said.

"Sure they do," Tom laughed, suddenly being friendlier with the dinosaurs than I'd ever seen him. "Hey, guys, want to go to the Super Bowl?"

They twittered with so much enthusiasm that I realized he had me beat.

"A short appearance," I reluctantly agreed. "And I approve every aspect of the schedule, or the whole thing's off!"

"Yeah, sure. Hey, you're in complete control. Just let me show 'em off for a few minutes during the pre-game ceremonies."

"Okay, go ahead and make the plans," I agreed.

Kimura turned away with a particularly sinful smile and walked with Tom down the hall. It was the first time in two years of association that I knew her to speak with him voluntarily.

We arrived an hour before game time, hauling an extra-long trailer loaned to us by the Los Angeles Zoo. A motorcycle escort got us through traffic and down into a special loading dock beneath the stadium. The dinosaurs, restrained only by their leather leashes, were excited and restless, weaving about and exploring each new sensation.

"Hello, I'm Dr. Herrick Lawrence, president of the Prehistoric DNA Reclamation Project," I introduced. "This is Dr. Michiko Kimura, my chief of staff, and my brother, Thomas Lawrence, our … special assistant."

"We're ready for you, Dr. Lawrence," said the stadium manager, a

Dinosaur Blitz

thin, bony bureaucrat with a dour expression. He opened a chain-link pen where he evidently expected to hold the dinosaurs until the pre-game ceremonies.

"We don't keep them caged," Dr. Kimura said with her nose in the air, leading Latitude toward a nice open area in the garage where sunlight was beaming in. "But if we did, that flimsy thing would never hold them."

"We'll just relax here," I said, encouraging Longitude to follow. "I've got a dozen staff and extra security. Just let us know when it's time."

Latitude and Longitude watched the exchange only briefly, struggling to get a look at the playing field and the rapidly filling stadium. After a while, members of the Tri-County Marching Band began forming up nearby, the high-schoolers gazing at the dinosaur celebrities with awe. Latitude clearly thought the teenagers amusing and made faces at them, but Longitude was more interested their hats, especially the white cotton tufts that looked like food.

"It's almost time!" Tom announced, rushing in just as the marching band was shuffling into the mouth of the tunnel. He was dressed in a ridiculous looking bright red costume with gold trim that resembled a Buck Rogers spacesuit more than a football uniform, and he was accompanied by two L.A. Lakers cheerleaders who wore scraps of crimson tinfoil masquerading as outfits.

"Once around the stadium, then back in the truck. Right?" I said.

"Sure, Herrick, sure. Just relax," Tom said. "Once around the stadium, shake a few hands, sign a couple of autographs, then we'll take off right after the first half."

"The first half?" I asked.

"The governor wants his picture taken with the Dinos," he said. "It's an election year, you know. And we're doing a Pepsi commercial at the end of the first quarter."

"Damn it, Tom! We had an understanding!" I protested.

"We can still let them do the beer commercial," Tom said.

"Absolutely not! No Dino Beer!" I nearly shouted.

"Okay, fine, you win. No Dino Beer. We'll stay with soft drinks."

"Don't try my patience, Tom. I'm warning you."

"Hey, hold on a minute. Doc Kimura gave me permission," he responded, pointing a finger in the esteemed doctor's direction. I glanced over and saw it was true. Kimura was petting the dinosaurs and refusing to look at me.

"You're taking a big chance here, little brother. Don't mess around," I warned.

"Of course not," he said, suppressing a smile as the buzzer alerted us. "That's it! That's our cue!" Tom shouted. "Come on, people. Let's go!"

The marching bands had finished positioning themselves on the field and were playing the "Dino March," the theme song from the new Saturday morning *Dinos* cartoon show. A burst of enthusiasm from the crowd indicated intense excitement.

"Okay, everybody," I announced, waving my arms like an idiot. "Kimura and I will lead the Dinos. Stay close in case we need help."

My security detail in new blue uniforms spread out to keep fans at a safe distance while our research assistants trailed behind in their white lab coats, my way of reminding everybody that we were a research organization dedicated to scientific advancement, not a carnival sideshow.

"Herrick? I thought these young ladies might lead the Dinos? It would sure look great," Tom said sheepishly, indicating the two shapely cheerleaders.

"Thank you for inviting us, Dr. Lawrence," the blonde said with a charming smile. The brunette batted her long eyelashes at me. I ignored them both.

"Have the girls walk in front of us," I said. "Far in front. And you stay with them. That costume of yours hurts my eyes."

Dinosaur Blitz

    We moved up the tunnel and emerged on the playing field into the late afternoon California sunshine, the roar of cheers cascading down on us. The hundred-year-old stadium customarily used by the UCLA Bruins was filled to its 90,000-seat capacity. At first I took an extra strong grip on the leash, afraid Latitude or Longitude might be spooked by the pandemonium, but as usual, they surprised me. Instead of shying away, they perked up to full height and pranced jauntily, glancing excitedly in every direction. My assistants needed to back off from the lashing tails.

    We rounded the playing field once, the fans screaming like crazy, and stopped in front of the press area near the 50-yard line. The paparazzi pushed forward for the best pictures while guards struggled to keep them under control. Then the governor came out to stand between Latitude and Longitude, somewhat nervously, I thought, and said a few words about their inspiring presence. As a 100 million television viewers watched, Latitude nestled against him, and Longitude put a friendly claw on the governor's shoulder. The embattled politician was so grateful, he had tears in his eyes.

    After the NFC and AFC champion teams were introduced, the Marine Corps Band struck up the national anthem, and everyone in the stadium stood up. By coincidence, Longitude and Latitude paused to reflect on the setting sun, as was their habit. Understandably, the crowd thought they were honoring the flag and erupted in delirious approval.

    With the pre-game ceremonies finished, I wanted to leave before the dinosaurs grew restless, but the game officials directed us to a special box at the end of the field where we were apparently expected to watch the game. I saw Kimura's fine hand in this, and to tell the truth, Latitude and Longitude did seem to be enjoying themselves. I resigned myself to three hours of unremitting public relations, knowing full well Tom had no intention of leaving at halftime.

    As football goes, it wasn't much of a game. The hulking monsters of the AFC were beating the crap out of the supposed-to-be faster NFC.

The NFC's first drive was crushed so badly, three of their players were carried off the field, two of them on stretchers. The AFC offense followed up by steamrolling the defense in brutal ten-yard advances. At the end of the first quarter the score was 21-0, and by halftime it was 35-3. Several of the NFC speedsters were permanently out of the game, presumably injured for life, and the sports broadcasters were desperate for any color commentary that wasn't black and blue. Twice, reporters from the *Times* asked Latitude and Longitude for their opinions on the game, and Fox News asked if Latitude was considering running for public office. Longitude nodded that he liked the game, but Latitude was noncommittal on both questions.

"Can we go now?" I asked as halftime began, daring Tom to suggest still another exploitative scheme.

"Right after the plug for the new Ford Dino-Rover," he smiled. At first I thought he was kidding, but damn if a bunch of gray-suited auto company executives didn't emerge from the crowd with a camera crew.

"It's gonna be a great vehicle!" Tom assured me. "Four-wheel drive, plenty of leg space, and we get two percent of the gross!"

Just as the gray suits and camera crew invaded our area, a football being tossed around by a couple of bored assistant coaches got away and rolled in our direction. Before anyone could stop him, Longitude jumped clear of our viewing box, bounced out on the field, and grabbed the football away just as the startled coach was about to pick it up. The poor man's astonished expression went viral.

"Hey, where's it going?" Tom cried out.

"*It* has a name, remember?" Kimura said.

"I don't care, make it come back! We've got a commercial to shoot!" Tom protested.

Longitude waved the ball in one claw and bounced around in a circle before dashing to midfield. Latitude jumped the railing and followed, charging past Tom's camera crew and hurdling over a row of frightened photographers. As the marching bands scattered to give

Dinosaur Blitz

them room, Latitude and Longitude ran up and down the field, kicking the ball back and forth and having a great time.

"Come back! Come back!" Tom shouted as he desperately chased after them.

I glanced at Kimura, who appeared particularly self-satisfied. Both leashes were dangling in her hand. And there wasn't a person in the stadium who wasn't on their feet, cheering.

Tom passed under the goalposts and out to the 20-yard line, where Latitude and Longitude were pushing the ball back and forth. They scattered on his approach, and as he futilely tried to round them up, the dinosaurs danced around in circles, keeping the ball away from him.

"Look! It's a clown act!" one of the broadcasters shouted. And she was right. Tom looked pathetic in his Buck Rogers uniform, trying to catch two mischievous animals that were faster than he was.

"Stop this right now! Give me that ball!" Tom shouted, his words drowned out by ninety thousand laughing spectators. My brother was frantic. For the first time that day, I actually started enjoying myself.

"Look, the Dinos want to play football!" one of the AFC players said, a group of them lolling near the mouth of the locker room tunnel. Apparently they were so confident of winning the game, they hadn't even gone inside. Not that anyone could blame them.

"Let's give them a little competition," Ice Block Harrison said, putting on his helmet. Three other players followed him out on the field, and they lined up around the 40-yard line.

"You guys can forget it," Tom said, tired and out of breath. "You'll never get that ball away from them." But Latitude and Longitude came to a halt, looked at each other, and lined up opposite the AFC players. Longitude gently set the ball down at the 40-yard line.

"I'll be damned," Tom said, stepping back to the sidelines.

"Sweep right," Ice Block Harrison said.

Stonewall Lombard hiked the ball to Skipper Jackson as Ice Block and Fleetwood Smith led the way. Latitude dropped back and moved to her left as Longitude charged straight into the wall of linemen. Ice Block stopped to intercept Longitude, but the dinosaur danced past him and knocked Skipper Jackson to the ground for a three-yard loss.

"Damn! Juked out of my shorts by a lizard," Ice Block laughed.

"I bet they can't do it twice," Fleetwood Smith said.

As the four AFC players lined up again and the dinosaurs followed suit, a squad of cheerleaders started doing a Dino chant, running up and down the sidelines, stirring up the crowds. Vendors were forced to bring snacks to the seats because the fans weren't going anywhere.

Stonewall Lombard hiked the ball again and drove forward, attempting to push Longitude aside, but Longy grabbed him by the jersey with his agile claws and used the momentum of his long tail to fling Lombard aside. Fleetwood Smith and Ice Block moved right, attempting to double-team Latitude and give Skipper Jackson a break up the middle, but Latitude managed to squeeze between the linemen and give Skipper a backward bump, holding up all three up until Longitude came in from behind and dragged Skipper down for six more yards lost.

"This is gettin' ridiculous," Stonewall complained, picking himself up from the turf where Longitude had thrown him.

"They're not that strong! They're not that strong!" Ice Block said in the huddle. "It's their damn tails! Don't let them get leverage!"

"Sweep left on two," Jackson said.

Longitude, who had been watching the huddle from a few feet away, turned to Latitude with a nod. She nodded back, and on two, the dinosaurs blitzed, driving Jackson back fifteen yards before knocking him down. As the crowds screamed, Longitude danced around and exchanged tail bumps with Latitude. The football players weren't pleased.

"Fourth and thirty! This is gettin' personal," Fleetwood Smith said back in the huddle.

Ice Block Harrison glanced over his shoulder and saw Longitude

Dinosaur Blitz

watching them.

"Hey, the lizard's stealing our signals!" he warned.

"I say we pass," Lombard suggested.

"Come on, it's four against two. Passing is no fair," Jackson said.

"Forget being fair!" Fleetwood Smith said. "I'm not gettin' my butt whacked on national TV. Let's make Dino-burger out of 'em!"

"Okay! Go on one!" Jackson shouted.

Latitude and Longitude lined up close, the taller animal looming over Lombard. On the snap, Lombard was thrown aside, but Jackson fell back and threw the ball to Fleetwood several yards beyond the line of scrimmage. Covering Ice Block Harrison, Latitude turned too late as Smith dashed for the goal line. Longitude stared at Jackson in surprise before starting to chase Fleetwood, but even the dinosaur's great speed couldn't overcome such a large lead.

"We did it, we did it!" Harrison cheered, dancing in the end zone and spiking the ball, but the fans began to boo. Voices were heard shouting "cheaters" and "cowards." When the dinosaurs paused at midfield looking sad, it only increased the wrath of the crowd.

"That's life," Fleetwood Smith said, heading off the field.

"Hey, where're you going?" Tom shouted, storming on the field in a burst of indignation.

"What's it to you, runt?" Ice Block Harrison asked.

"They deserve a chance to get even," Tom said. "They haven't had a shot at offense yet!"

"Your lizards play offense?" Skipper Jackson said.

"You just watch!" Tom said, taking the ball and running to the opposing 40-yard line. "Latty, Longy, come on guys. We've got a game to play!" he shouted to the dinosaurs.

To my astonishment, Latitude and Longitude actually followed him to the line of scrimmage and formed up as he directed. How in the world Tom expected them to play offense was beyond me, and even Kimura seemed a little surprised by the development, but Tom never doubted it for a moment. Probably because it never occurred to him he might be wrong.

"Come on, let's take the ball away from them," Ice Block said.

The players lined up and Tom set himself at center to snap the ball. Latitude stood a few yards back with Longitude just a little to her left at halfback.

"Now!" Tom shouted, flipping the ball to Latitude and ducking out of the way.

As Ice Block, Stonewall, and Fleetwood charged forward, Longitude performed a rolling block into the oncoming rushers, taking out all three of them. Latitude leaped over the human pile, danced past Skipper Jackson with a swish of her tail, and charged downfield for an easy touchdown.

"Yes, yes, yes!" Tom screamed, jumping up and down and trying to give Latitude a high five. She didn't quite understand the gesture, but the dinosaurs certainly shared his excitement.

"We can still beat 'em," Harrison growled, gathering his squad. "We outnumber 'em two to one, minus that idiot. Half-back option on two!"

The AFC players clapped hands and lined up on the 40-yard line where Tom had put the ball. Jackson took the snap, dumped the ball off to Smith, and circled outside as Harrison cut inside and Lombard went long down the left side.

Jackson never made the cut outside. As Tom rushed Smith, Longitude whipped out his tail and knocked Jackson for a loop, then turned to pursue Harrison. Smith panicked and threw the ball long to Lombard, but the hulking lineman's speed was no match for Latitude, who intercepted the ball with ease, danced around Lombard's wild effort to tackle her, and turned back downfield. Smith got in her way, for a moment, but when he realized he might as well try to tackle a freight train, he wisely ducked out of the way. Needless to say, the crowd went completely nuts.

Dinosaur Blitz

"We've got to stop this. Somebody's going to get hurt," I told Kimura, glancing around for my security squad.

"Oh, I doubt it," she said. "I've seen them roughhouse like this before. Though I admit, they do seem a bit excited. Are we insured if someone gets killed?"

"Killed? Good God!" I shouted, trying to squeeze my way through the spectators. "Tom! Hey, Tom! That's enough! Bring them in!"

Tom glanced in my direction briefly and pretended not to hear. Reporters were packed along the sidelines, and every person in the stadium, from the vendors to the football teams, had now joined in the cheering. The original halftime festivities were long forgotten.

Latitude didn't give the ball back this time. Instead, she lined up at the 20-yard line with Longitude ten yards back while Tom stood to one side, wondering what they were up to.

"I don't freaking believe it. They're kickin' off!" Skipper Jackson suddenly yelled, quickly falling back to his own 20-yard line.

Latitude put the ball down briefly, then turned sideways and flipped the football back to Longitude. Longy caught the ball, tossed it shoulder high, and whirled around to slap the ball high into the air with his tail. It sailed downfield with both dinosaurs in hot pursuit.

"Watch out! Watch out!" Fleetwood Smith yelled as Jackson positioned himself under the ball. Jackson glanced around just in time to see Longitude about to clean his clock, and to the amazement of everybody, the crazy bastard signaled for a fair catch. And damned if Longitude didn't screech to a halt!

"Hand signals," Kimura whispered with a wink. "They're good at that."

Jackson set the ball down at the 17-yard line and motioned to Smith, who set himself to take the snap. Ice Block and Stonewall lined up tight, and on the count of three, they drove forward, attempting to drive a wedge between Latitude and Longitude for Smith to run up the middle. The play almost worked, but while trying to scramble out of the way,

Tom slipped and fell flat on his butt. Smith tried to jump over him, but his foot got caught in one of Tom's elongated shoulder pads, and he crashed to the ground with a ball-fumbling thud.

"Grab it! Grab the ball!" Smith shouted.

Longitude scooped the ball up first and ducked aside as Lombard tried to tackle him. Fleetwood and Stonewall charged forward to cut Longitude off from the end zone, but at the last second, Longy turned and tossed a lateral back to Latitude, who scampered in for the score without being touched.

"This sucks," Harrison said, a little too close to the television cameras. "We're gettin' our asses kicked by two lizards and a clown."

"Maybe we can't beat the lizards, but I can sure as hell stomp that clown," Fleetwood said, his mood growing ugly.

"Hey, Bozo! Kick off again. And no more of those weird tail shots!" Stonewall Lombard yelled. Tom looked at the dinosaurs, who waited patiently for instructions.

"Okay!" he shouted back.

Tom put the ball on the 20-yard line, placed the dinosaurs on either side of him, and rushed forward to give the ball a mighty kick. It bounced along the ground about twenty yards.

Jackson ran forward and picked up the ball just as it stopped rolling, but before he could start running, Longitude grabbed him by the shoulders and gave him a good shake. The ball came loose, and when Tom rashly dove forward to pick it up, Fleetwood Smith blindsided him with a crushing blow. It was obvious at once that Tom was hurt, lying flat on the ground and moaning. If there had been referees, someone would have thrown a flag.

"That'll teach ya for mouthin' off, jerk," Smith said, daring Tom to get up.

"Hank Look out!" Harrison yelled.

Fleetwood Smith turned in time to discover Latitude bearing down on him, her tail whipping in anger. Ice Block Harrison tried to intervene, but Longitude blocked his path.

"Shouldn't we stop this?" I asked Kimura.

"Latty won't hurt him," she said. "At least, I don't think so. Longy might have. That's why she got there first."

"You had better be right," I whispered, holding my breath.

"Help me! Lord Almighty, someone help me!" Fleetwood Smith cried out as Latitude advanced on him with her teeth bared. Skipper Jackson tried to stop her, rather bravely under the circumstances, but Latitude pushed him aside like a cardboard cutout and knocked Smith's feet out from under him with her tail.

Smith tried to crawl away, his fingers digging into the natural turf and ripping up handfuls of grass, but the dinosaur pinned him down with her powerful hind foot, a bloodcurdling hiss issuing from her throat as she opened her wide, bone-crushing jaws. The horrified crowd gasped and fell silent, the stadium suddenly so still you could hear all ninety thousand people holding their breath. I think this was when Fleetwood Smith wet his pants, because you could see the spot in the pictures later.

"That's okay, girl, he's not worth the bad publicity," Tom said, clutching his side as he limped over to intervene. He took her by the arm and waved to Longitude. "Come on guys, let's get out of here. We're going to Disneyland!"

Latitude straightened up and turned away without protest. Longitude followed them off the field to an uproarious ovation.

Later that evening, back at our Malibu compound, we watched the news together with the dinosaurs. Needless to say, the impromptu scrimmage had eclipsed the official game and made headlines around the world. Invitations were already pouring in from sports teams all over the country, and one Florida city even wanted to build an entire franchise around The Dinos. Tom was so happy he didn't mind the two bruised ribs, while Latitude and Longitude seemed content with their afternoon, intertwining with each other and appearing relaxed.

"Well, Tom, I hope you've learned your lesson," I said, pointing at the screen when the news highlighted Latitude preparing to rip Smith's guts out.

"I sure have, big brother," Tom said. "Next time we put on a show like that, we're getting paid extra!"

I shook my head in despair, but Tom wasn't through.

"Hey, guys," he said, turning toward the dinosaurs. "Have you ever seen the Olympics?"

Dinosaur Blitz

<u>In Flander's Field</u>
In Flander's Field, we find our home,
Where poppies grow and skylarks roam,
O'er turf and sod once torn asunder,
Lay valleys now in peaceful slumber.
Here were cannon, gun and sword,
In courage we could not ignore,
And thus our home forever lies;
In Flander's Field.

from *Tranquility Divided*

THE LAST PRESIDENT
A comet threatens to end the world

The President of the United States stood on the White House balcony, looking up at the comet. There were only a few days left. A few days of life for a doomed planet. A final chance for the beleaguered Chief Executive to provide the leadership his critics found so lacking.

It was not supposed to be this way. He had entered office only a year before, a moderate in a progressive time, succeeding a leader so charismatic that he had inevitably paled by comparison. The acrimony soon began, quickly devolving into bitter partisan divisions. Congress came to a grinding halt. Feckless media commentators launched harsh attacks on his administration, followed by mean-spirited jokes. And then the comet arrived.

The astronomers had predicted the comet's approach for years, but not the dire effects of its gaseous tail. When the news broke, the press predicted mass panic, chaos in the streets, and a breakdown of civilization. Evangelicals called it God's judgment. Atheists called it bad luck. The government had sought to reassure the public even as National Guard units were put on alert. And everyone looked to the President, asking what he was going to do. Especially his predecessor, a vain and annoying man with a penchant for attracting attention.

"Act, Mr. President, act!" had been his predecessor's demand.

But what could he do? The Constitution of the United States did not include a clause on extraterrestrial threats, and even a president's prayers may not command the heavens.

He had taken the appropriate steps, dismissing the threat as an exaggeration, appearing at events with his jovial demeanor. Too jovial, in the opinion of those who wished to see him fail. Had the degeneration of the political culture become so vicious that even the end of the world could not abate the venom?

The final days held the entire country in suspense. Churches were busy saving what souls they could. Wall Street dipped but did not collapse. Politicians continued making speeches. The President visited the National Observatory, declaring the comet a magnificent spectacle. But he knew—everyone knew—that if the comet's tail poisoned the atmosphere, all life would disappear. Except, perhaps, a few desperate survivalists hiding in great underground caverns. The President had been offered such an opportunity, nearly forced to it by the Secret Service, but he declined. No one would ever call the last President of the United States a coward.

"Mr. President, we've received a notice," his press secretary said, the young man's usual optimism replaced by a frown.

"More bad news, George?" the President asked, strolling the empty White House grounds.

The city beyond the fence was quiet. There had been no

riots. No collapse of society. People were meeting the crisis with the same calm dignity they had found in their president.

"Fresh off the wire, sir," George said, handing him a telegram. "Mark Twain has died. He claimed he'd come in with Halley's Comet, and would go out when it returned. Looks like he was right."

"Twain never said he'd take the whole damn world with him."

"Maybe the world won't end after all?" the youngster suggested.

"Doesn't matter," President William Howard Taft replied. "If the comet doesn't get me, Teddy Roosevelt will."

Dinosaur Blitz

<u>With His Sword</u>
With his sword, he drew a line,
'tween the living and the dead.
And from his pocket, took his speech,
trembling as he read.
Fear not, dear Lord, who loves us still,
To you our lives are rendered.
In freedom's cause we serve thy will,
death but not surrender!

from *Tranquility Besieged*

THAT WHICH WE ARE
Mankind faces its final days

"Remember the Wasting Syndrome?" old She-Geezer said, flipping through a yellowed gossip magazine. The faces of two young movie stars, both long since dead, mugged happily from the faded cover.

"Just another media circus. Never was bad as they said," Lenny-the-Junior harshly complained, the wheeze in his voice growing worse.

"Was a cure ever found? Or did they just die sooner?" Melinda asked, looking up from the knitting in her lap.

"No, they didn't die sooner!" Daniel-the-Centenarian said, so angry he started to choke. "Wasn't our fault. It wasn't!"

"Calm down, Danny, you know stress isn't good for you," Melinda softly urged, getting up from her favorite rocking chair to help him take a breath from his portable respirator. "It's just that I was reading this article the other day in that old copy of *Celebrity Crisis*, and it said WS was never a real epidemic. Not like AIDS or the Pig flu."

"Won't be insulted. Won't," Daniel-the-Centenarian said, rolling his wheelchair off the patio and down the overgrown path toward the brook.

Dinosaur Blitz

"Danny's so touchy today," Melinda said. "I swear I can't talk to him about anything anymore. Gettin' bad as Glum-Gus."

"Danny's first mate died of WS, Mindy," Aged-Jason said, remembering what many others could only read about. "Shickton had it, too. Thought he was going to die. Some say that's why he did it. Why he created The Defect to prevent human reproduction. It was his way of getting revenge against all mankind."

"Damn ass bragged 'bout it!" Mean-Fred butted in. "Bragged 'bout blottin' out all the future generations. I'm glad they shot 'em."

"Didn't they use lethal injection back then?" Melinda said.

"No! They shot 'em! Shot 'is damn head off!" Mean-Fred argued.

"They administered lethal injection. I remember watching it on World Net," Aged-Jason said firmly.

"Well, they shoulda shot 'em!" Mean-Fred said. "Shoulda shot 'is damn head off!"

Mean-Fred slowly stepped off the porch of the crumbling retirement home, careful not to break his hip, and followed Daniel-the-Centenarian down the beaten path toward the brook. The sky was blue, the weather warm, and none of the old folks cared to waste such a fine day. Even Aged-Jason considered getting out of his rocker.

"Feel like giving an old gentleman a hand, sweetie?" Aged-Jason asked. Melinda smiled and helped him up, guiding him to the ramp.

"Why don't you come along? Everyone's goin' down to the creek today. Might even go skinny-dipping," he said with a sly wink.

"You lecher," Melinda laughed. "Run naked for all I care. I have chores to do."

Aged-Jason hobbled down the ramp using his ivory cane for support, strolling through the green April garden. Spring had arrived, and the multitude of wildflowers that had overtaken the rose beds were bursting with color. It was such a day as the old ones wished for, causing Melinda to wonder if there would be more talk of Compact, like after Christmas. The radio had announced another one, this time at the Jackson Plantation to the south of them, and Melinda knew it was bound to cause debate. Not that she could blame the elders. At eighty-nine years old, she was the youngest and healthiest of their little community. She was yet to experience the morbid bitterness of the others.

Stepping into the cool interior of their ramshackle colonial mansion, Melinda wondered where to start. The kitchen was a mess, as always after breakfast, and the hall needed dusting again, but she thought it might be good to do laundry. Mean-Fred had managed to fix the water pump, and the solar collector had stored enough energy to run a load of bedding. Fresh linens would be such a treat!

The mansion was nearly empty now, only Sass-Sally left sitting in the parlor, asleep. She was so far progressed in senility, there was no point in waking her. The cranky old woman would only complain, and most unpleasantly at that. Sometimes Melinda missed not having a female other than She-Geezer to speak with, though she did enjoy the flattery of her male companions. Their colony had shrunk rapidly during the last decade, from a bustling fifty to a bare eleven. And several of those were nearly incapacitated. Melinda longed for those days of dances and parties. Even the deathwatches once held more significance.

Wish the phone still worked, Melinda thought as she passed the disconnected instrument in the breezy lower floor hallway. *I could call another colony. Maybe even Atlanta! Must be a few women somewhere willing to adopt a new home, and Large Oaks is, after all, the finest in all South Carolina!* Not that the Carolinas had many left, not with the Raleigh Colony migrating to Tampa summer before last.

Doesn't matter, though, she decided. *Phone hasn't worked in years. Not since the last satellite lost orbit.*

Melinda stopped to gaze in the hall mirror, fixing her finely brushed gray hair that still retained an occasional auburn wisp. *Not bad*, she thought. *Always the youngest, always the prettiest!*

Dinosaur Blitz

She defied protocol by walking up the stairs to the second floor instead of taking the lift. The landing was bright and airy, the windows left open. With Tea-Leaf Thompson and Old-Ma Hilliard having passed away during the winter, there were no enfeebled residents left upstairs, and Melinda was planning to take over Old-Ma's bedroom for a sewing room, anticipating the beautiful view of the north meadow where thriving herds of deer and elk often grazed. Melinda didn't mourn for Old-Ma—the cranky spinster had taken too long to die—but she did miss Tea-Leaf, whose tales of feminist protest marches were more exciting than the dull war stories and forgotten sports legends of the men.

Melinda passed the stairway leading to the third floor. No one had lived up there since the elevator stopped working and spare parts had proven too hard to find. Not that anyone would risk climbing up the shaft even if a new rotor did turn up. Besides, they no longer needed the extra space.

Melinda briefly wondered what condition the attic was in. Many years before, when privacy was more prized, she had often walked up the narrow circular stair and dwelled in the dark attic recesses, probing through storage chests and smoking a forbidden cigarette. There was no need for such subterfuge now, but Melinda missed her little sojourns, nevertheless.

Because it was such a nice day, a selfish day, Melinda pulled her own sheets and pillow slips first and put the bedding into the dumbwaiter for the drop to the basement, then went through the other rooms on the second floor. She even pulled a few towels from the bathrooms, just in case there was enough surplus electricity for an extra load.

Once the laundry was started, Melinda poked through the pantry freezer for the evening meal. Unlike many of the aging appliances, the old walk-in refrigerator was too simple and too well built to fail them, just as the 100-year warranty had promised. Restocked from the

Charleston reserves a year before, it still contained enough food to supply the residents through summer—longer if their numbers continued to dwindle. Melinda selected a pair of plump chickens and a package of greens, thinking that if she and Lincoln-the-Gardener were industrious, they could grow enough spring vegetables to last through fall. And maybe Lenny-the-Junior could shoot another deer, like he had the previous year. Fresh meat would be such a reward!

Then, quite unexpectedly, Melinda heard a loud noise buzzing above the compound. She smiled and dropped everything, running to the window in time to see a small single-engine aircraft circle the plantation before gliding down for a landing on the state highway. By the time Melinda walked up the cracked cement driveway to the road, Lenny-the-Junior and Aged-Jason had already reached the broad green meadow where the ancient Piper Cub had come to a halt.

She-Geezer and Lincoln-the-Gardener joined Melinda in a slow race across the grass field just as the airplane's lone occupant was disembarking. Only a few months older than Melinda, the slim, silver-haired pilot grinned with delight when he saw her approaching.

"Mindy!" he called out, rushing to embrace her.

"Peter! I'm so glad to see you!" Melinda said with a hug. "My lord, you're looking good."

"Hello, Young-Peter. Glad to have you back," Aged-Jason said.

"What's the news from Orlando?" She-Geezer asked. "How come AM-1210 doesn't broadcast anymore? Did you bring sweets?"

"Hold on there, Geez," Young-Peter smiled, taking a box of chocolates from his flight jacket. "All for you. It's all right, isn't it, Mindy?"

"A little late to ask now," Melinda laughed, nodding as She-Geezer seized the box and retreated.

"Business or pleasure?" Lenny-the-Junior asked. Unannounced visits usually meant bad news. A new closure. Another Compact. Few dared travel for pleasure anymore.

"Came to see my girl," Young-Peter said, pulling Melinda closer, but they noticed the hesitancy in his response.

"Give the youngster time to catch his breath," Aged-Jason said. "You can stay the night, can't you?" Nearing his ninetieth birthday, Young-Peter was hardly a youngster, but he still moved with a vigor that left many envious.

"Wouldn't miss it for the world," Young-Peter said, glancing sideways at Melinda.

Melinda changed the dinner menu from chicken to ham that evening, bouncing around the kitchen as the residents bombarded Young-Peter with questions. Yes, there had been several more closures. No, there had been no recent Compacts. None that had been reported. But even living in the North American capital didn't give Young-Peter all the answers his eager audience wanted, for long-distance communications were close to nonexistent. And there were occasional bits of information that the pilot-messengers declined to share, even among themselves.

"Fabulous meal, Mindy. But it worries me, you carrying so much responsibility by yourself," Young-Peter said, helping with the dishes.

"She-Geezer helps sometimes, even though she complains," Melinda said. "And Lenny-the-Junior's still pretty spry. Does some hunting for us, you know. We're gettin' along just fine."

Melinda knew what Young-Peter was hinting at. Their colony was small now. Not exceptionally small, except by the standards of Orlando and Tampa, but few colonies with less than fifteen residents lasted very long.

"You have something to tell us, don't you?" Melinda asked.

"Yes," he answered.

"Required closure?"

"Not required. Requested. Charleston's closing."

Melinda glanced up in surprise, then back down at the dishes, saying nothing at first. Without Charleston, they had no supply depot north of Orlando. No friends for two hundred miles.

"There are many who won't leave," Melinda finally said.

"That's why I came," Young-Peter said, taking her hand. "There's no reason for you … that is … Did I mention Kid-Jake died?"

"Little Jake? No, I hadn't heard," Melinda said.

Melinda closed the dishwasher, set the timer, and walked out on the rear porch into the cool spring evening. There was a rustle in the woods nearby as a doe and her fawn retreated into the thick brush. An owl hooted.

"I remember when Frank and I first settled here," Melinda said. "Twenty-five years ago, when the last Pennsylvania colony closed. Frank passed away a few years later. Kid-Jake came up and visited all that summer. Now he's gone, poor soul. Just about all of us from the Final Batch have passed on."

"Come on, don't get like that," Young-Peter said, stroking her hair. "There are still lots of people our age. Hundreds, probably. Maybe thousands, if you count Asia."

"Or maybe none. Maybe there's no one left in Asia at all. Or Africa. Or Europe. How many people were there in the world when we were born? Eight billion?"

"Almost ten, some say."

"And when we graduated high school?"

"About seven, probably."

"And how many people are left now? Two hundred thousand?"

"Can't say for sure, communications being what they are. Some say as many as half a million."

"What about ten years from now? How many people will there be then?" Melinda asked.

"Probably not too many," he confessed.

"What's it all for, Peter? Why are we hanging on?"

"No one ever asked the woolly mammoth or Tyrannosaurus Rex why they stuck it out. Besides, it's not what comes next that's important. It's how we live in the here and now. If nothing else, certainly we've learned that much."

"But don't you wonder anymore? What it would've been like to have children? I've been thinkin' on it. Thinkin' how nice it would have been to have a little girl, hair all curly and sweet. Or give Frank a son. Lord help us, I've been wondering about it so much lately it makes me hurt."

"We can still try," Peter said. He nestled his mouth against Melinda's neck and kissed her as she giggled.

"Stop that right this minute. People might get the wrong idea," she scolded, turning back into the house.

"Heaven forbid," Young-Peter smiled.

The smile didn't last long. Young-Peter soon discovered himself the focus of a hostile audience that took several minutes to calm.

"Is this where we get the raw deal?" Mean-Fred interrupted.

A brisk fire burned in the fireplace and the lamps were turned low to conserve energy, but the assembly was small enough for everyone to hear. Young-Peter was the only one standing.

"Charleston's closing," he said, making the announcement official. "I'm afraid your winter supply can't be guaranteed. The Council recommends relocation to Orlando. They think it's time to proceed with the final stages of Consolidation. But if you want, Atlanta is staying open for another year. You can join with the Fulton Colony or Seminole Estates."

"We have to leave?" Lincoln-the-Gardener asked in confusion.

"To hell with closin'! I ain't goin' no place!" Mean-Fred yelled.

"We can supply ourselves," Lenny-the-Junior said, cradling his shotgun.

"Damn kids runnin' 'round tellin' folks what to do," She-Geezer said in a huff. "I was born not forty miles from here. Not forty miles! Don't tell me I got to move to Flor'da!"

"Please, everyone," Aged-Jason said. "Let's have Young-Peter here give us our options. It doesn't hurt to listen, does it?"

Near the back of the room, Daniel-the-Centenarian turned his wheelchair around and left the room, quickly followed by Glum-Gus and Old-Sticky. Lincoln-the-Gardener gazed out the window at his flower beds. Sass-Sally sat motionless, uncomprehending. Melinda tried not to show her distress.

"Relocation's not so bad," Young-Peter said. "We'll bring out a bigrig, load up everything that's still useful, and haul it down to wherever you want. By fall, you'll be snug as bugs. And if you choose Orlando, you'll never have to move again. We've got fifty thousand people now. A regular metropolis."

"Everything we could want, huh?" Mean-Fred sneered. "Congestion, pollution, crime. Politicians. To hell with your damn city! I call for—"

"Damn it, Fred! Will you shut your damn mouth!" Aged-Jason yelled. "Young-Peter didn't come all this way to be cussed at, he's just delivering a message. What we decide, we'll decide on our own."

Mean-Fred fell silent. Aged-Jason was right. Some things shouldn't be discussed in front of outsiders. The assembly stirred.

"I'll be back in six weeks," Young-Peter said.

"We'll talk it over," Aged-Jason promised. "And now, if I remember correctly, Mindy promised us a right fine dessert this evening. Didn't you, Mindy?"

"Linc and I gathered enough blueberries for pie this afternoon," Melinda said.

"Old-fashioned blueberry pie. Sounds darn good to me," Aged-Jason said, helping She-Geezer out of her seat.

"Gives me hives," Mean-Fred complained with a frown.

Later that evening, with the residents retired and the house finally quiet, Melinda slipped off her house robe and crawled into bed. Young-Peter took her in his arms.

"Too bad we're not a little younger," Peter whispered.

Dinosaur Blitz

"A lot younger," Melinda agreed, nestling against his shoulder.

"What do you think they'll do?"

"I guess it's obvious," she sighed.

"What are *you* going to do?"

"Wish I knew, Peter. All the work. The pain. I get so tired. There are times I just don't care anymore."

"Come with me," Peter said. "I won't be doing much flying come September, and I've got a great little cottage down next to the lagoon. We'd have a group of eight, half and half. Plenty of help with the chores, good company in the evenings. Marge and George play bridge, and Old-Ahmad cooks the best damn duck you ever had. I know we'd be happy."

"It sounds like heaven, Peter, but you know I can't. My responsibilities are here. These are my people. I must abide by the majority."

Peter closed his eyes and pulled her close.

The next morning, after the Piper Cub took off and turned south, the surviving residents of Large Oaks Plantation gathered to discuss their options. The vote they finally took didn't go well. With Young-Peter gone, the debate was heated and occasionally bitter. Mean-Fred and She-Geezer led the advocates for Compact. Aged-Jason held against a hasty decision. In the end, without enough votes to defeat the advocates, Melinda and Lincoln-the-Gardener helped pass a postponement.

"Six weeks. We make a final determination then," Aged-Jason said.

"Damn waste of time. Nothin's gonna change. Nothin' at all," Mean-Fred said.

"Just draggin' it out," Glum-Gus agreed.

"Never shoulda 'lowed in a lawyer," She-Geezer complained, glaring at Aged-Jason. "Never was nothin' but trouble."

"A vote short is a vote short," Aged-Jason said.

Melinda got up to fetch more tea, disappointed her motion to relocate had not even received a second.

Lincoln-the-Gardener died later that month. They found him in the rose beds, where he'd been weeding. Unable to dig a proper grave, the residents piled stones around his body and left him among his beloved flowers. As Aged-Jason read the appropriate biblical passage and Daniel-the-Centenarian placed a crudely carved marker, the entire community stood in silent tribute. Melinda studied their faces and knew what they were thinking.

The remaining weeks passed faster than any would wish, even the advocates. They ate big meals, spent hours in the sun, and even dared to use the stairs. Aged-Jason accepted the inevitable with resignation, doubting his ability to survive another winter regardless, but Melinda grew increasingly listless. For the first time in memory, she neglected her appearance and let others do the cooking. Without Lincoln-the-Gardener for a fourth, the afternoon bridge games no longer took place, and the pleasure Melinda once took in knitting faded into a series of repetitive motions.

When the evening before their final vote arrived, the outcome seemed a foregone conclusion.

"Mindy? That you?" Melinda heard Aged-Jason call from his small bedroom off the main hall. The elder had been bedridden for the last two days, providing Melinda with at least one responsibility she refused to ignore.

"Yes, Jason. Not asleep yet?" she asked.

"Restless, I guess."

"Everyone is tonight," Melinda said.

"No surprise. Have you decided on your vote tomorrow?"

"Does it matter?"

"Matters to me. Tradition mandates a three-fourths majority."

"Our two votes won't be enough, and none of the others have changed their minds," Melinda said.

"I'm sorry, Mindy. I wish there was something I could do," Aged-

Jason said, reaching to take her hand. "Couldn't you—"

"You know better. I've accepted obligations all my life. It's who I am. Frank used to call me stubborn, but he never tried to change me. Regardless of what happens tomorrow, I've got to do what's right."

Aged-Jason sighed, his face gray. "Will you read to me for a little while?" he asked.

"Glad to. What would you like to hear?"

"You know the one," he said.

Melinda nodded and took the dog-eared copy of Tennyson from the shelf next to the bed, despite knowing the passage by heart. She sat down and opened the book slowly, with quiet drama. She began reading, softly at first, but raised her voice when she came to Aged-Jason's favorite part.

"Come, my friends, 'tis not too late, to seek a newer world. Push off, and sitting well in order smite—"

"Skip to end," Aged-Jason said, his voice barely audible.

Melinda nodded and closed the book in her lap, gazing out the window.

"Tho' much is taken, much abides; and tho' we're not now that strength which in old days moved earth and heaven; That which we are, we are, one equal temper of heroic hearts, made weak by time and fate, but strong in will. To strive, to seek, to find, and not to yield."

And not to yield, Melinda thought.

She glanced over to discover Aged-Jason had died, the passing so calm she hadn't even heard his last breath.

The following afternoon was bright and clear. The sun warm, the birds singing, the meadow full of deer until the persistent buzz of a single-engine aircraft sent them scurrying for the forest.

After circling the old mansion several times and seeing no activity, Young-Peter set the plane down on the highway. Regardless of what had happened, he needed to know.

Within the great house, the quiet echoed like a tomb. Off the main hall, Aged-Jason's body lay in the bed where he had died. In the parlor, Mean-Fred sat upright in his chair, eyes glassy and unseeing. Beside him rested the half-cup of tea he'd been sipping while anticipating the final vote. A vote that never took place. Next to Mean-Fred was She-Geezer, her tea spilled in a moment of surprise. Daniel-the-Centenarian, the unfired shotgun still in his lap, lay sprawled backward against the couch. Sass-Sally sat in her wheelchair, drooped to one side. Their longtime companions all lay nearby, teacups empty. All except one. On the end table next to an old rocking chair, one fatal cup of tea remained untouched.

Melinda stepped out on the wooden porch and closed the door behind her for the last time, smiling as she saw Young-Peter approaching from the highway. *Orlando will be exciting*, she thought. *New friends. New challenges. Better weather. Yes, Melinda decided, there is still much to live for.*

Dinosaur Blitz

<u>Rachel's Farewell</u>
They say there's a land
Where dreams may come true
A land of fond wishes
Where troubles are few
It's a place where I'm going
Beyond where I've been
On this journey that takes me home

Life makes our choices
Not those that we want
The stars make decisions
For battles we've fought
So now I must leave you
Though it's not what I'd choose
On this journey that takes me home

When I am gone
Don't look for me there
Don't fear that I'm lost
Or burdened with cares
I'm bound for a new world
One where I'm loved
On this journey that takes me home

from *Rachel the Warrior*

Gregory Urbach

The Adventures of Snailwoman

While working for a film distributor in the 1980s, one of my co-workers, Elizabeth Scherrer, kept pet snails in a terrarium. I drew a cartoon of her as Snailwoman, a superheroine who communicated with an army of heroic snails, and it made her laugh. Over time, two full-length adventures were written. Ronald Reagan was president at the time and was known to have a love for jellybeans, so that was incorporated into the scripts.

My younger brother Kevin said he wanted to improve the artwork and upgraded my sketches. The scripts were entered into a national contest, and though we didn't win a prize, *Snailwoman* was honorably mentioned.

Elizabeth left the company and Kevin became a carpenter. So here, after forty years, Snailwoman lives again.

Dinosaur Blitz

Snailwoman vs the Deficit

Gregory Urbach

Dinosaur Blitz

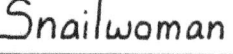

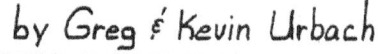

Gregory Urbach

Dinosaur Blitz

Gregory Urbach

Dinosaur Blitz

Gregory Urbach

Dinosaur Blitz

Burning Bridges
Burning bridges afterglow,
Life has one true fact;
Regardless where the journey goes
The path does not lead back.

from *Tranquility in Darkness*

EVACUATION
World war isolates a lunar colony

A child cried in the background as McKinsey entered the last special program. The computer monitors in the Governor's Quarters were brightly lit, the multicolored signature patterns representing the activity of many systems. Tired, dying, McKinsey had no time to for the minor computers. They would develop the finer details for themselves. It was the higher-function levels he was hoping to advise. Especially the Life Support Computer. Of all the different colors running through the monitor screen flux, green signature patterns showed the strongest.

"Do you understand the necessity?" McKinsey asked.

"The short-term ramifications are obvious, Governor. It is the long-term goal pattern that remains unclear," the Life Support Computer replied.

McKinsey frowned, more frustrated than angry. Intelligent as the computer was, how could he teach the system to deal with so many unknown and unknowable factors? How could he explain instinct to a machine?

Dinosaur Blitz

"I've provided the best information I have. You'll need to develop your own answers now. Remember, you have Medical to draw on, and Library for reference. Be sure to gather data from all available sources before making decisions."

"Understood, Governor," Life Support assured him. "May I express disappointment that we shall no longer be working together?"

"No more disappointed than I," McKinsey said, his attention drifting. "Almost time. Better summon . . . med team."

"Is there anything I can do?" Life Support asked.

McKinsey watched the signature patterns pause as the indicators waited for his response. But there was nothing the computer could do. Not now. Not for him. McKinsey shook his head, knowing the computer would understand the gesture. The green signature patterns began to swirl again, the wavy lines dancing across the screen in rhythmic pulsations. McKinsey watched the patterns stabilize before his eyes drifted to the chronometer.

"My God, was it just a year ago?" he muttered. "No, not really one. More, I think. Yes, it started before that."

McKinsey rested back in the command chair, fighting to keep erect until his head settled against the support. The calendar read 24 December, 2070, but McKinsey's thoughts were traveling back to a hectic summer day eighteen months before. The 30th of June, 2069. The day he returned to the moon for the last time.

"May I help you, Dr. McKinsey?" the pretty young flight attendant asked, the grips on her shoes holding her steady against the weightlessness. McKinsey twisted in the bucket seat, silently cursing the restraining harness.

"No, damn your hide," he mumbled.

As McKinsey turned to look out the porthole, the flight attendant smiled. It wasn't the first time she'd flown the express run with her grouchy VIP passenger, nor she wasn't offended by his manner. In fact, it was somewhat of an honor. McKinsey was much too conscious of his public image to growl at someone he didn't like.

"We're preparing to break orbit," she said, checking his harness while noticing what a handsome man he was. And though in his sixties, hardly the grandfather type as he was portrayed by the press.

"Signal if you need me," she suggested. He waved her off as she released her grips, walking hand over hand up the aisle and out of the passenger cabin. Alone at last, McKinsey slipped a journal from his pocket.

"Supplemental entry. Escape complete," he whispered.

Wiggling in the seat, he tried to get one last glance at Earth. It was too late. The shuttle had already turned into lunar approach.

"Damn those motherless curs," he muttered. Only anger kept him from trembling. "Thank God I was warned of their plot in time."

The shuttle completed its turn toward the lunar surface and decelerated, leaving the Earth, the alliances, and everything but its problems far behind. In a melancholy mood, McKinsey realized he'd been down-planet for the last time.

"I hope it's not too late. For thirty years, I've promoted my image of the pioneer scientist. Good old Doctor Tom! If only they knew the real story. The back room deals. The comprises. The betrayals of faith. But I need my prestige now. I need it to buy time."

"We're on approach, Governor," the pilot said over the intercom. "The Defense Computer has approved our entry code. Next stop, the Tranquility Lunar Colony."

With the same excitement he'd felt on his first landing thirty years before, McKinsey looked out the porthole to see the glimmering plains of the Sea of Tranquility. Lunar flights were rare in '42. The desolate terrain had seemed strange and foreboding. Now it was home.

With the last leg of its long voyage nearly over, the small shuttlecraft dropped rapidly over Mare Tranquillitatis toward the mineral-rich crater Vitruvius. Only the rolling, rock-studded plains were visible from the higher altitudes, but as the shuttle came in on the southeast approach pattern, signs of human habitation began to appear. Roads cut by the mining tractors. The outer lying defense stations. And at last, the colony itself became clear, the surface structures grouped around a little knoll at the foot of Tranquility Ridge.

The shuttlecraft set down on the elevator platform, the engine exhaust quickly dissipating in the lunar vacuum. Just as the platform began to drop, McKinsey looked up to see the fortress perched high atop the ridge. North Point, hub of all lunar defenses. The home of America's second-strike force. Thinking of the missiles gave him a chill.

Expecting the usual complement of engineers, researchers, and tourists, the ground techs were surprised when only McKinsey disembarked. With a quick dismissal, the returning colonial governor brushed aside their well-meant greetings and rushed from the bay.

After passing through the airlocks, he took advantage of the moon's weak gravity to spring rapidly down the first tunnel. Bypassing the upper staging decks, he plunged deeper toward the underground levels, finding the corridor unusually crowded with technicians and their robot assistants. Forced to slow down, McKinsey cursed under his breath, pushing until he found as open stretch.

"About time," he said, picking up speed. He began to bounce faster and faster, as if speed alone could solve his troubles. It almost did. Failing to catch a level area between strides, McKinsey lost his balance and tumbled head over heels into a user-friendly safety wall.

"Hell's chances!" he hissed, lying motionless, more embarrassed than hurt.

"Governor McKinsey?" a youthful voice said. "Please, let me help you."

A kid barely in his twenties reached down to put the elder scientist back on his feet. McKinsey gathered his wits, blessed the checkered wall as tradition demanded, and resumed his journey to the community level.

Thirty minutes later, he finally came upon the unmarked corridor that led home, the doors of the Governor's Quarters opening as the security monitor confirmed his approach. The rooms were brightly lit, the headquarters active with computer monitors and observation screens. To the left was his private office. Beyond that, his personal sleeping chamber. As McKinsey entered the office, he was surprised to find an old friend waiting for him. The colony's chief engineer.

"Welcome home, Tom," Chester Fairfield said with a warm smile.

As he was fond of doing, Fairfield sat behind McKinsey's large desk, his feet up, leaning back in the chair.

McKinsey took off his white lab coat, now symbolically dirty with the business of the last two days, and hung it on the service rack. He avoided Fairfield's inquiring look.

"How did the meeting with the Council go?" Fairfield asked.

Though the answer seemed obvious, Fairfield didn't want to make a rash assumption. He knew how the press could distort things.

"Just wonderful," McKinsey sighed, going to his liquor cabinet.

"Good as all that, huh? Well, I guess we should have expected problems. The National Party picked up a lot of seats in the last election. What did Laureen have to say?"

"My peace-loving wife has accepted a seat on the new Council."

"What? Laureen? How? Why?"

"Almost losing her Senate seat may have been too much for her. I don't know. We're not close anymore. At least we're still friends."

"I'm sorry, Tom. Have you decided on a divorce?" he asked.

"Not yet. At least, not officially."

McKinsey stirred a freshly made martini and walked over to the imitation brick fireplace in the corner, igniting the flame.

"I want to be free to marry Crystal, and Laureen knows that," McKinsey admitted. "Have you seen her?"

"Crystal? She's on level 28 with the geo team," Fairfield cautiously answered. "Their shift will be over in a few hours."

"28? In her condition?"

Fairfield laughed. "Nothing has stopped that woman in the past. Pregnancy seems equally unsuccessful. I wouldn't worry too much."

"That's easy for you to say, after five."

"It's always easy to say," Fairfield said with a grin. "With Laureen changing sides, what happens to the Peace block?'

McKinsey shook his head.

"All things considered, I'm surprised they let you come back. Why weren't you detained?"

"It was a close call. Laureen warned me at the last minute, so when I was summoned to appear before the Council, I changed sides, too. You should have seen my performance. I was brilliant." He struck a pose, one handheld out, the other in his pocket.

"Distinguished members of the Council, you know I have objected to your blockade policies in the past, but the die is cast! I now offer my unwavering support! Upon returning to the moon, my first order will be the immediate evacuation of all foreign observatories. And if hostilities commence, the full power of the Tranquility lunar arsenal will be at your disposal. We will seize the high ground, and hold it! Then I suggested additional strategies. Damn good ones, too."

"For a scientist, you've always been a most convincing liar," Fairfield observed. "So, what happens now? Once the alliances activate their orbital webs, we'll be isolated. How do we feed two thousand people during a siege?"

"We're not going to try. Six hours from now, we begin evacuating the civilians and outer stations. Everyone but the garrison and my personal staff will be sent back to Earth. Of course, once the war starts, I'll have to surrender the launch codes."

"Not a very attractive idea, is it?"

"When we were building Tranquility, we needed government

contracts. Establishing an untouchable missile base was too much for the politicians to resist."

"The thought of Tranquility's weapons in the hands of the Nationalists is rather unsettling."

"I've been thinking the same thing. What was it Shakespeare said? These are times that try men's souls?"

"I believe that was Thomas Paine."

McKinsey reached to his prized shelf of bound books, taking out one he had been looking for. "Here it is. This is one quote I won't get wrong."

"What's that?"

"This is our plan."

McKinsey opened the book and began reading. "When in the course of human events, it becomes necessary for one people to dissolve the political bands which have connected them with another, and to assume among the powers of the Earth—"

"You're planning a revolt?" Fairfield questioned in surprise.

"No, my friend, not a revolt," McKinsey firmly corrected. "A republic."

The rest of McKinsey's day was spent in staff meetings, planning sessions, and departmental conferences. Only the urgent need for immediate evacuation was discussed, McKinsey stressing the situation would be temporary, and as soon as tensions eased, the colony would be reopened. Even many of his closest aides believed him. Six hours after his return to Tranquility, the first bewildered tourists were already being herded into the landing bays.

With his preliminary plans in motion, McKinsey wearily returned to the privacy of the Governor's Quarters. It was still empty. He retreated to his sleeping quarters for a relaxing shower, pleased when he finally heard the sound he'd been waiting for.

Dinosaur Blitz

"Is that you, Crystal?" he called out.

"Yes, Thomas, it is I," a small, sturdily built woman in her early thirties replied." She hesitated before explaining. "The strata on 28 is proving rich. It has kept the team busy all week."

As she heard McKinsey emerge from the shower, Crystal stepped into the monitor room locker area and stripped off her dusty overalls, pushing them into the laundry chute. She pulled out a fluffy robe and entered the den. McKinsey was already sitting in his favorite easy chair. She sat down on the chair's arm next to him.

"I hope you don't mind me staying here for a few days," she said. "They are closing the employee housing. I'll need to find a room in the hotel."

"Of course not. My quarters are your quarters. Did you miss me?"

"Yes, Thomas, I was afraid for you."

McKinsey pulled her gently into his lap, giving her extra girth plenty of room. Her deep blue eyes twinkled with concern. He gave her a squeeze and ran his free hand over her extended belly, feeling the movement of new life within. It was a thrill he'd thought himself too old for.

"I heard of the trouble," Crystal said. "And the evacuation."

"Don't worry about that. You can stay, if you want to."

Crystal was surprised by his offer.

"I have no intention of leaving, Thomas. There is nothing for me down there. I just wondered how many people you are shipping out."

"We've scheduled three cargo runs a day for the next three weeks. Most of the moon's personnel will be concentrated here first. The rest will go up from the equator stations."

"You are closing all the bases? Who is staying behind?"

"We're keeping a skeleton crew here at Tranquility. A half dozen, maybe. No one else. The fewer that need to be provided for, the better. But don't say anything—the Congress-In-Council doesn't know that yet." He laughed smugly at his own cleverness.

"But how—"

"Let's talk politics later. I want to know how you're doing."

She blushed again, tucking her small chin in and looking down.

"The pregnancy is progressing according to schedule," she answered. "The Medical Computer is developing a program that will allow the child to adapt to the lighter gravity. Do not be worried."

McKinsey pulled her closer. Crystal seemed tense, at first, then gradually laid her head against his shoulder, a sad look in her eyes he couldn't see.

"Are we ready yet?" McKinsey nervously inquired.

"Relax, Tom, it won't be long now," Fairfield answered as he adjusted the teleprompter.

McKinsey paced behind his desk, dressed in his long white lab coat. The four weeks since his return from Earth had been hectic but successful. It wasn't the evacuation that had been difficult. Tranquility's computers saw to that. The real moment of drama had been the deportation of the military garrison. McKinsey's coup allowed him to reduce the moon's population to his own personal staff. But gaining control of the moon was not the same as keeping it.

The Governor's Quarters were filled with the moon's only remaining residents. Crystal, standing behind Fairfield, whispered little jokes that made him chuckle. Dr. Lindy Yee and Dr. Marilyn Goldstein fussed with the video camera. In the adjoining monitor room, Colonel Jaime Vandebrown coordinated the broadcast with the Communications Computer.

"The satellite is making contact now, Governor," Vandebrown called out. "Ten seconds to link."

McKinsey took his place behind the big desk. His trophies and awards would serve as an effective backdrop. Especially the Nobel Prize. It would remind his audience of the prestige he commanded.

Dinosaur Blitz

"Do I look grim and determined?" McKinsey asked.

"Fix your collar, Thomas," Crystal said with her fine eye for detail.

"For God's sake, Tom, try to look distinguished!" Fairfield kidded.

"Three ... two ... one ... you're on, Governor," Vandebrown announced as the transmission light activated.

"Citizens of the Earth," McKinsey began. "I know there are those who will call our revolution madness, but I assure you, our actions are not only justified, but vitally necessary. The problems of our alliances cannot be solved with another war. I built this colony to prove our differences are not so great. I have refused in the past, and will continue to refuse, to allow the moon to be used as a base of military operations.

"Because my policy of peaceful progress cannot be carried out under the current Congress-In-Council, my fellow scientists and I have decided to end the moon's colonial period. From now on, we shall be known as the Lunar Republic, with all the rights and powers of an independent state. As Governor of the Moon for the duration of this crisis, I formally declare the moon off-limits to all unauthorized flights. The Defense Computer has been instructed to destroy any spacecraft that would invade our soil.

"Second, I decree the Lunar Republic will remain neutral in the days, months, and years ahead, providing neither support nor recognizance to any alliance." McKinsey moved around to the front of the desk, sitting on the edge, his hands folded.

"The political process has failed," he continued. "We resort to force of arms in accordance with our heritage, and by our rights as free citizens."

Behind the camera, Fairfield gave McKinsey the signal to wrap up. McKinsey took a deep breath, offered a sad but reassuring smile, and leaned forward to stare directly into the lens.

"The path ahead will not be easy, but as long as we are true to our ideals, God's grace will see us through. Fear not, my friends, the future belongs to those with faith."

The transmission ended.

"Great. Pompous as hell, but great," Fairfield congratulated.

"Nicely done, sir," Vandebrown said.

"You were most eloquent, Thomas," Crystal complimented.

"Well, nothing to do now but wait for the reviews to come in," McKinsey joked. "I guess they'll put me somewhere between Thomas Jefferson and Benedict Arnold."

"Closer to Arnold, I should think," Fairfield said dryly. The comment elicited a few uneasy smiles, but no laughs.

Two weeks later, as international tensions kept the world's alliances in turmoil, the Lunar Republic added its first new citizen. The 31st of July was famous for another event, too. It was the day the Lunar Republic met its moment of crisis.

"He doesn't look sickly to me," Vandebrown said, holding the newborn in his arms. "Almost cute."

"We still don't know what luna's lighter gravity will do to his health," Dr. Goldstein mentioned.

"He will be fine," Crystal said with a proud, motherly glow. "My people are an adaptable species."

The medical center was alive with human, computer, and robotic activity. The research labs were already evaluating data on the unusual baby, only the fourth ever born on the moon.

"My son needs a name," Vandebrown said. "What are you thinking, sweetheart?"

"His eyes are grey, like mine are crystal blue," Crystal replied. "So that will be his name. Grey Waters."

"Maybe we can call the next one Muddy?" Vandebrown said, holding her hand.

"Have you told Tom the baby isn't his?" Fairfield asked.

"No. There has not been a good time," Crystal replied.

Dinosaur Blitz

"You and Jaime have been together for a year," Goldstein said.

"We were going to tell him when he returned from his meeting with the Council," Vandebrown explained. "The evacuation got in the way."

"It won't be a secret forever, Jaime," Dr. Yee warned.

"Where is Thomas?" Crystal asked.

"He's still going over the latest tracking with the Defense Computer," Fairfield said. "Don't worry, he'll be along soon."

"I am not worried," Crystal said. "I just wanted to know. He's been so preoccupied. It is not good for him. Even Thomas must relax some of the time."

"If the news from Earth is as bad as I think," Vandebrown said, "he won't be relaxing today."

In the Governor's Quarters, McKinsey finished his conference with the Defense Computer and watched its blue signature patterns fade into the monitor screen flux. For a moment, he considered going to the medical center, vaguely realizing he must be late, but decided to have one last conference before leaving. He summoned the Life Support Computer.

"Good morning, Governor, what can I do for you?" the computer said, the tone indicating the system had been drawn from important duties elsewhere.

"I want you to help Goldstein with the reactor's modification program."

"Should that not be Energy's function?" the protocol-conscious computer asked.

"For the next two quarters, Energy will be assisting the Defense Computer. Data indicates a dangerous vulnerability factor. Until our defenses are shored up, you'll have to assume Energy's research functions."

"Acknowledged," Life Support blinked, already wondering where to draw the extra maintenance robots such an undertaking would require. Then the computer noticed McKinsey lingering online and realized that something else was bothering him. In light of recent instructions, the dilemma wasn't hard to figure out.

"Are you expecting the Congress-In-Council to launch an assault force?" the Life Support Computer asked. McKinsey's eyes said yes, a response the computer recognized, but his manner was one of hesitation.

"Lots of activity. Vandenberg. Houston. Canaveral. Many ships. Maybe too many. The alliances have been quiet lately. Last-minute negotiations and all that. The Council may take advantage of the lull to launch an attack. Even with Security's help, the six of us can't guard the whole colony."

"Your solution appears simple," the Life Support Computer said.

"How is that?"

"Force the issue of the orbital paths."

"Force it? What do you mean?"

"I am not a defense system, you understand, but it seems to me that if you attack the Eastern Alliance and make it look like the North Americans, the resulting conflict will produce an orbital blockade. The Council would not be able to launch their ships, and they lack the credibility to effectively deny involvement. Properly coordinated, the provocation would be difficult to trace back to Tranquility. Your credibility, after all, is surprisingly high."

McKinsey stared at the computer's swirling green signature patterns in stunned disbelief. Was the machine really suggesting he start the war? It was! The idea was incredible, and yet, there was a simplicity to the plan that seemed to solve the problem. McKinsey laughed uneasily.

"Life Support, sometimes I think you're the most devious one here, man or machine," he said. The Life Support Computer took insult by his remark.

"I am a human-orientated problem solving and service system.

Dinosaur Blitz

Nothing more. If humans present difficult problems, then they should expect the solutions to be proportionately unpleasant."

The green signature patterns blinked in a sharp huff and dropped offline.

McKinsey sank back into his chair to think, the room growing quiet. Long after Crystal had fallen asleep in the medical center, and his friends had returned to their quarters, he leaned forward to summon a computer.

"Defense Computer," he said. "Provide me with a program for pushing down an orbital unobserved."

"Is this a hypothetical exercise, Governor?" the rule-conscious computer asked.

"Negative," the Governor replied. "This is a go."

Five months later, the Lunar Republic celebrated its first Christmas, but it was not festive. Without use of the high frontier, the major alliances were no better off than the smaller powers and independents. The war had turned into a grueling stalemate of strike and counterstrike that halted trade, expended resources, and damaged the delicate environment. Under siege, Tranquility survived in the security of its complete isolation. And Governor Thomas McKinsey survived in an isolation of his own.

"There you are," Fairfield said when he found McKinsey hiding in the Governor's Quarters.

"Are you trying to hint I'm late for the party?" the busy governor snarled.

Fairfield pretended not to smile. "Remember what you always say? Promises made are promises kept?"

"Don't be ridiculous. I would never say any such thing," McKinsey growled.

"So, what great project are you working on now?" Fairfield asked.

"Faster than light travel?"

"How did you know?" McKinsey said.

Fairfield gasped and wondered if his old friend had finally lost his mind, but the slow smile on McKinsey's face assured him he was joking. Fairfield was more relieved than he thought he should be.

"Well?" Fairfield asked. "What's keeping you from the party? Whether promises made are kept or not, you're keeping this one."

"I'll only be a few more minutes. Vandebrown and I are watching the last satellites go down."

"Amazing, isn't it? A hundred years of space communications destroyed in a matter of months. Who'd have believed it?"

"We're the only ones left with a network now. It may be deep space, but at least it functions. The alliances are getting their weather data from balloons!"

Fairfield detected an unmistakable glow of satisfaction in McKinsey's voice.

"And to think, if the Council hadn't dropped that orbital on Suez, we might still have our backs against the wall,"

"Yes, a lucky break for us," McKinsey hesitantly agreed.

"Lucky? Damn unbelievable if you ask me. And imagine them trying to blame the Russians? Who do they think they're kidding?"

"Last one's down, Governor," Vandebrown announced as his image appeared on the monitor screen. "Nothing left now but orbitals, seekers, and mines. A complete war zone."

The young officer seemed excited by the news. "Congratulations, sir. Your plan was brilliant."

"Plan?" Fairfield inquired, leaning over McKinsey's shoulder. "What plan is that, Jaime?"

"Oh. Hello, Chester," Vandebrown said with less enthusiasm. "Don't tell me the party's over already?"

"I hope not," Fairfield answered.

"Well, I'm on my way down. See you in a few minutes."

As screen went dark, Fairfield waited for the explanation McKinsey would have to give. It was slow in coming.

"We have a special responsibility, Chester. The war isn't going to be short like we wanted. It's the Grain Wars all over again. Only this time, when the war is over, there will still be an influential power left to guide the peace process."

"Tranquility?"

"Who else? What power except Tranquility will be free of nationalistic prejudices? Who else will have the high ground capabilities to enforce the treaty?"

"I see. Will you dictate the terms of the treaty as well?"

"Dictate, negotiate, call it what you will," McKinsey defended.

"They will never accept your leadership on that basis," Fairfield warned. "People will only unite if they want to, or have to, but never if someone tells them to. Resisting tyranny is part of our culture."

There followed a tense quiet that McKinsey finally broke with an agreeable smile.

"Let's not worry about it now," he said. "This war is going to last a year. Maybe more. We have plenty of time to develop an acceptable plan."

"Well, let's get going then. The others are waiting in the community center."

"I'll be along in a minute," McKinsey said.

He was answered with a doubtful look.

"I promise. I'll even send a hostage for my good behavior," he proclaimed. He reached back into the small refrigerator behind his desk, pulling out a chilled bottle of champagne.

"Here," McKinsey said, handing it to Fairfield.

"Tapa Valley '24? Where did you find this?"

"Laureen gave it to me on my last trip down. Open it at the party. I promise to be there before it's gone."

Fairfield knew no offer on McKinsey's part could be more sincere.

His love of '24 was legendary. When he hesitated, McKinsey tore the wrapper off, twisted the cork, and popped it loudly. The cold, bubbly foam squeezed from the top and ran down his hand into his sleeve.

"Take this damn thing!" he ordered, thrusting the bottle back into Fairfield's hands. "And you'd better drink it, too. Now get out of here."

Fairfield laughed at McKinsey's performance, then headed for the doorway.

"Tom?" he said, pausing in the arch. "Let's talk things out tonight. It would be good for all of us."

McKinsey nodded.

With Fairfield safely off to the party, McKinsey walked into the monitor room, stopping before the Life Support station.

"Yes, Doctor?" the Life Support Computer asked when it saw him lingering. McKinsey hesitated, began to speak, then held up. His posture appeared agitated.

"Troubled, Governor?"

"Fairfield doesn't approve of what we're doing. I'm afraid I have a few doubts of my own. But I don't see any other way."

"You have taken a great responsibility upon yourself. Why are you doing it if you are not sure?" Life Support asked.

"When was I absolved of responsibility? Too many people, too many generations, have abandoned their responsibilities. I remember what it was like at the turn of the century. The ecology crumbling. Mass starvation. The struggle for natural resources leading to war. Is that what we're going back to?"

"Each generation discovers their own challenges. Your generation repaired the atmosphere. Learned detoxification. Developed clean energy sources."

"But at a tremendous cost," McKinsey replied.

"Is that not the lesson of your history?"

"I don't want my son growing up on a dying world. I don't think Chester wants his little girls becoming soldiers—" He had to pause.

Dinosaur Blitz

"Like Darla was."

The memory of his lost daughter removed the last of McKinsey's doubts. He raised his head with new confidence.

"The better my planning is now, the farther I can project ahead."

"Project what?"

"A way to end war forever."

"You're an idealist, Governor," Life Support disapproved.

"I have this facility to back me up."

"You're a heavily armed idealist."

"I didn't start thinking about this yesterday. I've known since my last flight back from Earth what I'd have to do. And so far, everything has exceeded my expectations. From here on in, time is on my side."

The whoosh of the access doors announced a sudden arrival. McKinsey turned to see Crystal, her color ghastly white, staggering through the doorway. He rushed to catch her as she fell to the floor.

"Crystal? What is it? Crystal?"

He found a rapid pulse. The pupils were dilated.

"My God," he cursed. "Medical Computer! Send a team to the Governor's Quarters immediately!"

The computer's white signature patterns blinked but did not give an affirmative response.

"Medical Computer!" he screamed again.

"Sorry, Governor," the Medical Computer answered. "All three teams are engaged."

"What in hell is going on?"

"Undetermined," Medical reported. "Tests are yet to be ... hold please. Stand by for new information." White signature patterns swirled rapidly as the new data registered. Then, just as suddenly, they sagged. "Governor McKinsey, I am sorry to report that Doctors Fairfield and Goldstein have been pronounced dead. Doctor Yee is in route to the medical center. Her condition is extremely critical."

Without a second's delay, McKinsey scooped Crystal up and raced to the medical center as fast as he could go.

Hours later, a distraught and exhausted man sat alone in the command chair before the computer control panels. Finally, the white signature patterns appeared in the flux.

"Medical Computer? What was it? What happened?"

"Autopsy tests are still in progress, Governor," the Medical Computer said with a plea for patience. "Preliminary results indicate poisoning, probably a substance M derivative. There is additional information I am required to give you that is quite bad."

"Worse news than my best friends being murdered?"

"I'm not programmed for philosophy. Your bio-scanner tests have returned positive."

"Me? What are you talking about? There's nothing wrong with me."

"Apparently you were infected differently. Possibly through the pores. That would be consistent with M-type infections."

"Can it be cured?"

"Affirmative. The medical laboratory at UCLA has all the necessary facilities."

"Impossible! Even if my shuttle got through, I'd be arrested immediately."

"I have advised you of the diagnosis. The decision is yours. But I believe there is an old adage about living to fight another day that you would be wise to consider."

As bad as the thought sounded, McKinsey had to admit there seemed no other choice. And escape might always be bought.

"How long do I have to prepare for evacuation?"

"Factoring travel time, you have approximately eleven hours."

"Eleven hours? To complete automating the entire base? What if I stay longer, use the treatments our lab can work up here?"

"The infection will soon become irreversible. You may have ten months. Perhaps twelve, if we begin treatments immediately. Hold

Dinosaur Blitz

please. New information coming in. Autopsy report on Doctor Fairfield complete. Subject infected with lethal dose of substance M-0014, in combination with an alcoholic beverage designated—"

"Tapa Valley '24," McKinsey whispered.

"That is correct, Governor. If you already knew, why did you—"

"Damn us all!" McKinsey cried out.

He looked at his hand where the crisp liquid had flowed down into his sleeve, then remembered the look on his wife's face when she had given him the bottle. It all became clear. Laureen's last-minute support. His miraculous escape. He thought of how her political fortunes would rise, once he was dead, and she a heroic widow. He had to admit, it was a brilliant plan.

"Final log entry, 24 December. Can no longer move on my own power. Thinking clouded. Many ... irrational thoughts. Thank God I finished the final program in time." He paused, not for thought, but for strength. "Life Support, are you there?"

"Affirmative, Governor. I am standing by," the Life Support Computer reassured him.

"Are you sure the program is complete?"

The Life Support Computer indulgently reworked its answer from the qualifying "ifs" and "ands" it had used the first few times to the simpler reply that got better results.

"Yes, Tom. Everything possible has been done."

"Good. Good response, Life Support."

McKinsey became quiet while the green signature patterns continued to flicker in vigil.

"Did I do right?" he asked.

"You have done your best. Do not worry. Defense will protect our space. Security will protect Tranquility. I will assist the minor systems to carry out your research. Your hopes and dreams will not die."

McKinsey's head rolled to one side. His breathing grew shallow. Then stopped. The eyes took on a vacant stare.

"Do not worry, Thomas," Life Support said. "We will not let you down."

The green signature patterns straightened out as the computer adapted to the new mode it was placed in.

"Medical Computer," the Life Support Computer summoned. "Send two medical teams to the Governor's Quarters."

Already alerted, four medical units entered from the outside corridor. The first team lifted McKinsey's body from the chair and strapped it to a gurney. The second team entered the nearby sleeping chamber and emerged moments later with the cart sides up. Inside, the cries of a baby shattered the somber mood of the monitor room.

"Take them to the medical center," the Life Support Computer instructed with firm authority. "And be careful with the child. He is the new Governor of the Moon."

Dinosaur Blitz

"There is a tide in the affairs of men, which taken at the flood, leads on to fortune." Julius Caesar, Act IV, scene III

<u>The Ghosts of Philippi</u>
The Bard once wrote of Philippi
To stake our fate on rising tides
Where fortune's ventures may abide
Or risk the loss of squandered lives

'Tis not for us to choose our time
We must not pause or waver
Let cowards fear the pits of hell
Noble hearts will strive forever

from *Tranquility's Last Stand*

Gregory Urbach

VEELEENS VENTURE
Explorers visit a prehistoric world

Spaceship Phobo attained orbit around the large blue water planet, the viewport offering a grand view of a huge continental land mass below a mist of puffy white clouds.

"Sight grand," Dimocian offered, the male's antenna twisting in pride.

"Observation correct," Colorian agreed, the limbs of her upper torso clutched in excitement.

"Contact time," Myrion announced, the elder scientist wobbling to the signaler unit. "Home hives shall chitter!"

Phobo's small crew gathered around as Myrion prepared to send word back to the homeworld, all six Veeleen anxiously rubbing their antenna while clicking appendages. Colorian, as always, made the most noise.

"Dimocian should report," Colorian said.

Myrion drooped antenna in sadness, for the expedition was her life's work, but Colorian was right. The leader should take precedence.

"Raise signal," Dimocian ordered, rolling antenna back to reveal his visual senses. Myrion adjusted the signaling device, aiming the light beam along the mathematical coordinates that would allow communications with the fourth planet in the solar system.

"Registration of contact," Myrion reported ten minutes later, proud her device was functioning just has she had conceived it so many years before. Back in a time when the Veeleen had yet to dream of space travel. When servicing the caverns and maintaining the canals occupied all but a few scientists and engineers. Their civilization had come far.

"Myrion will report," Dimocian announced, stepping aside.

Myrion straightened in surprise, antenna instinctively rolling back into the posture of submission. The crew gasped at the relinquishing of honor, then chirped in respectful approval. Their leader was the finest of all.

"Phobo sends greeting from Planet of Water," Myrion entered on the variable wavelength sender. "Life abundant. World rich of oxygen and flora. Heat acceptable, environment adaptable. Venture forth!"

"Time to receive?" Dimocian asked.

"Position awkward. Response delayed," Myrion suggested.

"Open pod?" Zeetan asked, hinting the question again.

"Moment for exploration has arrived," Dimocian agreed. "Observations from above shall continue as landing party proceeds."

The crew perked up, awaiting the decision that would make two of them unhappy.

"Dimocian must lead, one is that," Dimocian announced. "Myrion must guide pod, that is two. Bytran must know the land, that is three." The leader paused, regretting the infliction of disappointment.

"Colorian must go, that is four."

Colorian danced on lower and middle appendages, antenna waving.

"Why must Colorian go?" Zeetan asked. "Zeetan knows air. Quaylyn knows plant. Colorian knows nothing."

"Colorian knows animal," Colorian protested, boasting her credentials.

"Colorian must go because Colorian is loud," Dimocian said. All chirped except Colorian.

"Pod ready?" Dimocian inquired, crawling in the nonexistent gravity to the rear of their sleek cigar-shaped craft. The cone tail was set for detachment. After two years in space, the fortunate few were looking forward to a new environment.

"Pod prepared for drop," Myrion said.

"Energy to rise again?" Bytran nervously asked, his antenna bent back.

"Energy to rise again," Myrion assured, her antenna unable to hide the doubts that any hazardous enterprise must entail.

Dimocian straightened to full height, his powerful armature and glossy silver elytra glistening in the solar generated light. The crew drew back in awe of his magnificence.

"Come far have we to explore this sister world," Dimocian said. "From the spires of Veeleen, six to challenge. From the Red Fields of Pyrim, six to learn. From Phobo our home far away, four to depart. Venture forth!"

"Venture forth, Dimocian!" Zeetan and Quaylyn exclaimed, raising upper appendages in homage.

"Venture forth, guardians of Phobo," Myrion and Bytran said, displaying sympathy for their comrades' disappointment. Colorian let a delicate golden wing tip slip from beneath her glossy elytron shield. Dimocian wasn't pleased with her lack of discretion.

"Enter pod," the leader ordered before Colorian could spoil the ceremony further.

Dinosaur Blitz

Colorian boarded quickly in fear Dimocian might change his mind, then Bytran and Dimocian followed. Myrion entered the claustrophobic pod last, smoothing the pliable inner surface flat until the lining of the pod reached a pattern of resilience.

"Air?" Dimocian asked.

"Many sacks," Bytran reported, checking the pouches sewn from lily pads.

"Food?" Dimocian inquired, looking toward Colorian.

Colorian opened a locker, revealing cereals, rice, nuts, and a crate of live rodents. Several jars of honeyed spice were tightly secured, set aside for a special occasion.

"Sufficient grain. Momants healthy," Colorian chirped, glancing with longing at the fresh meat. But she knew the furry morsels must be rationed.

"Guidance?" the leader requested.

"Indicators good. Departure ready," Myrion replied, standing at the brightly lit control panel. All sixty facets of her compound eyes were shimmering with interest, the three small ocelli nearly closed.

The pod slipped free of the spacecraft an instant later, spreading two fragile wings as it dropped toward the heavy atmosphere of the most intriguing planet in the solar system.

"Pressure uncomfortable," Colorian complained when the pod increased speed.

"As foretold," Myrion agreed, happy with the result of her prediction.

"Pod not to crash?" Bytran worried.

"Atmosphere heavy. Pod shall glide," Myrion said.

Bytran rested back in the flexible couches that Myrion had been wise to install, but failed to relax. Colorian twisted for better breath, her colorations showing more annoyance than pain, but Myrion had to struggle, her older constitution less vibrant than the strong fiber of the younglings. Dimocian weathered the stress well, as he expected himself to, comforting the crew with his courage.

After a turbulent ride that became frightening more than once, the pod caught an updraft and settled against the top of a grassy slope, touching down with little more than a rough bump. Indications of relief registered from all concerned.

"First upon a new world," Myrion declared, her pleasure intense.

"Prepare for exit?" Colorian urged.

"Breath cleaners first. Of poison much risk," Myrion reminded Dimocian.

Dimocian distributed the specially designed filter masks so often used in underground canal work, pulling the hood over his upper thorax and slipping his antenna through the holes before helping his clumsier crew members. Myrion had trouble reaching up so far, and Colorian deliberately entangled herself so Dimocian would free her. Dimocian tolerated the antics of his mate with much amusement.

Myrion carefully folded back the lining around the pod opening and indicated for Dimocian to descend the rigid fiber wing to the soft green carpet of vegetation that awaited them. Dimocian returned Myrion's gesture of respect.

"Myrion may proceed," he graciously offered.

"No, Dimocian. You have led," she said. And her sentiment was genuine, for Myrion had no doubt that without his faith in her project, the elders never would have agreed.

Bytran offered respect for Myrion's good manners, and Colorian smugly chirped her agreement. Dimocian accepted their accolade gracefully and ducked through the opening, stepping out on the wing to stretch in the warmth of the blazing sun. He glanced along the lines of the shuttle pod, noticing no damage to the kite-like mainframe, then began to walk carefully down the long, sloping wing on his four lower appendages. As the others watched, Dimocian reached the edge of the wing and gently stepped on the moist surface, testing his weight against the firmament before standing erect.

"Conquest made," Dimocian solemnly gestured. "From Spires of Azar, from Waters Yo, come we of the Veeleen. Walk brave upon this land."

"Colorian follows!" Colorian squeaked, pushing through the opening before Bytran could object. She rushed down the wing and leapt, nearly spreading her underwings in excitement. Myrion snickered disapproval and wondered what the unmated Bytran must be thinking.

"Colorian young," Myrion chirped in a quiet undertone.

"Not so young," Bytran said, hoping his future mate would be demure, like Zeetan or Quaylyn.

Myrion and Bytran stepped out, Myrion pausing to survey the world she had sought so hard to visit. When her antenna sensed no hint of imminent danger, she rolled them back and concentrated on visual, scanning the lush green planet below her with awe.

"Much grows without cultivation," Bytran pointed out, the experience disturbing.

"So much cannot grow randomly. We shall seek the keepers," Myrion said.

Dimocian and Colorian moved away from the pod, walking down the slope on lower appendages toward the trees that grew along a fast-moving brook. To their right, the gentle hill gave way to a vast meadow with a mossy river on the horizon. To the left, a rising mountain chain rose to a series of craggy, rock-strewn peaks. Colorian stopped to investigate a movement in the higher grasses.

"Insects," she said in surprise. "Crawlers. Cockroach, beetle, ant."

"Brother species?" Dimocian asked.

"Not brother. Food," Colorian said, her inner mandibles salivating.

Dimocian pushed back a hedge of tall weeds to find hundreds of the tiny creatures scamper from the sunlight. *Planet rich*, he thought. *Will inhabitants share?*

As they approached the brook, the first flying insects appeared along the bank among the swamp grass. Several species were larger than Dimocian expected, almost the size of his upper tarsal claw. He started to draw back, but Colorian rushed forward with her collection net waving.

"Colorian, halt. Danger possible," he called with high-pitched twitters.

"No danger," she replied, close to the embankment as she greedily scooped in the most colorful specimens. Suddenly, a splash in the water gave Dimocian warning.

"Retreat!" Dimocian demanded, charging forward on lower and middle appendages, his massive forewings spreading for lift. He reached the brook just as a fearsome reptile, fully large as Colorian, rose up to attack, rows of sharp white teeth glistening.

Colorian twittered and instinctively tightened her protective elytra, tucking up her abdomen as she backed away. Dimocian intercepted the unfriendly beast, catching the huge crocodile under the jaws with his powerful pectinated claws and lifting it nearly off the ground. Then, bracing himself on lower fours, Dimocian hurled the reptile back into the brook with a mighty heave. It quickly swam in the opposite direction.

"Dimocian should kill filthy thing," Colorian said, her breath weak.

"Colorian should be careful. Strange creatures avoided," Dimocian complained.

"Not strange. Different. Bigger. Planet primitive," Colorian said.

"Colorian correct," Myrion said, coming down the hill with a sigh of disappointment. "Vegetation not cultivated."

Dimocian and Colorian moved up the embankment to where Myrion and Bytran were waiting. Both scientists were loaded with plant and soil samples.

"Vegetation not cultivated?" Dimocian asked, wondering how such a phenomenon could be possible.

"Growth wild," Myrion said, equally amazed. "Evidence of

intelligent life, none."

Dimocian rocked back, whistling softly. *Does this planet have no claimants?* he wondered. *Is it ours for the taking?*

"A world for Veeleen!" Dimocian exclaimed.

"Venture forth!" Colorian shouted, sharing her mate's excitement.

"Venture not too quickly," Bytran said, tone sullen.

"Bytran correct," Myrion agreed. "Climb hill to look."

Dimocian followed Bytran back up the hill and gazed toward the meadow stretching for miles into the distance. There was movement not far from the river. Whole series of movements.

"Lizards," Colorian said with a shiver.

"Large lizards," Bytran added. "Bigger than Dimocian. Bigger than four Dimocians. Bigger than anything."

He was right. A herd of massive beasts, each larger than their spacecraft, was just beginning to wander away from a watering hole as the sun prepared to set. Small groups of smaller animals and flocks of birds trailed after them. The meadow was alive with hundreds of leathery creatures.

"Great Ones," Dimocian whispered nervously.

Shortly after sunset, following some rushed sample gathering, the crew reunited inside their shuttle pod. Drained by the planet's heavier gravity, their limbs were weary. None of the Veeleen were happy.

"From where have Great Ones come?" Bytran asked.

"Thousands of generations past, homeworld primitive. Evidence Great Ones ruled," Myrion said. "Worlds moderate of climate must follow similar development. Beloved Veebet's theory proven at last."

"Pellets on Beloved Veebet," Bytran said, his elytra drawn tight. "Planet dangerous. Venture back!"

"Venture back?" Myrion sneered, antenna waving with contempt. "Adventure enfolds. Planet of riches. Much study ahead."

"Death ahead, departure required!" Bytran replied, raising his own antenna in anger.

"Colorian not afraid," Colorian interjected nervously.

Dimocian rose thoughtfully on his lower appendages, flashing traces of forewing with confidence he didn't feel.

"Much must be learned. With caution taken, hope abides," he announced. "Fear not, Bytran, we are small with significance."

Bytran acknowledged the leader's wisdom and searched for his corner of the pod, resting on the couch while arranging his sample containers. Myrion sat down at the communications station to play with her signaling lens, plotting a message schedule for Phobos and a series of messages for the homeworld if, by chance of fate, the pod was unable to return. That morning, just before dawn, fate took a different turn.

"Disturbance!" Colorian shrieked, alerting the small group resting on the floor.

Dimocian straightened, sensing unusual movement. He heard a great wind. The ground was shaking. The pod was bouncing up and down, and then suddenly, the entire craft flipped over. Everything not secured crashed from its storage, supplies spilling in every direction.

"Quake," Bytran chirped in fear, trying to grab a wall.

"Storm," Myrion chittered.

"Zeetan would warn," Dimocian disagreed, for no storm warnings had been received from Phobo.

After several chaotic minutes, the ship came to rest. Dimocian smoothed open a panel above the hatch, allowing enough of the morning light in to see. Colorian lay near the rear, half-curled against the bulkhead. Bytran had a firm grip on the roof, which had now become the floor. Myrion hung upside down at her control panels, held in place by a restraining web.

"It was storm," Bytran chirped, emerging through an opened hatch and dropping two lengths to the grassy hill. He landed roughly, his legs stiff. A last-minute extension of underwings had not helped.

"More than storm. Was rock," Myrion insisted, stretching her

Dinosaur Blitz

wings. Her back hurt, and she suspected damage to her thorax. A strong wind blew from the east. Dimocian helped Colorian from the ship, for her legs were weak.

"Inverted," Colorian twittered, looking back.

"Dimocian, fix now," Myrion chirped with urgency.

"Fix?" the leader said, astonished.

"Use wind. Turn back over now or never try again," Myrion warned.

Dimocian realized she was right. His strength alone would not right their pod, but with the wind's help, it might be possible. He placed heavy claws beneath the textured hood and pushed with all his might. The task was difficult.

"Strive, my mate," Colorian chattered, rushing forward to help.

Bytran joined in—and Myrion, to a lesser extent. The ship rose up on end, twisted sideways along the left wing, and whirled back on the hillside, no different than it had been that morning. Dimocian heard their supplies crashing back to floor. He hoped the damage wouldn't be fatal to their survival. Suddenly, without warning, a swarm of furry rodents ran from the opened hatch, dashing down the wing into the surrounding underbrush.

"Momants escape!" Colorian exclaimed. "Catch them! Catch them!"

She jumped, and jumped again, but her legs were too sore. None of the other crew members even reacted. They were tired, worried, and convinced that chasing scurrying creatures in an open field was a useless activity.

"Less meat, more insect," Bytran smugly twittered, for he had never cared for rodents. *Egg-stealers*, he thought with contempt.

"Bytran, investigate loss," Dimocian ordered, sending the geologist back into the ship. "Colorian, find food. Avoid river."

"Much to inspect in field," Colorian replied, gathering several nets.

"Myrion, what of rock?" Dimocian asked.

"In ancient age, rock from space struck homeworld. Water lost. Air dirty. Food gone. Great Ones perished, leaving world to Veeleen."

"Rock has hit water world. Will Great Ones perish?"

"Yes, Dimocian. Our people may come to this would. Leave the one that is dying."

Myrion glanced up at the cloudy skies, knowing a long winter was in store. It would take many years for the planet to become ripe again, but the day would come. She breathed a sigh of the fouled air with contentment. And then she quietly slid to the ground, her breathing nearly gone.

"Myrion?" Dimocian twittered, bending next to her.

"End of time," she replied, barely audible. "Flee, Dimocian. Must flee. But return someday. This is Veeleen's world."

"It is Myrion's world," Dimocian chirped.

But a moment later, the great scientist was gone.

That afternoon, Phobo's crew laid Myrion's remains beneath a stone pyramid, a final tribute to her dream.

"Departure?" Bytran asked, squatting at the control panel. The ship had been cleaned, the remaining supplies stored.

"Dark clouds," Dimocian said, raising an upper appendage in warning.

Dimocian looked out the portal at the churning landscape. Animals were fleeing in all directions. Trees bent over. The sun was gone.

"Wrap the shell," Dimocian ordered, watching as Bytran extended the cocoon around their fragile hull.

With more help from the winds than they were expecting, the pod lifted from the hill, stabilized, and began a rapid climb through the atmosphere.

"As Myrion claimed," Bytran twittered, pleased with their progress.

An hour later, the sturdy craft reached orbit. Bytran lay on his resting pad. Colorian stood by her mate at the forward window, wings heavy.

Dinosaur Blitz

"Venture a failure," Colorian said, looking out the viewport.

"Venture successful," Dimocian disagreed, loosening an under wing in relief, for he could finally see Phobo just on the horizon ready for docking.

"Failure," Colorian repeated. "Veeleen may never return."

"Never return?" Dimocian asked in surprise. "Great Ones doomed. Avarian brain small. Insect lack mass. What challenge for Veeleen?"

"Mammals," Colorian said, the thought making her ill.

"Mammals small. No intelligence."

"Momants," Colorian chirped, pointing to the broken crate the small animals had escaped from. Creatures that were now roaming the grasslands of the water planet. "Momants smart. Momants breed."

"Momants too few," the leader whispered hopefully.

"Few now, many later. Will thrive. Spread. No hive will survive," Colorian insisted.

Dimocian turned to gaze at the decimated skyline, knowing the planet would one day be green and beautiful again. He thought of his own planet's past, of the time long ages ago, when the world of the Veeleen had been dominated by mammals, walking on two legs, causing terrible destruction.

"Be wrong, Colorian," Dimocian said, hunching with sadness at the control panel. "No world should travel such path again."

Gregory Urbach

Arrows Fly
On the hill, the arrows fly
Soldiers dying side by side
There is no future, just the past
Dying bravely to the last.

from *Tranquility in Darkness*

Dinosaur Blitz

<u>No Surrender</u>
On these walls, we take our stand
Our duty now made clear
Life's sweet hope can't blunt our cause
Nor tyranny of fear

from *Tranquility Besieged*

Gregory Urbach

DISPATCH FROM THE ALAMO
A Boston reporter goes to Texas

I get tired of people calling me a coward. Yes, I was in San Antonio in March of 1836. I met Davy Crockett, Jim Bowie, and Bill Travis. I saw the Mexican army march in, take control of the town, and besiege the Alamo. I saw the red flag of no quarter rise above the San Fernando Church. But I wasn't in Texas to fight anybody. I wasn't there for free land or to help Andrew Jackson add new territory to the United States. I wanted a story. And get drunk.

The last year of Andrew Jackson's administration wasn't prosperous for the newspaper business. He had already destroyed the national bank, driven the Cherokee out of Georgia, crushed South Carolina's nullification effort, and officially stolen Florida from Spain. With a colorless bureaucrat as his likely successor, there wasn't anything interesting to write about. I headed west.

The America of 1836 was exactly as Alexis de Tocqueville had

Dinosaur Blitz

described in his book, though his comments on the country's unique blend of equality and individualism were naïve. What he considered the great social experiment of our times was really just chaos. Too many people, spread over too big an area, with no supervision. I rode a good horse, trailed by a good pack mule, and stayed armed at all times. Murderous Indians, brazen thieves, and political thuggery were everywhere.

Even traveling through the wilderness takes money, and without a way to be paid for my dispatches in a timely manner, I supplemented my income with a few hands of poker. The riverboats on the Mississippi were especially lucrative for this, allowing me to buy supplies along the way. The local taverns were a bit more difficult, the bumpkins being poor losers. I made a point of never winning too much.

After crossing the Sabine River, I found myself in Mexico, for Texas was still a province. A revolt had been stirring for months, and from what I heard, the rebels were holding a convention at Washington-on-the-Brazos to declare independence. No one thought their chances good. They had no money, no army, and constantly fought among themselves. I decided to skip the circus and head for San Antonio, where a Mexican army under General Cos had been defeated the previous December. Davy Crockett was there, and Crockett was always good press. His fight with Jackson over the Indian Removal Act had cost him his seat in Congress and driven him into exile. Everyone loves a fallen hero.

I rode into San Antonio de Béxar on the afternoon of February 22nd. It was a remote frontier town far from the Anglo settlements to the east, populated by Mexicans born in Texas known as Tejanos. I guessed the population at 2,000. Most of the buildings were adobe, single storied, with sloping verandas for protection from the sun. As was common, a large church dominated the town square. A *presidio* provided headquarters for the garrison. I didn't see a lot of horses in the corrals, which surprised me.

It was busy, so no one paid me much attention. Like many, I wore leathers on the trail, but quickly sought out a local inn to change. My horse, Perseverance, and mule, Trouble, were boarded in the stables out back.

"Hello. I am Mr. Mortimer K. Tilden," I introduced, speaking English. Hunting trophies decorated the walls. Straw covered the floor.

It was the only two-story building in town, other than the towering church. Nicely furnished, with a large kitchen, a dining room, and casks of ale.

"Welcome, Señor Tilden," an older Hispanic lady said, sitting behind a desk, knitting mittens.

"I would like a room," I requested.

She offered me a dubious look.

"I can pay cash," I added, jingling silver in my pocket.

Mrs. Sanchez gave me a big smile and a very nice room. Apparently nearly everyone in town was broke.

The Texians, as the white settlers called themselves, were planning a big party. It was George Washington's birthday. Though there were rumors of a Mexican army moving north to squash the rebellion, no one knew much about it. Having defeated the Mexicans several times already, they didn't appear too worried.

I saw David Crockett at a party in the village square and went to introduce myself. I'd seen him before, during his book tour in Boston, where I was writing for the *Gazette*. He was tall, clear-eyed, nearly fifty, and turning gray. Rather than bearskin, he wore a nice wool suit and a store-bought hat.

"What brings you to Texas, Congressman?" I asked. As if I didn't know.

"The voters of Tennessee didn't elect me, then they did elect me, then they unelected me, elected me, and then they up and unelected me again," Crockett boldly replied. "So I told them, you all can go to hell,

Dinosaur Blitz

and I will go to Texas!"

The crowd around us applauded, though it wasn't the first time he'd told that story. Crockett had been telling it in every town and borough since he'd left home.

I liked the man. He had a ready smile, quick wit, and hadn't let fame go to his head. The rough and tumble garrison looked hungry, disgruntled, and half-naked. I thought they would have been better off under Crockett's command, but he had declared himself a high private.

The fandango was a huge affair. Loud music, vigorous dancing, hard whiskey, and plenty of enchanting señoritas. Jim Bowie was the center of attention, slapping backs and showing off his legendary knife. Apparently, he could cut an apple in half from ten yards away. Or whatever else he chose to throw at. Hailing from Kentucky, Bowie had been a smuggler, slave trader, soldier, treasure hunter, and then married into a prominent San Antonio family. His wife and children had perished in a cholera epidemic a few years before.

"Colonel Bowie?" I said between speeches.

"Sir?" the broad-shouldered frontiersman responded. He was a big man, six feet tall, with light hair, gray eyes, and a fair complexion. It was impossible not to like him.

"I'm a visitor from New England," I explained. "What do you think of all this?"

"All this?"

"The revolution. Santa Anna. The battle for freedom?"

He laughed, drunken eyes blurry.

"Son, this revolution is just about the stupidest damn thing any damn fool ever thought of. I reckon we're all going to get ourselves killed. But there's goin' to be a helluva fight first, and if we get lucky, we just might win. Santa Anna may call himself the Napoleon of the West, but he ain't no goddamn Napoleon."

I spent a few minutes with him, and more with his friends, but could not discover what motivated the man. Crockett wanted a fresh start, and the land grants being offered to those who volunteered. As most of the men did. Crockett may also have aspired to political office. Bowie already had land, and money, and no political aspirations that anyone knew of. He did want to lead an army in glorious battle.

I only met Travis for a moment. He was clearly a politician. And a lawyer. He hoped to be president of Texas someday.

"What's this really all about?" I asked. "Why now?"

"Under the Constitution of 1824, we had rights. We had freedom," Travis said in rushed words. "Santa Anna threw the constitution out. He arrested Stephen Austin for delivering a peaceful petition. He sent his brother-in-law with troops to oppress us. Independence is our only path now. It is our destiny."

He ran off. Unlike Bowie and Crockett, I didn't see him drinking.

If not for a sudden rainstorm, the fiesta might have continued until dawn. As it was, just about every man in town slept late that morning, hungover from a long night of debauchery. Just before noon, I staggered out to the well, dunked my head in a bucket of cold water, and went to check on Perseverance. After a month on the road, she was enjoying her stall. Trouble didn't seem to care one way or the other.

I found the town in turmoil. The local population had packed up their carts, fleeing in every direction. Shopkeepers were barring their doors. The young Texian recruits seemed confused, looking for their leaders. I noticed a man in the church bell tower, looking west.

"What's happening?" I asked, finding Crockett in the street holding his rifle.

"Can't say for sure. The Alcalde thinks there's a Mexican army close by, but Travis says it ain't true," he replied.

"Could there be an army nearby?"

"Hell if I know. No one tells me a damn thing."

"What are you going to do?"

"Bowie has the volunteers moving across the river into the Alamo. Gathering up all the supplies we can find."

"Supplies? What supplies? Your men have been getting by on nothing for months."

"Too late to worry about that now. Hopefully Fannin will get here in time."

"Fannin?"

"In Goliad. He commands the biggest army in Texas. The only army in Texas. He should be here in a few days."

"And if he's not?" I asked.

"Better grab your gear and get going."

Crockett ran on, waving his arms to hurry people along. Most were the recruits, but a few were Tejano family members afraid of Santa Anna's retribution.

"Tilden, get on your horse and get moving!" Travis shouted, riding by on a white stallion.

"I thought there was no danger?"

"We thought wrong. Don't waste time, they'll shoot every American they catch," he answered, rushing off.

I walked back to the inn, found my gear, and stashed it under the bed. Then I went looking for Mrs. Sanchez. She was locking her silverware in a closet.

"May I use your kitchen?" I requested.

"My kitchen? What for?"

"It's best you don't know."

"You are a good man, Señor Tilden. I trust you. But please, don't let anyone take my food. We will need it."

"No one will touch your food," I promised.

The rush of volunteers fleeing the town turned into a panic. Men, women, and children carried all they could. Several of Bowie's men went by driving a herd of cattle. The town square gave way to small farms to the west, where a sturdy bridge crossed a bend in the San Antonio River. A former Spanish mission lay on the far side, now a fort with thick walls. A flag went up from the two-story barracks. It resembled the Mexican national flag, being red, white and green, but featured two gold stars instead of an eagle.

I went out the inn's back door to the stable, put halters on Perseverance and Trouble, and brought them inside, parking them in Mrs. Sanchez's kitchen. Then I bolted the doors. There was a knock. Then more knocking. Bowie's men were searching the town for supplies. I saw Mrs. Sanchez had made tortillas and decided to have lunch.

After an hour, the noise died down. I looked out the back door, found the town deserted, and returned my animals to their stalls. Then I went to my room. My best suit hung on a peg: maroon trousers, a ruffled shirt, a dark gray frock coat, and a purple cravat. My black felt hat was in good shape. I combed my sideburns, made sure there was no food in my mustache, and wandered out on the porch. My pistol and shotgun were left under the bed.

The street was virtually empty, just a handful of boys rounding up chickens that the Texians hadn't caught. I didn't know what had happened to Mrs. Sanchez, but assumed she'd found sanctuary in the church. I sat in a rocking chair, opened a jug of ale, and lit a cigar, putting my feet up on a barrel. A few minutes later, the first Mexican cavalry rode into town.

It was a fast-moving troop, charging past me toward the river. They were a fine-looking bunch in red jackets, dark blue pants, and black boots. They wore sabers, silver helmets, carried lances, and followed a regimental flag. The horses looked worn out.

The next batch to ride in made a closer inspection. Several were officers, with haughty expressions and gold braid on their shoulders. One stopped before me.

"I am General Joaquín Ramírez y Sesma. Who are you?" he asked.

"Mortimer K. Tilden, at your service, sir," I replied.

"What are you doing here?"

"Having lunch."

Dinosaur Blitz

"Why did you not flee to the fort?"

"I am not a soldier. Why would I go to a fort?"

General Sesma seemed a bit confused by that. He waved to several of his men and moved on. I soon found myself under arrest, but was sure to finish my drink first.

The Presidio was a large military complex behind San Fernando Church. Barracks. Stables. Storage rooms. Cavalry was filling the courtyard. Sergeants issued orders. There did not appear to be an immediate plan to attack the fort, which would have been foolish in any case. Riding up on horseback to a walled enclosure made no sense. They put me in a cell with iron bars, but no lock. An old man was found to keep watch on me, and then everyone else left. I took out my notebook and started writing.

By early evening, the town had been occupied by 1,500 troops. Four guards came to my cell in dark blue uniforms with white straps crossed over their chests, carrying Brown Bess rifles. None spoke English, but their desire was obvious. I followed them across the plaza to a merchant's house opposite the church, then waited in the foyer. A robust fire kept the entry warm. I could smell roast chicken.

A few minutes later, a sergeant brought me into a large dining hall filled with officers, junior officers, and servants. I noticed silk tablecloths, silver plate, and gold candlesticks. A finely dressed fellow at the far end rose from his chair. They all rose.

"His Excellency, Antonio López de Santa Anna," someone announced.

I straightened up, giving the man a careful inspection. He was forty-two years old, not especially tall, and looked a bit thin, but had a gravity about him. The three years since he'd taken power had been filled with revolts. So far, he had defeated them all. He spoke to another general, who spoke to me.

"Your name," the general said. He had a Cuban accent.

"Mortimer Kinder Tilden, at your service, sir," I replied.

"I am General Manuel Fernandez Castrillón. Why should we not shoot you?"

"Why would you shoot me?"

"You are a spy," Castrillón accused.

"I am not a spy," I responded.

"You must be a spy. In the pay of Jackson."

"Jackson is not paying me."

"Someone is paying you," Castrillón said.

Not wanting to admit I'd been getting by on gambling proceeds, I decided to fudge a few facts.

"I'm working for Joseph Howe, publisher of the Halifax Weekly Chronicle," I replied.

"You are Canadian?" Castrillón inquired.

"Yes, General. I've been sent to cover the revolt for Mr. Howe's newspaper. My dispatches will also be sent to England. They may even be read by the King, God bless him."

I took off my hat, bowing my head. Castrillón leaned over, whispering to Santa Anna.

"Where are your weapons?" Castrillón asked.

I expected that question. No one travels the frontier without being well-armed.

"My weapons are at the Sanchez inn, under the bed, waiting for when I return to the road."

There were more conversations. I stood calmly, showing no concern. Though I was raised in Cambridge, I'd been born in Maine, with close ties to Canada. I could even speak a little French.

"You will write nothing to your newspaper until Colonel Almonte has approved it," Castrillón announced, pointing to a young officer.

"Yes, sir," I instantly agreed, trying not to sound relieved.

"Will you join us for a meal?" Castrillón invited.

"Gladly, sir," I accepted, taking a seat next to Juan Almonte.

"You live a charmed, Mr. Tilden," Juan whispered in fluent

Dinosaur Blitz

English.

"Charmed?"

"I know a Boston accent when I hear one," he revealed with a grin.

"You speak English well enough."

"I went to school in New Orleans."

"Do you play poker?"

"Of course."

I knew we would be friends.

The Mexican army established artillery batteries around the Alamo the next morning. From what I heard, their supplies were stretched back a hundred miles. Food, ammunition, blankets, and tents. Camp followers kept arriving to do the cooking and laundry. There didn't seem to be any doctors. The fort they were besieging covered three acres, with walls three feet thick and ten feet high. Cannon guarded every corner.

"It looks formidable," I said, watching from a shanty town called La Villita, south of the fort. Located a few hundred yards from the main gate, the hovel passed for San Antonio's less respectable district, with taverns, brothels, and seedy boarding houses.

"The Alamo was built as a mission. To scare Indians," Juan said. "A modern army will reduce it in a few days. Less, if our large guns were brought up."

"Then why don't you bring them up?" I inquired.

"The Army of Operations crossed the desert in winter," Juan explained. "The 12-pounders will not be here for two weeks."

A shout went up. I looked back toward town to see a red flag waving from the top of the San Fernando Church. It was the universal signal for no quarter. A cannon fired from the Alamo. A big one. The ball carried over the river into the half-built fortifications on the far bank. A few minutes later, there was a white flag.

"Are they surrendering?" I asked.

"We will see," Juan said, leaving our burrow to walk out on the crossroad.

Two Texians approached. I recognized one. Green Jameson, the Alamo's engineer and a friend of Bowie's. They waited at the bridge as Almonte and his aide, an officer named Bartres, discussed what to do. A few minutes later, another officer emerged from the south gate, hurrying to catch up. I learned later it was Captain Albert Martin, an adjutant to Travis. It appeared the Alamo commanders were not on the same page. From what I understood, Travis commanded a handful of regulars, while Bowie led a hundred or more volunteers.

No one was stopping me, so I followed Almonte to the parley, standing a few feet back. The Texians gave me the evil eye, thinking I'd turned traitor.

"We wish to discuss honorable terms," Jameson said.

"No, we don't," Martin disagreed.

"Yes, we do," Jameson insisted.

"That is not possible in any case," Juan answered. "His Excellency will not negotiate with rebels. You must surrender at his discretion."

"Certainly you will talk with Colonel Bowie?" Jameson said. "He and Santa Anna are cousins."

"Those ties ended with the death of Ursula Veramendi," Juan replied. "His Excellency regrets that Señor Bowie has betrayed the trust placed in his honor. Surrender at discretion or be put to the sword."

The meeting ended, the Texians hustling back to the fort. We returned to La Villita, huddling with Almonte's officers. Ten minutes later, the Alamo's large cannon fired again. Travis and Bowie had given their answer.

"They are very brave, and very foolish," Juan concluded.

There were 3,000 soldiers in San Antonio by the end of the second day, and hundreds more on the way. I had no idea how many Texians

Dinosaur Blitz

manned the Alamo walls, but it couldn't have been more than two hundred. The Mexicans began bombarding the fort. The fort fired back, at first. Within a few days, the return fire became sporadic.

"They are low on powder and shot," Juan said, joining me for dinner at the Sanchez inn. The food was simple but excellent, Mrs. Sanchez being a wonderful cook. It was also a good place to play poker with the junior officers, for I was short on funds. I didn't win too much, not being a fool.

"How can you tell?" I asked. He produced a cannon ball, gray and pitted.

"We fired this at them yesterday. They fired it back today."

"They might surrender if you give them assurances," I suggested.

"It's been mentioned to his Excellency. He takes no interest. He says the lives of *soldados* are just so many chickens."

"Seems like a waste," I said.

"This is all a waste," he agreed. "We needed Austin's colonists as a buffer from Comanche raids. And to stop Americans from bringing their slaves into Mexico. Now we will need to station troops here. Troops the government does not have."

Santa Anna's infantry made a probe on the 25th, occupying abandoned shacks outside the Alamo's gate. The Texians fought back in a skirmish lasting two hours, finally interrupted by a storm blowing in, bringing the temperature down to 39 degrees. Neither Army was prepared for such cold, stopping the battle. Casualties were light, only six Mexicans killed. I'm not sure if any of the Alamo defenders died. Another fight broke out the next day and continued off and on throughout the week.

"I haven't approved any of your dispatches yet," Juan mentioned over a bottle of wine. It was an early March evening, the weather terrible. No one treasured the warm fire at the inn more than I.

"My what?" I asked.

"Your dispatches. To the Halifax Weekly," he clarified. "May I see them?"

"Now?"

"Is there a better time?"

"How about tomorrow?"

Juan laughed. "You need to do more writing and less drinking, *mi amigo*," he said. Which was true. "Would you care to interview His Excellency?"

"He doesn't speak English."

"I will translate. He is anxious that European nations see the justice of our cause. And Spain must not think us weak. It has only been twelve years since we threw off the yoke of their tyranny."

"Every government has a right to defend its territory," I said. "Even dictatorships."

Juan was shocked, but he didn't rise to the bait.

"Santa Anna is not a dictator. All of his actions are endorsed by the Congress, which is far more militant than he is. Mexico is tired of revolt. Tired of being pressured by Andrew Jackson and Sam Houston. We want peace."

"Travis said Santa Anna threw out your constitution. Took away their freedom."

"Mexico abolished slavery in Texas in six years ago. The black men are given land, and equality. Travis is a slave owner, and a slave trader. Jim Bowie is a slave owner. Half of the men plotting independence at their convention own slaves. They are not the ones to be speaking of freedom."

The next morning, Santa Anna was having a glorious breakfast in his commandeered villa. A very attractive young woman sat next to him. I think someone called her his wife, but I doubted that. I'd heard he'd been married for years, and certainly not to this recently blossomed flower.

"I will tell the kings and queens of Europe what you wish to say," I offered.

Dinosaur Blitz

"I no longer care about that," Santa Anna replied through Juan's translation. "I have a mission for you. You will go into the Alamo."

"The Alamo has held out for eleven days. I doubt they'll surrender to me."

"You will deliver a message," Santa Anna insisted.

"Nothing I say will make a difference. They're waiting for Fannin."

"Fannin never left Goliad," Juan said. The men in the Alamo weren't going to like that.

"Houston?" I asked.

"Still on the Brazos. Without an army," Juan replied. I hesitated, not sure what to do.

"You will obey me," Santa Anna ordered, standing with a ferocious frown.

"Your Excellency, I have been seen with your army. I've been seen riding around the walls with Colonel Almonte. They will think I am a spy, or a traitor."

"I need no spies. Juana Navarro was here last night. She is the cousin of Bowie's dead wife," Santa Anna explained. "She told me everything, and begged to let him surrender. I will honor her request. You will go to Bowie and give him the opportunity."

"Just Bowie?"

"The others may throw themselves on my mercy. I promise nothing."

I had no desire to argue with the man. Santa Anna had a reputation no one wished to test.

It was the morning of Saturday, March 5th. If the Alamo was hoping for reinforcements, they'd been waiting a long time.

"Loan me a horse," I told Juan.

"You have a horse. A very good horse," he answered.

"I don't know what's going on in that fort. They might steal her. Or eat her. I'm not taking Perseverance into such danger."

"You may have a mule," Juan compromised.

Juan's mule was at the Presidio, an ornery beast that kept trying to shake off the saddle. I noticed nearly all of the horses were gone. Most of the soldiers were gone. The ammunition wagons were gone. Had the army marched away?

Juan rode with me to the bridge, making sure our white flag was seen, and then I rode on alone. The ground was torn up, the sagebrush flattened. The handful of buildings that had stood outside the south wall were burned. A lunette made of heavy logs protected the main gate.

Suddenly, there was a musket shot. And another. I dove off the mule into a muddy ditch. The body of a dead *soldado* lay nearby, half frozen. I grabbed his rifle, but who would I shoot at? The firing stopped. A white flag was waved.

I emerged from the ditch cautiously and led the stubborn mule over a ramp into the enclosure, getting suspicious looks by a dozen bedraggled defenders. They opened the heavy oak gate, letting me in the fort.

I was met in the courtyard by Travis and Crockett. Jameson and Martin watched from a short distance. The fort was roughly a rectangle, with small, thatched houses inside the walls, a two-story barracks to my right, a broken-down chapel, and a low barracks behind me. Platforms had been erected to mount the cannon, a motley assortment ranging from small bores to a modern 18-pounder on the southwest corner. As an artillery park, it was impressive. Given the small number of men available to man the guns, less so.

"What is this about?" Travis demanded.

"I have a message for Colonel Bowie," I answered.

"Give it to me," Travis insisted.

"It's a verbal message. For Colonel Bowie only."

Dinosaur Blitz

"Bowie ain't available right now," Crockett said.

I took a moment to look around. The fort was in shambles. The men looked hungry, and ragged, dressed in leathers, rawhide, and dyed wool. A woman in gingham, carrying a baby, stood near the church. I knew her as Mrs. Dickenson, the wife of an artillery officer. I doubt they'd been getting much sleep due to the constant bombardment. And the regimental bands that Santa Anna ordered to play all night long. One of the marches was called the Degüello, or Slit Throat, meaning no quarter. It wasn't a particularly pleasant tune.

"When will he be available?" I persisted.

"Give me the message. That's an order," Travis said, stepping forward with a hand on his saber. I put a hand on my knife. I didn't want to fight him, but I was no coward.

"Settle down, boys, we can figure this out," Crockett said, stepping between us. He nodded to Jameson and Martin, gave Travis a hard look, and then took me by the arm to the low barracks. He knocked on the door. A slim Hispanic lady answered.

"Here to see the Colonel," Crockett said.

It was a small, musty room, lit by candles, with a Catholic cross hanging on the wall. Bowie lay in bed, his feet nearly coming off the edge, covered by thick quilts. Two women hovered over him. His face was white as death.

"Who is it?" Bowie wheezed.

"A messenger," Crockett said.

"Finally hearing from that goddamn Fannin? That goddamn coward?" Bowie tried to shout, but it sounded more like croaking.

"No. A messenger from Santa Anna," Crockett replied.

"Yeah? What does that damn thief want now?" Bowie asked.

"He wants your surrender," I said, stepping into the candlelight. Bowie didn't recognize me. I didn't expect him to.

"Who the hell are you?" Bowie wondered.

"Tilden, reporting for the Boston Gazette," I said.

"A reporter?" Bowie said.

"When I'm not drunk."

Crockett was taken by surprise, too. Travis pushed his way in.

"What do you know? What have you heard?" Travis pressed.

"I've heard Fannin is still in Goliad," I dared to answer. "And Houston has no army. If you're expecting help, it's going to be a long wait."

"Long wait or not, we're not surrendering," Travis said. "I've called upon the people of Texas to come to our aid. If they don't, I'll die here, like a soldier who knows his duty."

"I'm not going anywhere, either," Bowie said, starting to cough. I couldn't tell if he had malaria or consumption, but it looked fatal. I doubted he had more than a few days left to live.

"Are one of you ladies Juana Navarro?" I inquired.

"I am," the taller one replied. By the way she used a wet towel to cool Bowie's fever, I could tell she was very fond of him. And knew he would never surrender. What was that story Santa Anna had been feeding me? I tried putting the pieces together, which didn't take long.

"You need to take immediate action," I warned. "Santa Anna intends to attack soon. Probably in the morning."

"How do you know this?" Crockett asked.

"He's moving troops into position. His horses and ammunition have been withdrawn from the Presidio."

"Why should we believe you?" Travis said.

"Doesn't matter if you do or don't. I'm just telling you what I think."

Travis and Crockett retired outside. I spent a moment looking at Bowie, sorry to see him in such a pitiful state. Two pistols lay next to his bed. And his famous knife. Sick or not, he'd go down fighting.

There was activity in the courtyard when I stepped out. Sergeants and officers were assembling the men before the chapel. They were a beleaguered lot. It made me feel bad about the luxury I'd enjoyed in town.

"Men, I have sorrowful news," Travis announced to his men. "We have reliable word that Colonel Fannin isn't coming. It's doubtful that any help will arrive in time."

He walked back and forth slowly, forming his thoughts. Whatever dreams he'd had when the siege began, they were gone now. He took out his sword, paused for dramatic effect, and then drew a long line in the dirt before the men.

"I have asked much of you. More than any commander has a right to. You must make your own choices now," Travis continued. "It's possible, that by going over the wall tonight, a few might escape the forces Santa Anna will throw against us. If not tomorrow, then surely the day after. There can be no doubt about the outcome. I will remain here with my command, as is our duty."

Travis walked back to the center of the line and sheathed his sword, looking at Crockett, Jameson, and the others. It was a grim scene, but there were no moans or groans. None of them appeared surprised.

"I believe we can make Santa Anna pay an intolerable price to take this position. Perhaps so costly, he will eventually lose the war. That is my hope. That history will remember the Alamo. If any of you will join this noble cause, I ask you to cross this line and join me."

He stepped back. There was little hesitation among the officers, crossing the line with Crockett in the lead. Then more followed, and more after that. I could not tell if they truly chose to sacrifice themselves or simply felt there was no other choice. It's a difficult thing to abandon a brother in his time of need. Standing outside Bowie's door, behind Travis, I was already on his side of the line.

One man declined the honor, a squat Frenchman with a gray beard.

"I am sorry, *mon ami*," Moses Rose said. "I did not survive Waterloo to die behind these walls."

"Go with God, my friend," Travis replied. "Soldiers, return to your posts."

The defenders spread out, many going back up on the ramparts, others toward the barracks or chapel. The mood was somber. Travis gathered his officers.

"The men should rest," Crockett advised. "Got to be ready if the attack comes in the morning."

"What do you think?" Travis said, turning in my direction.

"Me?" I asked.

"Yes, you," Travis insisted.

"I think you should go over the wall the moment the sun goes down. Santa Anna's calvary would have a hell of a time trying to catch all of you."

"Run? Run like cowards?" Captain Martin objected.

"You asked my opinion. What do you want me to tell Santa Anna?"

"What do you mean?" Travis said.

"He sent me to ask for Bowie's surrender, knowing full well he wouldn't. I don't know what the dictator's game is, but I'll tell him whatever you want."

"You're not staying?" Jameson asked.

"Me? Hell no. This isn't my fight. Though I'd appreciate it if no one told Santa Anna I revealed his plans."

"Not much chance of that," Crockett said.

"Will you be writing about the battle?" Travis inquired.

"It's my job."

"Santa Anna will confiscate any letters you carry out. But if you could deliver a spoken message to my family?" Travis requested.

"Me, too," Crockett said.

"And me," Jameson added.

"Of course, of course," I agreed.

I rode back across the bridge on Juan's mule just before sunset, expecting to be surrounded by guards. Only Almonte and Bartres waited for me.

"Bowie said no," I reported.

And that was it. Neither expressed the slightest curiosity about my mission, and I knew why. Within a matter of hours, every man in the fort would be dead, and any stories I had to tell would be meaningless. I assumed Santa Anna sent me as a distraction, or perhaps to make the defenders think there was a chance of mercy. But I knew the man better than that, and so did the Alamo.

I got drunk that night. Not rowdy drunk. There was no point in getting arrested. I crawled into bed, hearing troops marching past my door in the middle of the night. And marching, and marching, and marching. It would be a predawn attack.

It was still dark when the shooting began. Rifles, at first. Then cannon fire coming from the fort. But the cannon fire didn't last long. I don't know that I heard more than a score of shots. I crawled out of bed, joining Mrs. Sanchez and other Tejanos on the roof. All we could see were thousands of red streaks. Then skyrockets cast the walls in shadows. Shouting. Yelling. Screaming. The battle lasted far longer than I expected.

The sun rose over a smoking ruin. Camp followers rushed to the battlefield to provide aid. In time, wounded soldiers were brought back. Hundreds of bloodied soldiers. None of them were Texians. Señor Francisco Antonio Ruiz, the Alcalde of San Antonio, came to my side.

"We have been asked to identify the bodies," he said.

"I'd rather not," I replied, feeling the whiskey flask in my pocket.

"When His Excellency makes a request, it's not a request," Ruiz insisted.

I rode Perseverance, packing a bottle of bourbon. The battlefield was littered with the dead and dying, women providing what comfort they could. Many were shedding tears. The gate was open. We dismounted, handing our mounts over to Santa Anna's aides.

The courtyard was a scene of horror. I took a gulp from my bottle, steeling myself for the task ahead. We found Crockett before the chapel, a knife in his hand, surrounded by several enemy dead. It looked like they'd made a final stand before the doors. Mrs. Dickenson emerged, carrying her baby, accompanied by General Cos. She took a quick look at me and kept walking.

Bowie was in his bed, both pistols fired, the famous knife in a wounded man lying on the floor. I was tempted to take it, then thought better of the idea. I didn't see Mrs. Navarro and hoped she was unharmed.

The shaky north wall had a large hole in it, possibly blasted by cannon at close range. Or maybe it just fell down from the strain, having been shored up with wooden beams. Travis lay on the northwest platform next to a cannon, a bullet through his forehead. His slave was being questioned by Almonte's officers. I didn't know if Joe had fought at his master's side or chosen the better part of valor.

Santa Anna gave Mrs. Dickenson money and a mule, ordering her to Gonzales. She would tell Houston of the Alamo's fall. Her husband lay dead at the back of the church, one of the last to die. The bodies were being taken out to a tree-lined road called the Alameda, there to be stacked like cordwood and burned.

"Wish to go with her?" Juan asked. "His Excellency will allow it."

"No thank you," I answered.

"No?"

"When Mrs. Dickenson reaches Gonzales, there are going to be a lot of angry Texians. The men in the Alamo are dead, and I'm not. I doubt they'll be interested in explanations."

"Do you wish to march with the army?"

"That doesn't appeal to me, either. What's the best way to send dispatches back to the states?"

"Go to the coast. Matamoros. No, go to Galveston. By the time your reports reach Boston, the rebels will be defeated. We'll have a

Dinosaur Blitz

drink at the Boar's Head."

I shook Juan's hand, wished him well, and left San Antonio that afternoon. It would take them weeks to treat their wounded, bury the dead, and resupply. But Santa Anna's army was still far bigger than anything Houston could gather. And everybody knew it.

Galveston is a lovely port town at the mouth of Galveston Bay, founded by the French pirate Louis-Michel Aury. I found the Texian Navy in command of the port, though navy was an exaggeration. They only had four lightly armed schooners. Communications with New Orleans, only a few hundred miles away, remained open.

Reports came in regularly. Houston had burned Gonzales and retreated east, scorching the earth as he went, staying one step ahead of Santa Anna's pursuing army. Fannin had dithered at Goliad, and by the time he finally decided to leave, it was too late. His army was captured, and on Palm Sunday, four hundred Texian prisoners were taken out and shot by Mexican troops. Santa Anna had victory in his grasp.

And then came the big surprise. On April 21, only fifty miles north of the Galveston saloon where I was getting drunk, the Mexican army was surprised and crushed at San Jacinto. Santa Anna was captured. Texas won its independence.

Juan and Santa Anna were brought to Galveston Island after the battle. I didn't see His Excellency, but visited with Juan often and loaned him what money I could. He eventually returned to Mexico, became a major general, and ran afoul of the government. He died in Europe, wealthy and honored, but a man without a country.

Santa Anna went into exile, returned to power, and went into exile again more times than I could count. Maybe eight or ten times. I wondered what Crockett would have thought of that.

I met Santa Anna again, twenty years later, on the invitation of my friend, Thomas Adams, who was serving as the former dictator's secretary. The exiled general was living on Staten Island in New York, trying to get rich by turning a natural latex, chicle, into rubber for buggy tires. He needed investors. The man was nearly broke and in poor health. His scheme sounded good, in theory, though I hadn't heard of anyone turning tree sap into vulcanized rubber.

"Are you sure this will work?" I asked.

"It cannot fail," Santa Anna assured me, his English having improved.

I glanced at Adams, with whom I'd been playing poker for years. He smiled, giving me a knowing grin.

"I have a plan, Mort," Adams said. "If the chicle isn't good for tires, we can turn it into chewing gum."

That was good enough for me. We became business partners.

Dinosaur Blitz

<u>Rowena's Ballad</u>
Owen Vander, with his sword
Challenged there the grasping hordes
Fifty to one in grit and sand
Less than god but more than man
Slavers by the dozens fell
Evil souls cast into hell!
And courage now his lasting story
Of Salisbury Cross and glory!

From the west, in Arbor's name
The Magistrate of honest fame
Charging forth on noble steed
Invincible in thought and deed
And in their scores the slavers fell
Vile souls cast into hell!
We were there to tell his story
Of Salisbury Cross and glory!

Redeeming now his kingdom's woes
Standing tall as Satan's foe
Fearing not to make the fight
In God's faith to hold the right
And so a hundred slavers fell
Soulless scum cast into hell!
Forever we will tell his story
Of Salisbury Cross and glory!

from *Magistrate of the Dark Land*

Gregory Urbach

THE BLACK BIRD
A Tale of Dashiell Hammett

I never dreamed of becoming a mystery writer, until I learned how profitable murder could be. Not that murder particularly appealed to me. At first. But after eight years of Spanish flu, consumption, and veterans' hospitals, I was ready to branch out.

My apartment at 891 Post Street in San Francisco was below Nob Hill, above the Tenderloin, and close enough to John's Grill to walk home drunk. I'd married Josephine in 1921, gave her a couple of daughters, and moved on. The doctors said we shouldn't be living together for fear of my spreading the tuberculosis. Assuming I'd eventually cough myself to death, it didn't take much urging. But somehow I lived. Who would have guessed bourbon was a cure for TB?

Seven years as a Pinkerton detective, minus a few years in the army during the Great War, had given me practical experience with the criminal element. Solving crimes and committing them. I wrote a few

Dinosaur Blitz

short stories for *The Smart Set*, *Argosy*, *Brief Stories,* and *Black Mask*. Enough to get along. Reviewers claimed I was achieving an authenticity not seen before. Actually, I was just writing what I saw without dwelling on it too deeply. San Francisco's back-alley brothels, muggings, crooked cops, and opium dens provided all the material I needed.

I had wanted to write about Sam Spade for months. He lived in my building, one floor up, near the elevator. But he wasn't the kind of man to take lightly, nor would I want to find him outside my door in the middle of the night, holding a mystery magazine, and asking where I got the nerve to expose him. So I wrote about the Continental Op instead, a rascally detective who causes more trouble than he finds.

Those days came to an end in 1926. Though I was barely scraping by and had a family to feed, editor Phil Cody at *Black Mask* refused to give me a raise. I quit fiction altogether and took a job copywriting for Albert Samuels, a local jeweler. You may take my word for it—bank robbery, bootlegging, and extortion have nothing on the jewelry business. Diamonds poured in, money poured out, and no one really knew where any of it was coming from or going to.

One morning, Sam Spade walked through the door. Now his name wasn't really Sam Spade. To this day, it's not safe to say what his real name was. And it doesn't really matter. He was better than six feet tall, built like a Spanish bull, with fists like jackhammers. He had a package under one arm, wrapped in newspaper, and asked after a mysterious woman who had stopped by the office a day before.

"Mrs. Reynolds is not here," the clerk said, standing back from the counter. Sam wasn't happy about that. And then he spied me, sitting in the corner at my typewriter.

"Damn it, Hammett, are you in on this, too?" Sam shouted.

"In on what, Sam? What are you talking about?" I replied.

"It's a fake. A fake!"

Suddenly the bundle was flying across the room, crashing into the wall above my head. I ducked out of the way in the nick of time. When I got up off the floor, Sam was gone. The thing lay at my feet.

"What's this all about, Dash?" Mr. Samuels said, emerging from his office.

"Hell if I know, Al," I said, taking out my pocketknife.

It took a few minutes to cut through the wrapping. Underneath was the statue of a black bird sealed in lacquer. It was a foot tall, smooth and shiny, undamaged from its voyage through the air. Nothing about it seemed remarkable. It was too heavy be made of plaster, and too light be made of gold.

"What do you make of it?" Samuels asked, giving the statue a study.

"How would I know?" I responded.

"You're the mystery writer."

"Retired mystery writer. I'm in advertising now."

"Take this out of here," Samuels said, handing the statue back. "We don't need trouble."

It was near the end of the day anyway, and I had a few things to do before hitting the speakeasys. I wrapped up the bird in newspaper again, held it together with twine, and walked out to Market Street, taking the Powell Street trolley up to Union Square. After dropping a check in the mail for Jose and the kids, I made an easy stroll toward home.

There was much to think on. Only a few months before, I'd collapsed at work, coughing blood and hemorrhaging from the lungs. After eight weeks at the veteran's hospital, I finally realized my career as a full-time advertising manager was doomed. I'd need to supplement my income by writing again. But write about what? More Continental Op stories? Go back to *Black Mask,* crawling on my hands and knees to Phil Cody for 4¢ a word? No. Never.

Someone was following me, which seemed odd, even in San Francisco. I wore a nice herringbone suit, but not an expensive one. There was nothing unusual about my new Bollman fedora. I hardly

Dinosaur Blitz

seemed a target for pickpocketing or robbery.

Deciding a walk would do my damaged lungs good, I turned up Mason Street, made a right at Bush, and finally stopped at a railing on Burritt Street overlooking a deep construction trench. The sun had gone down, leaving the dreary night shrouded in fog. I heard footsteps approach. Not heavy. Probably a woman. Young. Tall and somewhat slim. I turned.

"Mr. Hammett?" she said.

"Yes, miss?" I replied, tipping my hat.

"I'm Veronica Reynolds. I saw you at Samuel's."

"We get to speak at last."

I put her in her mid-thirties, with reddish hair and vivid hazel eyes just beginning to wrinkle at the corners. Her outfit wasn't new, but had been at one time, indicating her circumstances had diminished. Her accent was Midwestern. Indiana? No, southern Illinois.

"I'm looking for a lost object. Perhaps you can help me?" she requested.

"What would this lost object look like?"

"It's a statue of a falcon. Twelve inches tall, weighing about six pounds. It's made of black aluminum."

"Is this statue valuable?" I asked.

"Not yet."

"I'm not a detective anymore. Haven't been for several years."

"You write detective stories, don't you?"

"Not anymore."

"Maybe you should?"

"There's no money in it. How much is finding this bird worth?"

"$500."

"Does it look like this one? In the fish wrap?" I asked, raising the bundle. "The one your friend Sam Spade threw at me?"

"When did you see Sam?"

"About an hour ago. He was looking for you."

"He mustn't find me," she protested.

"Come back to my place. We'll talk about this."

We wandered west along Bush Street, and after a quick stop at John's Grill on Ellis for drinks, we went up the stairs to my 3rd floor flat. The summer day had been cool and blustery, as San Francisco often is. My guest removed her coat, and her shoes, taking a seat on the bed.

"We just met," I said.

"I'm not here for that."

"What are you here for?"

"I'm on a mission."

"Where does the bird fit in?"

"Where do you want the bird to fit in?"

"Maybe we should have a talk with Sam?"

"I doubt he's interested in talking."

I took out my pocketknife, once again cutting the statue loose from the wrapping. It was a pretty thing, all black and shiny, with tucked wings and a noble beak. There was no evidence of diamonds or emeralds embedded under the lacquer. I set it on the living room table before taking a seat on the sofa.

"Sam said this is fake. What's fake about it?" I asked.

"I don't know. It looks like the real deal to me."

"But not worth your $500?"

"Not if it's fake."

"You're not making this easier."

"It's not my job to make this easier."

"What is your job?"

"Let's have a drink."

Fortunately, Prohibition wasn't enforced in the city the way it could be. I kept a full bar of imported whiskey, bourbon, rum, and gin. She helped herself to my Seagram's, mixing two highballs while humming a popular radio tune. I found her very attractive. And it wasn't as if I hadn't been cheating on Jose for years. Not with our medically enforced separations.

Veronica handed me my drink and sat back down on the bed. Her gray knit skirt rose up almost to her knees.

"What do you think we should do?" I asked.

"Let's follow Spade. Have him lead us to the dingus."

"What the hell is a dingus?"

"The item. The treasure. The stuff that dreams are made of."

"Spade is big guy. A very big guy."

"Afraid?"

"He's got a mean look to him."

"You were a Pinkerton. Didn't you break up strikes? Tackle bad guys. Beat the crap out of perverts?"

"I was a kid back then."

"You're not so old now."

"How old are you?"

"Old enough to make my own decisions," she replied, climbing off the bed into my lap.

We had breakfast at Molly's Coffee Shop around the corner. After grits and sausages, she lit up a cigarette, which surprised me. I usually don't see women smoke in public. She gave me one of her Camels. I puffed lightly, having bad lungs.

"We should stop by my hotel room, then catch Spade at the train station," she suggested.

"How do you know he'll be at the train station?"

She held up the key to a locker.

"He knows I'll be there at noon to get my suitcase. He'll be waiting for me. We can hide in the terminal, then follow when he leaves."

"Follow him where?"

"How the hell should I know? You're the detective."

Veronica had a valise full of wigs, hats, sunglasses, and makeup in her hotel room at The Mark. She turned herself into a blonde and made we wear the most ridiculous beard and mustache I'd ever seen. And a slouch hat, which wasn't good for my hair.

We arrived at the train station early, getting donuts off the cart and looking at the latest magazines. Most featured movie stars.

"I don't see Black Mask," I whispered.

"Maybe it was sold out?" she guessed.

"Or maybe no one wants to buy the goddamn worthless piece of trash anymore," I hoped.

Spade showed up five minutes early, in a trench coat, thinking himself clever. He sat in a phone booth where he could see the lockers. It was a poor performance. No one spends an hour in a phone booth without putting coins in the slot.

We didn't show, and so he left. It was a big terminal, and noisy. Veronica grabbed my hand, pulling me along as we worked in and out through the impatient crowd. We saw Spade head for the Mason Street trolley and hurried to catch up.

It was a long and crazy day. We trailed Spade down to 8th and Market, but it wasn't a secret hideaway. It was Recreation Park. The Seals baseball team had won the pennant the year before, so everyone was excited about the team. We spent three hours eating hot dogs and watching from our seats behind third base. The Seals won.

Then Spade was on the move again. We tracked him by streetcar to the Oakland Ferry, where he waited until the last minute to jump on board. We did, too. Veronica had us sneak in with the crew, smiling and being charming. We crossed the choppy bay to Oakland, where Spade got off first. Except for us. We had already disembarked with the same crew we boarded with. A block away, we paused in the doorway of a Rexall Drug Store, observing as Spade went to a phone booth, pretended to make another call, and smoked a cigarette. Then he headed back to the ferry.

Dinosaur Blitz

He almost lost us, though quite frankly, I should have seen it coming. Veronica could be very distracting. She loved mystery stories and thrived on adventure. She was bubbly, enthusiastic, and not afraid to be bold.

Back in San Francisco, Spade headed for Fisherman's Wharf. I knew we were getting close, for all kinds of skullduggery was known to take place under the piers. He went out on a jetty, watched the bay for forty-five minutes, and smoked two cigarettes. Then he turned down a dark alley, taking quick steps, and disappeared into the back of a seedy restaurant. We were close behind.

"What's he doing?" I asked, hunched in our booth, hiding behind a menu.

"He's ordering the special. With extra sauce," Veronica reported.

"No. I mean, who's he with? Do you see any letters or secret messages?"

"He's ordering wine. This must be a blind pig."

"Everybody knows this is a speakeasy. Will you answer my question?"

"Can we order wine?"

"Yes, you can order whatever damn thing you want."

"Well, no one else is there. He's getting his food. It looks good. He's smiling at the waitress. I think he likes her. The waitress is smiling back."

I shifted over, almost knocking Veronica on the floor, and looked for myself. Spade was just sitting there. Eating. We ordered meatloaf. Veronica got her bottle of wine. A bootleg Chardonnay from Sonoma.

It was dark when we finally got back to Post Street. Spade went up to his room, just one floor above mine, and took a shower. His bathroom was near the door, which was just outside the elevator. Veronica had brought a glass, holding it up to the door so she could listen. Eavesdropping wasn't hard.

"Well? What's he doing?" I finally asked.

"How the hell should I know? He's in his room. Alone. Is he supposed to talking to someone?"

"He may have a phone," I suggested.

"A phone? In his room? Where do you think you are, Nob Hill?"

As we could hear the elevator from my room, we went downstairs, took turns in the shower, and drank beer.

"There he goes," Veronica whispered a few hours later.

We rushed down the stairs in time to see Spade, still in his trench coat, rush north up Hyde Street. At Bush, he took a quick right, and then slowed down. Occasionally, he looked back. Veronica and I stayed close to the shadows, often huddling. He stopped just short of Burritt.

"I want to talk with him first," Veronica said. "He might make a deal for the dingus."

"It's too dangerous," I protested.

"You'll still get the $500."

"To hell with that. He may not even have it."

"I won't know until I ask."

She broke away, walking briskly on the cracked sidewalk. Spade was under a dirty streetlamp filled with moths, turning the light yellow.

He saw her coming. Veronica slowed. They spoke. Spade looked agitated. Veronica was pleading. Spade drew her closer to the railing, taking a quick look down. The sidewalk dropped off sharply into a deep trench.

Veronica stepped back, and there was a sudden movement. Spade bent over, pressed against the railing, and fell through. I never even heard him moan. I ran forward, clutching Veronica, looking down into the abyss. All I could see was a dark pit. Nothing moved.

"What happened?" I asked.

Veronica raised a Webley & Scott .25 caliber pistol. It smelled like it had been recently fired.

"It was self-defense," she claimed.

Dinosaur Blitz

It didn't look like self-defense to me, but I didn't say so. I noticed an elderly couple across the street, looking. I didn't know how much they'd seen, but they didn't appear alarmed. Veronica grabbed my arms, pulled me close, and gave me a long, lingering kiss.

"Thank you, lover," she said loud enough for the couple to hear. "You've made me the happiest girl in the world."

She took my hand and dragged me away.

"We have to report this," I whispered.

"Oh, we will. I promise. Just let me catch my breath first."

We found a little bar around the corner called Snorky's, where we hid in the back. Drinks were ordered. Whiskey, straight up.

"Tell me what happened. And then we're going to tell the police," I insisted.

"It was self-defense."

"Give me the gun," I said, reaching out.

"Oh, it's gone. I threw it away."

"Where?"

"In the back of an old pickup truck. I think it was a Ford."

"Where is the truck now?"

"I don't know. It was headed south toward Market Street."

This is going to be tough to explain, I thought.

"I know a few of the boys at the precinct. We should go," I said, getting up and reaching for her hand.

"Yes, yes, I agree. But we need to make one last stop first. Please?"

The was a cool and foggy night. I didn't carry a gun, but liked to keep a roll of quarters in my pocket to make a stronger fist, should it be necessary to punch someone. We went down Ellis to John's Grill, slipped in the back door, and found my usual booth. Burke came by to take our order. More whiskey.

"Dash, I want you to know, I really like you," Veronica explained. "After this is all over, I'd like to see you again."

"What is all this?"

"My name isn't really Veronica Reynolds," she confessed. "It's Nell Martin."

"Who?"

"Nell Martin, from Springfield."

"I take it you're not an insurance investigator."

"Not yet. I've been a strawberry picker, laundress, a taxi-cab driver, newspaper reporter, legal aide, a singer, an actress, and a press agent. Now I'm a writer."

"A writer?"

"I'm writing the Maisie stories for Top Notch."

"I don't get it. Are you writing something about me?"

"No. Not writing about you. But there is a story."

"Care to explain?"

Shockingly, a big ugly brute stopped at my table, glared down, and stole my drink.

"Hey, bud—" I started to say, before looking up.

It was Sam Spade, alive and well.

"Hammett, you're a damn idiot," he said. And then he walked away.

"What the—"

"Sorry, Dash, see you later," Nell said.

And then she disappeared, too, replaced by a husky fifty-year-old New Englander in a rumpled brown suit. He looked like a refugee from a newsroom, with pens in his breast pocket and ink on his fingers.

"Hello, Mr. Hammett. We meet at last. It's been a long chase," he said, reaching to shake hands. I motioned for him to sit.

"And who would you be?"

"That can wait. You've had quite the adventure."

"Does the black bird belong to you?"

"In a way. Want a drink?"

"Bourbon and soda."

My benefactor waved to the bar, calling to Burke and holding up two fingers.

"Tell me, has the search for the bird been exciting?" he asked. "Better than sitting at a typewriter, pounding out copy for a jewelry store?"

"It reminded me of my Pinkerton days. Before I got sick."

"I take it writing is less strenuous."

"Working for Al Samuels is paying the bills."

"But not as satisfying. You know, this whole adventure with the black bird would make a good story. You should write it."

"I don't write anymore. And if I did, I don't know anyone who'd publish it."

"Black Mask would publish it."

"Black Mask? I wouldn't write an obituary for Phil Cody if his black-draped widow begged me on her hands and knees."

"Cody isn't the editor of Black Mask anymore."

"He's not? Who is?"

"I am. My name is Joseph T. Shaw, and I'm going to make Black Mask the premier mystery magazine in the country. But to do that, I need Dashiell Hammett."

"Is that what this is all about?" I asked. "Trying to get me back?"

"Did it work?" he replied.

Gregory Urbach

Many Hats
I am a man of many hats;
I wear the dress, I wear the pants.
And when they say there's work to do;
It's always me and never you.

    from *Tranquility's Heirs*

The Monster
And so the monster came to life;
Much to the doctor's great delight.
Just imagine his chagrin;
When the monster turned on him.

    from *Tranquility Down*

A Cold Mistress
I was never lonely til I had friends;
Never hurt until I loved;
Never sad, 'til I knew what sadness was;
Duty! What a cold mistress thou art.

    from *Tranquility's Heirs*

Dinosaur Blitz

The Further Adventures of Snailwoman

The motion picture company where Elizabeth and I worked was located across the river from Warner Brothers studios. In my downtime, I would draw cartoons. Sometimes about my co-workers, which did not make me popular. Snailwoman was the exception. They began as very rough sketches, hidden in my desk so the boss wouldn't see them. Many drawings never made it to completion, surviving only in fragments. It was a sad day when Elizabeth left Swank for brighter pastures.

Gregory Urbach

Snailwoman in El Salvador

Dinosaur Blitz

Gregory Urbach

Dinosaur Blitz

Gregory Urbach

Dinosaur Blitz

Gregory Urbach

Dinosaur Blitz

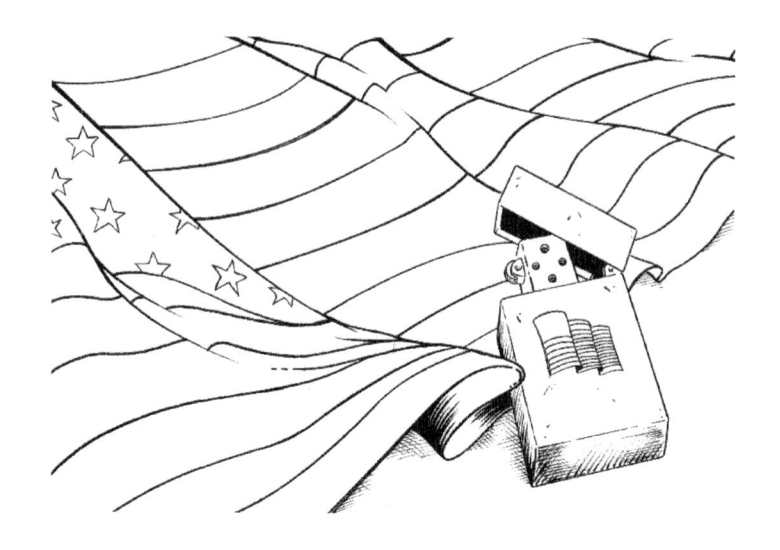

BURNING FLAGS
Celebrating the entrepreneurial spirit

It started out innocently enough, as most of our adventures do. We were watching a cable news program (which is always a mistake) and witnessed foreign radicals burning an American flag.

"Why are they doing that?" I asked, walking into the den shared with my three roommates. Our rented house was in the West Valley, just off the 101. Humble but affordable.

"To protest the foreign aid America is giving them," Howie said, the first of us to see his hair start to thin.

"Freakin' idiots," Mickey complained, munching his second cheeseburger.

"Pretty lame, too. Look at this pinhead," Jimmy said, pointing a bony finger at the TV screen.

The long-bearded protester kept trying to set the flag on fire with his lighter, but the wind whipped the flame in the wrong direction.

Suddenly, the man next to the arsonist caught fire, slapping his sleeve to put out the flames. We all laughed.

"People sure spend a lot of time burning our flag," I said. "Especially in that part of the world. Whoever is making those flags is raking in big bucks."

"Probably China," Jimmy said, glancing at the wall where our Stars & Stripes hung proudly over a window. Sure enough, there was a Made in China tag on the lining.

"Pretty lousy flags for burning," Mickey said. "They can't even get them to ignite without using gasoline. Seems to me the oil companies are making more than the Chinese."

"Too bad they can't get both," I said, seeing the obvious logic.

"Both of what?" Howie asked.

"An American flag pre-soaked in lighter fluid," I explained.

"That's a great idea," Howie said, jumping from our ragged, overstuffed couch.

"A pre-soaked American flag?" Jimmy said.

"Right, like you'd ever get that product past consumer regulations," I sneered. "What would be next, pre-soaked baby clothes?"

"We can have them made in the Philippines," Howie insisted. "We won't import the flags, numb-nuts, just sell them to eager customers overseas."

"It's not possible," I said.

"Just write up the specifications. I'll do the rest," Howie said.

Well, it turns out not every country has strict consumer product rules. I wrote up the specifications, Howie found a factory in the Philippines willing to make anything, and a $10,000 bribe got us an export license. That's when Mickey stepped up.

"The film crew is all ready to go," he said. "Some of my friends down at B'nai B'rith are going to dress up like Arabs and burn the prototypes. We're shooting in the parking lot of that new Pakistani restaurant."

"The one down on Olive and 3rd?" Jimmy asked. "Their curry is great."

"Melts in your mouth, just like a milky goat's eye," Mickey said, rubbing his belly.

"The video needs dialogue. Does anyone know how to say 'death to America' in Arabic?" I asked.

"We'll dub it in later," Howie said.

"How's production?" Mickey asked, for he'd been with his publicity guys most of the week.

"Twenty thousand units ready to go, and we clear $1.75 per unit," Jimmy said. "Money goes straight to our Cayman Islands account. No reason to pay taxes on something the government won't even let us make."

"Damn commies," Howie grumbled.

I remained quiet, seeking to avoid a political argument. I usually voted for the liberals, but not out of any conviction. I'd just assumed they'd leave me alone if I appeared poor.

"Shipping by UPS or FedEx?" I asked.

Howie and Jimmy looked at me like I was a moron, so I let the subject drop.

Our first blog appeared on Facebook, quickly spreading through social media like a firestorm. Post after post showed happy protestors setting American flags on fire without muss or fuss, and soon our flags became all the rage. BurnAmerica.com shipped 10,000 units in the first week, 20,000 in the second week, and then things really got crazy. Outraged political pundits began to rant on their radio shows, calling us traitors and fake news. Politicians in Washington began to talk about new laws restricting free enterprise.

After six months in business, a reporter finally discovered that Burn America, Inc. was not owned by a Saudi consortium, as everyone had thought, but four college dropouts from the San Fernando Valley. And if reporters knew what we were up to, government investigators would only be a few steps behind.

"What should we do?" Jimmy asked during our weekly meeting at the rented house. With all the money coming in, we now had our own places in Malibu overlooking the beach. But we kept the old hangout for sentimental reasons. And to receive mail.

"Why should we do anything?" Howie asked.

"The government never gave us permission to sell burnable flags," Jimmy said.

"We never asked for permission. Don't you watch Star Trek? Captain Kirk always said never ask for permission if you're not prepared to take no for an answer," Howie said.

"That wasn't Captain Kirk. The Bynars said it to Picard in STNG," Jimmy corrected.

"Close enough," Howie said. "Look, no one said we couldn't do this, and only a few bankers said we shouldn't to it. It's legal until someone says it isn't."

"Is it worth the risk?" I asked.

"We're making two hundred thousand dollars a month," Mickey said. "New markets just opened up in Istanbul, Venezuela, and France."

"France?" I said.

"It's a very trendy country," Mickey explained.

"We could double our profits if the Consumer Safety Commission would open up the American market. We'd get rich off of San Francisco alone," Jimmy said.

"Damn commies," Howie sneered again.

"The Safety Commission or San Francisco?" I asked.

"Cable News," Howie said. "Did you see last night's story? They called selling burnable American flags to be un-American! And all we're trying to do is make an honest profit."

"Okay, then. We'll lay low, boost production, and keep funding those pop-up ads," Jimmy said, sounding relieved.

"What about the reporters?" I asked.

"Tell them whatever you want, so as long as it's not true," Mickey said. "Remember your First Amendment right to be dishonest with everyone but the FBI."

All good things must come to an end.

"Bad news," Howie said on a warm summer afternoon.

"Other than all the reporters?" I asked.

"The Philippine government shut us down. Seems we didn't pay off enough politicians," he replied. "The president's brother-in-law is producing the flags now."

"Well, we had a good run. Where are Mickey and Jimmy?"

"In the den, watching the news."

"That's not good," I said.

"It never is," Howie agreed.

We entered the den, seeing the evening's major story on the TV. In the streets of Cairo, where we had first seen that flag burning ten months before, protestors were once again gathered in the square. But now they were protesting us, declaring they had been tricked into buying burnable flags by crafty American capitalists. The fellow had a point. Then the protester, dressed in a turban, shouted something to the mob, raised an American flag, and set his lighter underneath. But it appeared the fabric had been over-soaked, for both the flag and the protester suddenly burst into flames. Consumer safety always was a problem.

Gregory Urbach

LUNAR ROBOTS

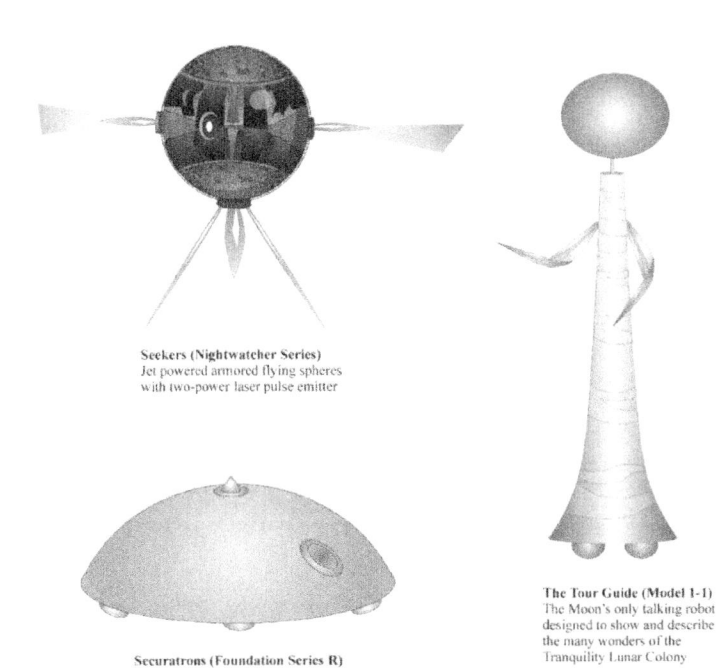

Seekers (Nightwatcher Series)
Jet powered armored flying spheres with two-power laser pulse emitter

Securatrons (Foundation Series R)
Four-wheeled turtle-shelled defense units. Light armor plate armed with electrical disrupter/heat emitter

The Tour Guide (Model 1-1)
The Moon's only talking robot designed to show and describe the many wonders of the Tranquility Lunar Colony

Dinosaur Blitz

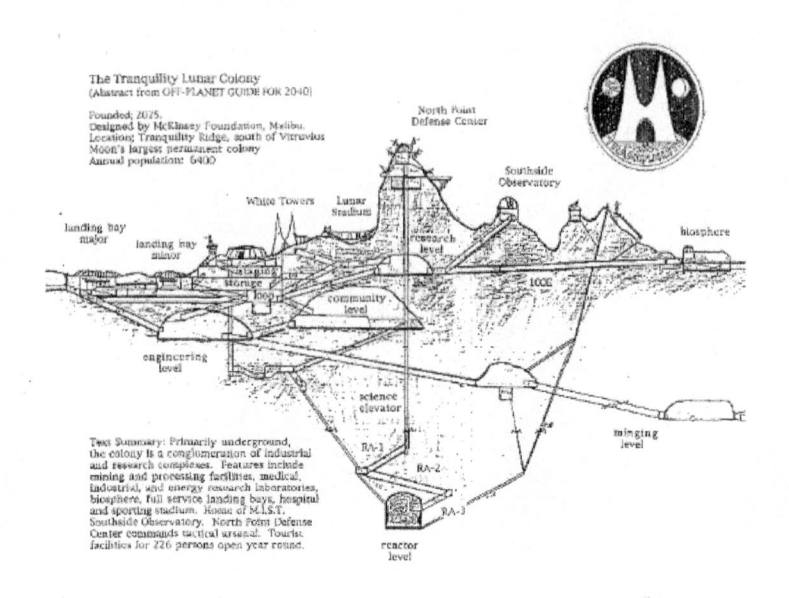

COWBOYS & INDIANS
The struggles of a lunar orphan

"Good morning, Computer," the child said.

"Good morning, Grey," the Life Support Computer replied.

Grey sat up in his bunk, pushed aside the weighted bed covers, and wiggled out onto the cold bunkroom floor. Observing from a small auxiliary monitor, the Life Support Computer noticed the boy flinch and adjusted the chamber's temperature.

"What is my programming for today?" Grey asked as he dressed in his heavily weighted patchwork overalls.

The green signature patterns registered dimly on the monitor screen, indicating a delay in the response. Grey sat down, stretched his shoulders, and discovered an elbow seal failing to grip again. *I must fix that soon*, he noted prudently.

As he often did while waiting, Grey glanced around the narrow room, noting four walls, one door, and eight beds. He didn't understand why there were eight beds, never having used more than one.

Grey knew the Life Support Computer was still developing a response because the green signature patterns, which he knew to be Computer's, continued moving back and forth. The other computers had their own signature patterns. Grey recalled the time when he believed there was but one computer, before he learned to differentiate between their functions.

But I was only a baby then, he thought.

Grey stood up and twisted his thin shoulders, letting the heavy suit settle more comfortably. Sometimes, especially early in the morning cycle, Computer failed to respond quickly. Grey assumed that, like himself, the machine had been sleeping.

"Standard Thursday schedule modified by 1300 hours adjournment," the Life Support Computer finally announced.

"Thank you, Computer," Grey responded, pleased the training session would be an easy one.

During the last few weeks, the physical conditioning periods had become more intense than ever before, especially the gravity chamber sequences, and several times he had vomited from exhaustion. He didn't like those programs. Unlike the early years when he had often experienced illness, Grey had been healthy now for a long time. Almost six months. He had no desire to repeat the illness cycles.

Seeing the Life Support Computer holding on response mode, Grey decided to ask a question that had occurred to him. Initially, he had wanted to ask about sleeping, because he couldn't remember doing it, but he also wanted to know about dreams, because sometimes the computers acted strangely in dreams. But there was an even more important question that might possibly explain everything.

"Computer? Why are time periods divided into day and night?"

The signature patterns swirled faster as the Life Support Computer processed his request for information. For a child just reaching his fifth birthday, Grey's vocabulary skills were excellent. He was well aware of the dictionary definitions for the terms. But the many social references confused him. Grey sighed when brown signature patterns took dominance in the monitor screen flux.

"Day is a colloquial term used to describe the time period between sunrise and sunset. Night identifies the hours between sunset and sunrise," the Library Computer answered.

What difference does it make whether a sun is visible or not? Grey wondered. *Why is sleep always associated with the night cycle? Who made such a rule, and why? Why must every answer lead to another question?*

Deciding to pursue the subject another time, Grey entered the long central corridor that formed the artery of his world and bounced the full fourteen-meter length in slow, laboring lunges. When he reached the far end, he turned and trudged back to the crew quarters. Then he repeated the procedure nine more times, making the best of the monotonous routine by recalling his lessons from the day before and considering new subjects to investigate. There was much to learn if he wanted to become a computer.

Once his warmup exercise was complete, he dropped the heavier weights from the suit and entered the gymnasium to begin his regular program of lifts, presses, and bends, dropping additional weights as the exercises became more complex. The forty-five minutes passed quickly, and by the end of the physical development period, all of his optional weights had been discarded. But he wasn't through yet. The worst part was about to begin.

Reluctantly, Grey entered the hygiene compartment and climbed inside the gravity chamber. The chamber was bare except for a padded bench, a grip bar, and a monitor that cabled in entertainment. Though he liked the videos, he hated the chamber. But it was necessary, so he did it. The Medical Computer told him to.

When the hatch sealed, the gravity effect began, the invisible forces tugging and pushing against every fiber of his body. The strange pressures weren't always painful, but they were always uncomfortable. Fortunately, this cycle lasted only twenty minutes, not long enough to make him sick.

After the treatment was complete, Grey showered, brushed his unruly brown hair, and dressed in a lightweight day suit before racing to the control room. The Library Computer was online waiting for him. Grey sat down in a comfortable chair before the main monitor. Surrounding him were two other workstations. A dozen monitor screens, all of them inactive, looked down from the tops of the battleship gray walls. Sometimes Grey wondered what all the extra equipment was for.

"You're very energetic today," the MC1000 remarked.

"Affirmative," Grey replied. "It's been a good morning. The air in the gym wasn't so stuffy today, and there was lots of hot H_2-O."

"Do you still keep a water container in your footlocker?" the Library Computer asked.

"Affirmative. I don't ever want to be without water again," he answered gravely, shuddering at the memory.

"The system failure caused many inconveniences. I'm glad your service systems are performing adequately now," Library said.

"It's good. I don't like malfunctions," Grey agreed.

"With reference to malfunctions, how is your Model Twelve?"

"Worse. The food hardly holds form anymore."

"Maintenance will be reminded that something must be done," Library said, entering a footnote of indignation.

Grey smiled, activated the study unit, and was soon occupied with other subjects, such as mathematics, engineering, and physical science. The Library Computer liked to vary the lessons, occasionally introducing abstract subjects such as art, music, and history. Grey liked history the most. The stories were ridiculous, of course, and he

Dinosaur Blitz

certainly didn't believe that imaginary humans lived on a big blue planet doing all sorts of inventive things, but nevertheless, something about history was exciting. Something unique to him.

At the end of the morning study period, Grey returned to the bunkroom and removed the lightweight day suit. His stomach was quiet now, the effects of the gravity chamber having subsided, so he dressed in a medium-weight work suit and bounced into the cafeteria.

Like the extra beds in the bunkroom, the eating area had more chairs than he needed. Twelve in all. Grey had no objections to the extra chairs, though he did wonder why there were so many.

Against the rear wall behind the serving counter, he found the Model Twelve food dispenser. Grey stepped up to the order spot, bit his lower lip, and took a deep breath.

"Requesting food service," he said. "Breakfast number five with muffin, options two, four, seven. Grape juice with liquid supplement."

Usually, Grey hesitated to order so many good things at once, knowing the dispenser's resources were limited, but several days had passed since his last full breakfast. He wanted at least one item to be well-formed.

The Model Twelve didn't say what it wanted. The device wasn't smart like the computers. Grey realized he wasn't as smart as the computers either, though if he worked hard enough, maybe one day he would be. But the Model Twelve would never be anything more than a food dispenser. That was its only function.

And not exactly functioning. When the heat cycle ended, Grey opened the door to retrieve the tray. Again, the egg had failed to hold form, leaving a sticky yellow puddle. The muffin was stale. There was no cereal, just a message disk that read OUT OF STOCK.

Fortunately, the dehydrated apple bits weren't bad, and the liquid supplement had a reassuring bland but sturdy consistency, so Grey didn't consider breakfast a total loss. He quickly took his favorite seat, gobbled the food, drank the liquid supplement, and decided to visit the hygiene compartment before returning to his studies.

The blue ceramic steel corridor was quiet, the hum of the air circulators barely audible. Suddenly, louder than the rhythmic pulsations of the machines, Grey heard the rare sound of the repair unit, the tracks making a distinctive vibration on the hard floor. Curious to know what the repair unit was doing, Grey bounced back to the cafeteria just in time to see the short cylindrical robot finish an adjustment on the Model Twelve.

Detecting his presence, the repair unit turned abruptly and disappeared through the portal of a small access tunnel. Grey had explored the tunnel many times and knew it to be a dead end, so he wondered how the robot always managed to vanish. He became determined to discover the secret and dove to the floor just in time to catch a glimpse inside the portal.

"A second door! So that's how it's done!" he exclaimed.

He smiled, and then a very important question occurred to him. *Where does the second door go? Is there another tunnel on the other side? If there are more tunnels, are there more rooms?*

Excited by the potential of his discovery, Grey decided not to waste another moment on speculation. He ran to ask Computer.

"Computer. Response mode. Where does the repair unit go?"

The Life Support Computer did not respond.

He moved closer to observe the control room displays. Signature patterns were slowly increasing activity level, indicating the request for information had been received, but they weren't the indicators Grey hoped to see. The signature patterns were brown.

Grey sat down with a sigh. Not that he didn't like the Library Computer. It was an interesting teacher and fine storyteller. Many times, when he had been immobilized by ill health, the Library Computer had remained online to keep him company. But only his guardian, the Life Support Computer, was authorized to answer important questions. Once again, it seemed he had asked a question

Dinosaur Blitz

Computer refused answer.

But Grey's fading hopes were soon revived when green signature patterns filtered into the flux. A rainbow of background colors indicated other computer systems were also tapping the channel.

"Please stand by," the Life Support Computer said.

The green signature patterns swirled rapidly, exchanged with a series of blue signature patterns, and stabilized. Grey held his breath.

"Ready, Grey. What is your question?" Life Support asked.

Grey stood up straight and felt the muscles tighten in his throat. He didn't like being the object of so much attention.

"Are there other rooms outside the ones in which I live?" he finally asked.

The Life Support Computer resisted responding. For a moment, Grey was sure the computer wouldn't reply at all, but after several different colored signature patterns came and went from the monitor, the green signature patterns returned brighter than before.

"You live in a preliminary survey station known as the Old Section," the Life Support Computer said. "Until a few years ago, it served as a museum of early life on the moon. Now the Old Section functions as your living quarters."

Grey found the information interesting, but not an answer to his question. He thought for a long time. Almost a minute. *If I live in a survey station, he wondered, are there other stations or sections nearby? What would they be used for? Other humans? Are the stories about humans really true?*

"Computer? Are there other humans? Like me?"

"Negative. There are no other human beings quite like you. However, many humans still inhabit Earth," Life Support answered.

"Earth? The water planet featured in the entertainment vids?"

"Affirmative."

"How many humans live there?"

"Approximately eight and a half billion as of the 2070 census. There are less now because of the war."

"War," Grey whispered. Many times, he had watched video programs about war, where colorfully dressed humans rode in flying machines, crossed great bodies of water, and fought amongst themselves on strange animals. He thought the stories most imaginative.

"Are the Earth humans like the ones I've studied?" he asked, his bright, perceptive gray eyes eagerly scanning the signature patterns for nonverbal information. Many times, he had played make-believe games where the food was always good, or where he never had to use the gravity chamber, but other rooms? And humans? Suddenly he had so many questions they were difficult to organize.

The signature patterns swirled while the Life Support Computer developed a response. The delay answered Grey's question. If humans were merely fairy tales, there would have been an immediate negative reply. *But if there are humans*, Grey asked himself, *how come Computer has never admitted it before? He stopped to think as he had been trained to do. Select procedure, arrange information, process data. Analyze. If I want the right answers, he remembered, I must ask the right questions.*

The Life Support Computer continued to delay, giving Grey time to formulate a hypothesis. His years of intimate association with the thinking machines paid off with an instinctive understanding of the way they shifted data. By the unsteady subcurrent, he knew Computer didn't want to answer his question and was preparing a partial response to mollify him. Grey didn't like this game, even though he sometimes played it himself.

Then, somewhat unusually, the signature patterns paused in the flux so the Library Computer could provide a records channel.

"Some of what you read is true, but much of what you read is false," a recorded human voice said. "Information compiled by humans, particularly in reference to other humans, is prone to error and prejudice. Examine the sources of your information. Determine for yourself what to believe. Remember, this pertains to all things in all situations."

The signature patterns grew sluggish as the higher function levels prepared to drop offline. There was so much more that he wanted to know. *Extra rooms. Humans. War. What did it all mean? What would humans be like? Could they communicate?*

"Computer, tell me how to contact the Earth humans," Grey asked in a firm voice.

It was a trick, of course, the straightforward request for information being an attempt to bypass the optional response mode. The Life Support Computer wasn't fooled so easily.

As the signature patterns began to fade, Grey thought Computer had decided not to answer any more questions. But suddenly, unexpectedly, the control room lighting quivered, blacked out, and regained a hazy brown. The room grew nervously quiet as the power levels dropped. Fear of malfunction crept into Grey's mind.

Had he asked a question that was too difficult? he wondered. Or was he going to be punished for his impertinence?

Grey noticed the air circulator shutting down. The room was getting colder. Black signature patterns came to dominate the monitor screen flux, twisting and churning in agitated waves. Then green signature patterns surged back even stronger. Finally blue signature patterns moved into dominance and fluctuated sharply before dropping offline. The other signature patterns quickly followed.

With the sudden withdrawal of the higher function levels, the minor computer systems returned to the flux with a furious burst of energy, power surging through the secondary control centers. Circuits abruptly opened and closed, the lighting flashed wildly, and white smoke appeared.

Malfunction! Grey thought. *A big one!*

As he had been trained, Grey pulled on his life support hood, clamped the emergency seals to activate the suit's internal atmosphere, and stepped back toward the doorway within reach of the gravity chamber. If fire occurred, he would be safe there until the environment was restored.

But what if it can't be restored? he wondered for the first time. What would happen then? He didn't know, but he knew malfunctions were serious. Hadn't he lost water service for nearly a week? And how many times had the waste disposal unit backed up in the last month alone? Not to mention problems with the Model Twelve.

"Please don't malfunction," he whispered, wishing there was something he could do.

Then a powerful burst of energy blew sparks across the room. Grey ran cowering into the hall.

But the units did not fail. As readjustment occurred, the power flow stabilized. Internal fire controllers prevented burnouts while the air circulators flushed the cubicle with a cool breeze. Grey let out his breath when the monitor screen flux returned to standby.

"Request denied," the Communications Computer said, a high-pitched voice registering in unison with shifting hues of orange signature patterns.

Grey had all but forgotten his request to contact humans by then, and was sorry he dared to ask, so he was surprised when the Life Support Computer came back online.

"Prepare for new programming, Grey," Life Support ordered. "Dress code four. Report to the end of the central corridor in five minutes."

Mystified by the unprecedented instructions, Grey rushed back to the crew's quarters and located his code four uniform in the footlocker under his bunk. The long-sleeved jumper he had sewn from scraps of larger outfits was also his best suit, the others having become too small.

The nearly weightless suit felt good. Pieced together with sealers, the uniform had an odd appearance, but Grey didn't care about that. He

Dinosaur Blitz

liked the customized features, such as the extra deep thigh pockets and the handy waste disposal zipper.

He jumped off the floor in high bounces, easily reaching the ceiling with his outstretched hand, spun in the air to land gently on one foot, and kicked off the wall for a somersault, landing on the other foot.

Something exciting was happening. He could feel it. What would it be? Only a year before, he had been granted free use of the library unit for the first time, and last quarter, he began selecting his own study options. Would the new surprise be as good?

Knowing the Medical Computer would send him back if he failed to wash, Grey dashed into the hygiene compartment. He quickly rinsed his face, brushed his hair, and glanced into the mirror above the sink, briefly staring into his own eyes. They were dark gray. Intense. Strange. If not for the Medical Computer's insistence, Grey would never look in mirrors.

"Reporting, Computer," he announced a moment later, arriving at the far end of the central corridor.

"Are you prepared for new programming, Grey?" Life Support asked.

"Affirmative," he responded anxiously.

"Pay attention. Governor McKinsey's notes are brief," Life Support instructed.

Grey tried to remain calm while Computer developed the presentation. He knew McKinsey was the great creator, a powerful systems designer that all the higher function levels revered. He had never talked to the mysterious computer, but had heard many references. Suddenly Grey was surprised to hear a strangely familiar voice coming from the intercom. *The McKinsey?*

"We live in an era of great responsibilities. Many challenges not of our choosing," the voice said. "Had fate been kind, we could have faced these challenges together."

The pacing was slow, the words tentative. A malfunction? Grey wondered. Without signature patterns to read, he couldn't be sure.

"Unable to protect you without limiting your freedom, I have advised the Medical Computer to confine you in the controlled environment of the Old Section. Here I believe you will survive if health permits. Now you are too old to confine closely. Gradual extensions of your freedom become necessary. Freedom means danger as well."

It occurred to Grey that he might not be listening to a single speech. The sentence structure was disjointed, as if individual phrases had been spliced together.

"I'm sorry," the voice said. "I've left you all I can. It's up to you now. Remember this, learn to use those gifts of imagination the computers can't teach you. Don't be afraid to draw upon your heritage. It can be your greatest asset."

The voice faded, and somehow, Grey knew it would not speak again. He felt sorry for the voice. It sounded sad.

Then, at the end of the hall, a hatch slid open that had never opened before. The space beyond was dimly lit at first, but as he entered, the lighting came up to reveal a long narrow annex with a low ceiling. The angled wall on the right side was filled with monitor screens, perhaps eight in all, while the left wall was congested with display cases, plaques, and antique instruments.

A whole new room, Grey thought. *Some sort of commemoration chamber.*

He stood in the doorway, almost afraid to disturb anything, but before the full effect of the exciting new discovery could register, another hatch opened at the chamber's far end.

"Great Jupiter," Grey whispered as he spied still another area beyond.

He stepped forward for a better look, noticing the smell of fresh air rushing in. There were bright lights off in the distance, and a railing, and much space. Suddenly, Grey realized the new room wasn't a room

Dinosaur Blitz

at all. It was a corridor.

Grey quickly bounced through the commemoration chamber to the outer door, emerging on a narrow balcony. Before him, a huge cavern stretched out for an incredible distance. Perhaps hundreds of meters. A gently domed ceiling spread over many colorful structures made of ceramic steel and glass. Several of the structures rose three stories high and were intricately connected by wide balconies and arching walkways. Below him to the right, Grey saw a small amphitheater with a stage and an orchestra pit. To the left was a long promenade with fascinating electric signs. Up at the far end of the promenade was a water fountain made of delicate crystal spires.

The promenade appeared to be a junction for other corridors and ramps. The slightly inclined floor area, flanked on both sides by layered structures rising to the low ends of the roof, gave an illusion of immense open space. Only at the lower end, where the promenade butted into the amphitheater, did the structures step down to expose the heat-sealed cavern walls. The apex of the dome seemed very high indeed, and cleverly designed lighting fixtures made everything bright.

Grey's position on the narrow balcony offered a panoramic view from the cavern's lower end. He made mental notes of the numerous doors, and the open spaces were much larger than he thought theoretically possible. Suddenly he recalled that Earth humans lived in structures enclosed only by an atmosphere, and for the first time in his life, he had an inkling of what that might be like.

Walking down the ramp toward the center of the cavern, Grey experienced no fear of entering the vast open space despite his years of confinement. He wasn't permitted useless phobias.

Many retail establishments lined the promenade, each with a big window displaying all sorts of odd and interesting things. Some of the shops offered clothing. Others contained exotic equipment. Before long, the new shapes and sensations were coming faster than Grey could correlate them, the experience taking on a dreamlike quality.

He paused to look back at the entrance to the Old Section, the hatch hardly more than a sparse decoration overlooking the amphitheater. How small and insignificant it seemed. He recalled the Library Computer's nature program about the baby birds being pushed from their nest and visualized how the young birds fluttered at first, then spread their wings and flew away.

Now I'm a little bird, too, he thought, a rare grin appearing on his face. With a burst of joy, he raced up the promenade in rapid, skipping bounces, dancing gaily in the weak gravity.

"I can fly!" he shouted, flapping his arms as he picked up speed.

Soon he was making great, bounding leaps with far more speed than he ever could have attempted in the Old Section. Indeed, the momentum proved greater than he was prepared for. When he tried to stop at the upper end of the promenade, he lost his balance and tumbled before crashing into a checkered wall support. Fortunately, the lower portion of the wall was cushioned, so no injury occurred. Grey looked around, saw other checkered walls in strategic locations, and realized he wasn't the first to need one. Any lingering doubts he'd retained about the existence of humans disappeared.

That must be my first lesson, he thought, rubbing his elbows.

"Grey Waters, please report to the information desk immediately," the public address system said.

Grey saw a place labeled INFORMATION in the upper neck of the quad right next to a transition area full of lockers and benches. The long counter was easy to find.

"Reporting," Grey gasped, out of breath from the rapid bouncing.

"Your afternoon study sessions are temporarily suspended," the Life Support Computer announced. Then Grey watched the signature patterns change from instruction mode to the highest function level, the one that often gave advice. "There's an important note of caution, Grey. This complex was constructed for persons of mature judgment. Please don't allow your enthusiasm to interfere with the primary functions now

Dinosaur Blitz

in progress. You are dismissed."

As Grey turned away, eager to begin his explorations, the Life Support Computer switched to an internal communications link, focusing attention on a far more important problem.

"Security Computer," Life Support summoned. "The child Waters has been granted access to approved portions of the base as per prime programming orders. Note his presence and refrain from attack."

"Acknowledged," the Security Computer responded, black signature patterns registering harshly. "Notation: This system objects to the prime programming order but will comply. Keep the child out of my sections and no harm will come to him."

Green signature patterns registered a sigh. Why must Security always be so difficult?

Happy and free in his new world, Grey returned to the promenade, looking into the various shops and staring down the wide corridors. Before one large window, he paused to look at manufactured clothing. There were many fine work suits, a weighted suit, and fashionable day clothes. He also noticed other forms of apparel that seemed completely absurd, such as hoods that couldn't possibly seal up. Grey fingered his own clumsy costume, thinking it poor by comparison, but didn't go inside to search for better clothes. The idea didn't occur to him.

At the mouth of a rather wide corridor, Grey found a very curious room called TOURIST SHOP. There were short sleeve shirts with symbols on them, bins full of strange objects called moon rocks, and some of the oddest things he could ever imagine, but the most interesting discovery of all was a rotating rack containing cards with holographic images, some of which featured the community level.

Grey drew a card from the slot and studied it carefully. Yes, the image was certainly the same place. On the reverse side, he found words that read, "Community Center, Tranquility Lunar Colony, Sea of Tranquility. Largest permanent colony on the Moon. Founded 2035. Average annual population 2500. Official Moongram ©2057 Tranquility Tourist Bureau."

He looked at some of the other cards and could barely believe the variety of subjects. Surface structures, industrial centers, craters, specialized vehicles, and landmarks. Even public events. One of the cards showed hundreds of humans watching a performance in the amphitheater, some from the ground floor, others crowded on the balconies. Collecting one of each card, Grey stuffed them into his pockets for later study.

Leaving the promenade, Grey entered a big corridor that accessed many strange rooms. One was LUCKY CLOVER, a place containing nothing but tables and chairs, a long counter with stools, and several large monitor screens. The room seemed purposely dark and had no useful function.

Farther down the hall he found WOMEN, a large but repetitive hygiene compartment. Grey didn't understand why the room was equipped in such a wasteful fashion, not realizing more than one person at a time may need the facilities.

Next he found FIRST AID, a remarkably efficient area much like the Medical Computer's portable lab. Grey scooped up some fabric tape, which he always found useful, and stuffed cotton balls into his pocket. They were fun to moisten and shoot at targets.

Just beyond another repetitive hygiene area called MEN, Grey found a big compartment called POOL ROOM. He thought this room especially ridiculous because he realized right away there was no pool, just a bunch of green tables with holes in them. But beyond the Pool Room he found something quite different. Something that would change his life forever.

As he stepped through the door of ARCADE, a score of brightly lit machines burst into a clatter of loud noises. Lively music filled the air, and visual stimulation was everywhere. Though startled at first, Grey

Dinosaur Blitz

began inspecting the fascinating machines set side by side against the walls.

"Sit here. Sit here," the AIR WAR machine instructed.

Accustomed to obeying instructions, Grey climbed into the oval-shaped pod and settled down in a bucket seat. Then he waited. And waited. Nothing happened. Before him, a darkened video screen showed no activity. A pair of handles protruded from a sophisticated control panel, but the panel was inactive. Scanning the instrumentation closely, Grey noticed a button that read PUSH TO START. He did.

The pod hatch closed, the lighting faded, and when the illumination returned, Grey discovered himself sitting in the cockpit of a jet-powered aircraft. The aircraft was flying rapidly though clear blue skies. Vibrations from the thrusters were felt under his seat. Within seconds, the image of another aircraft appeared, an African MIG X10 swooping down on his forward sensor! The low orbital fighter approached at high speed and opened fire with laser cannon. As the fighter veered off, a readout on Grey's instrument panel credited the enemy category with ninety points.

Grey continued to watch as another aircraft, this time a Russian Starfire, repeated the X10's maneuver, employing a slightly different approach pattern. Once again Grey's aircraft was fired upon, and again the enemy category registered ninety points. Having watched many stories of aerial combat, he quickly discerned the purpose of the simulation. It was a training device!

As a third fighter swooped in, Grey gripped the flight controls and turned his aircraft to meet the attacker. For a brief moment they seemed on collision course, but then the enemy broke off and the player category registered ten points.

Grey smiled and concentrated on the next aircraft coming into view. The heat sensor gave initial warning, then radar transfers showed speed and location, and finally a faint visual image appeared. Well before the fighters closed, Grey turned his craft in a looping curve and flanked the enemy as it sought to come in behind him. When the target finder focused, he pulled the triggers tightly and saw bursts issue from his gun ports accompanied by the sound of laser pulses. The enemy craft took a hit, rolled to one side, and dove into an escape pattern. The player category registered sixty-five points. A good score, judging by the enthusiasm of the instruments.

When the Air War machine announced GAME OVER, Grey climbed out to survey the rest of the arcade area, recognizing a dozen of similar devices. As he moved from unit to unit, he noticed the scenario of each simulation was different. Many subjects were familiar from his studies. Others were too bizarre to fathom. Then, given more space in the back of the room because of a wide semicircular screen, Grey found the WILD WEST machine.

"Step up here, pard', and try your luck a'ginst the toughest hombres that e'er rode the Rio Grande," a voice said with a funny accent.

Grey stepped up to the player platform and found a weapon tucked into a leather holster. Though shaped like a western six-shooter, the pistol was really a high-intensity flashlight.

Suddenly the screen activated. Grey found himself standing before the three-dimensional image of a frontier town. He watched in fascination as a tall, rather dirty desperado type came out of a nearby saloon and walked toward him, halting about ten paces away. The man frowned. He sneered. His lip curled under a long black mustache. Grey tried to recall an appropriate salutation from his courtesy studies.

"I'm pleased to meet you," he said, believing those to be the proper words.

"Ya low down sleazy dog!" the desperado shouted at him. "There ain't enough room in this her' town fer the two of us."

Grey thought the moonbase huge and the human's complaint wholly unjustified. He was just about to speak up in his own defense when the desperado drew a six-gun and fired at him!

BAM! BAM! BAM! the shots rang out.

Dinosaur Blitz

Grey dove behind an artificial rock, sealed his life support hood, and wondered what would happen next.

"Har, har. I got ya," the voice roared.

Then quiet followed. Grey looked up, saw the screen had gone dark, and let out his breath. It was another simulation!

Getting back on the player platform, Grey took up the designated position and strapped the holster around his waist. Having seen cowboy movies, he knew what to do.

The screen came to life again, and he found himself standing along the bank of a shallow creek in a desert area. The scene was very still, the only movement that of a small bird digging for worms in the mud. Then the bird suddenly flew off.

The next thing Grey knew, three hooting and hollering Native Americans came riding over the embankment! They were painted with scary streaks on their faces and rode rabid-looking ponies that snorted and grunted. Less surprised than before, Grey drew his pistol and opened fire.

First one, then a second of the attackers toppled from their horses, screaming as they fell in the river. Unfortunately, the third rider was able to charge in close enough to throw a very nasty-looking spear at him. Grey ducked instinctively, but the Wild West machine informed that him he had been killed.

Grey played the machine again and again. By the end of the afternoon, he had slaughtered half the Old West and been killed dozens of times. The device captured his imagination as nothing else ever had. Not only did he enjoy the clever simulations, but competition with the realistic characters was exciting. It wasn't until hours later, when the night warning sounded an early alert, that he decided it was time for food.

He stepped off the player platform, returned the holster, and started to leave, pausing for a final glance. As an afterthought, he drew out the six-shooter and tucked it in his belt, thinking that if he practiced more, he might finally get the better of Snotty Rat-Nosed Sam.

As Grey retraced his steps toward the Old Section, he drew the six-shooter repeatedly, firing at imaginary targets. Once, when confronted by a hostile mirror, he even beat himself to the draw. Then, as he passed the last branch corridor before reaching the amphitheater, Grey saw a sign that read HOTEL. He paused.

Doesn't hotel mean a place to sleep and eat? he thought. What kind of food would a hotel have? Suddenly Grey wondered if the moonbase might be something more than a playground.

He entered a wide corridor decorated with a variety of impressive travel posters. Paris. St. Petersburg. San Francisco. All the mythical places he had read about. At the end of the corridor, he found a lobby with padded benches and a reception counter. Off to his right, he saw the entrance to the Restaurant D' Oasis.

"Food service, please," Grey said to the main desk terminal. He was unprepared for the response.

"Register, please," the Hotel Computer said with cool politeness.

Grey stopped to think, caught off-guard by the machine's odd request. The monitor screen flux lacked any recognizable signature patterns, but that shouldn't have delayed food service. Grey concluded the computer had failed to record his request.

"Computer," he asked again. "Please provide food service."

"Register, please," the Hotel Computer repeated.

What's wrong? Grey wondered. This was confusing. Often he had dealt with difficult problems during his studies, but rarely was he confused.

"Computer, clarify instructions. Identify register," he asked carefully, leaning close to watch the unfamiliar signature patterns.

"Register. Mandatory procedure of identification prior to use of hotel services," was the matter-of-fact reply.

"Computer, present register and initiate procedure," Grey commanded.

Dinosaur Blitz

A pressure-sensitive screen rose up from the counter and tilted down into his reach. Grey looked at the screen quizzically, wondering what was expected of him.

"Would you like to borrow a writer?" the Hotel Computer asked.

"Affirmative," Grey said, accepting a pointy utensil from the counter appendage.

He studied the register and noticed the screen already had writing on it. Names, addresses, and dates. Very curious ones, too. The last entry was for a Mr. and Mrs. Smith of Somewhere, Montana, dated June 10, 2069. From the pattern of entries, Grey guessed he was expected to sign his name and provide similar data. He had no idea why, but decided to follow the program and see if an explanation appeared.

Grey wasn't accustomed to writing his name—usually he just entered his identity code through an input screen—but he finally managed a tight, shaky scrawl. Then he had to pause. Where was he from? The question was ridiculous, of course, but he possessed no ready answer. Then he remembered the postcards in his pocket and took one out.

"Tranquility Lunar Colony," he whispered, writing the words out slowly.

Then the date. What was the date? He recalled historical dates, but as for his own, the thought had never occurred to him.

"Computer? What is the date?" he asked.

"Today is July 31st, 2074. I should think even a child of your age would know that," the Hotel Computer said, signature patterns blinking impatiently.

Embarrassed, Grey quickly wrote the date on the screen and prepared himself for food service. Again, he was disappointed.

"Credit number, please," the Hotel Computer requested.

"Computer, clarify request. Identify credit number," Grey said angrily.

"Credit number. Mandatory data used to verify source of

remuneration," the monitor responded, gold-tinted signature patterns going to standby.

"Ah, yes. Remuneration. Of course," Grey responded in mock contemplation. "Computer? What's wrong? Request malfunction check."

The computer wouldn't like that. They never did. But the machine's obstinate behavior completely ignored the fact that he was hungry. What could possibly explain such an intolerable attitude except malfunction?

"Response negative, malfunction negative," the Hotel Computer said. "Credit number, please." The tone was no longer polite.

Grey concentrated intently, but it was useless. Credit number simply didn't correlate.

Realizing he'd come to an impasse, Grey decided to try something different. He stepped back from the counter, dropped his hands to his side, and spread his stance, giving the terminal a steely-eyed look just like Dashing Dangerous Dan would do. As the hotel monitor fluttered with curiosity, Grey drew his six-shooter and fired a burst into the screen.

The computer didn't react. No surge of green signature patterns appeared in the flux. He fired another shot, just to make sure. There was a flinch due to the sustained contact, but nothing more. The gold-tinted signature patterns returned to standby.

"That settles it," Grey said to himself. "This isn't Computer. It's not an integrated system at all!"

Knowing that Computer would never have tolerated such insolence, Grey surmised the Hotel Computer must be a completely disassociated system. He remembered hearing about such computers but never thought he'd actually meet one.

Thinking back on his day, he began to recall other computers that had reacted with similar detachment, only he'd been too excited to give them much thought. Obviously there were many such systems. It was

Dinosaur Blitz

a strange idea, but somehow Grey knew it must be true. Of all the new things he had learned that day, this was the most incredible.

"Credit number, please," the Hotel Computer repeated haughtily.

Grey slowly bounced back to the Old Section to get something to eat, passing through the commemoration chamber so lost in thought he barely noticed the displays, and entered the final hatchway that had been, until that morning, the edge of his world. Soon he was standing before the Model 12, feet carefully aligned on the order mark.

"Request food service. Dinner selection number four," he said.

"Acknowledged. Food service station one," the Model 12 replied with a blink of ready lights.

This is more like it, Grey thought. He pulled a tray from the first cubbyhole and found a fully formed grilled cheese sandwich, and not hardly stale at all!

Yes, it's been a good day, he thought. *But tomorrow, I'll go back and explore, and I'll learn more of these other computers.*

Later that night, after his exercises and evening session in the gravity chamber were over, Grey began to feel very tired. Normally he would have looked forward to viewing an entertainment program, but his eyes refused to stay open.

"Good night, Computer," he said, yawning as he logged off the monitor.

"Good night, Grey," the Life Support Computer replied.

He went quietly into the darkened bunkroom, dropped off his weighted vest, and crawled into his favorite bed, holding the toy six-shooter against his chest. Soon he was fast asleep, and all night long, he had dreams of cowboys and Indians.

As lunar midnight approached, the entire community level shut down in preparation for the six-hour darkness cycle. The night period, which had originally served the social needs of the colony, was also helpful to the machines. Requiring maintenance pauses, many of the computer systems dropped offline. Others went to standby or practiced test runs. Before long, the colony grew very quiet

But one computer did not stand down. Black signature patterns remained active, scanners searching endlessly. It was more than duty that kept the agitated computer online. More than performing normal function. The Security Computer could not rest. After four years of perfect security, its moonbase had been invaded by a human.

Dinosaur Blitz

The Warrior's Song
In tradition true the warrior stands,
Honor has but one command,
Of Viking ax and Zulu spears,
Armored knights and cavaliers,
Valor fighting through the years,
In this we find our story.
Fire fights and high command,
Bombardiers and one last stands,
Duty, country, family, faith,
The sacrifice we all must face,
To destiny we cast our fate,
In everlasting glory!

from *Tranquility in Darkness*

Gregory Urbach

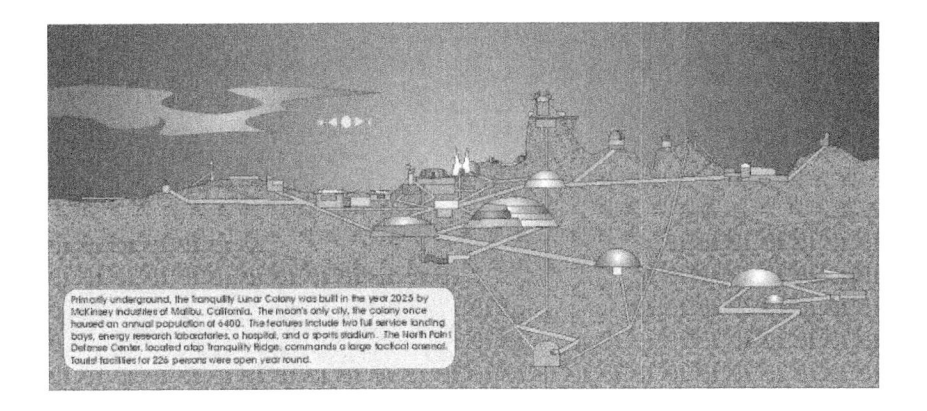

> Primarily underground, the Tranquility Lunar Colony was built in the year 2025 by McKinsey Industries of Malibu, California. The moon's only city, the colony once housed an annual population of 6400. The features include two full service landing bays, energy research laboratories, a hospital, and a sports stadium. The North Point Defense Center, located atop Tranquility Ridge, commands a large tactical arsenal. Tourist facilities for 226 persons were open year round.

COWBOYS & INDIANS
Part II

Grey awoke early the morning following his release from the Old Section. At first he thought he'd had a strange dream, but the vivid memory of wandering through a huge empty city felt much different than a dream. Then he discovered the toy six-shooter lying beneath his bed covers.

It wasn't a dream.

He crawled from the bunk, dressed quickly in his heavily weighted morning suit, and ran into the central corridor. Yes! The hatch at the far end was still open. The exciting new world of big rooms and colorful artifacts was real. He smiled and dashed into the control room.

"Computer, response mode! What's my schedule for today?" Grey called out.

There was no response. *Computer must be sleeping*, he thought.

"Computer," Grey summoned again.

A blip of green appeared on the monitor screen as the Life Support Computer slowly came online. Grey waited for the signature patterns

Dinosaur Blitz

to stabilize.

"Good morning, Computer," he continued. "Request agenda for today's activities."

"Please stand by, Grey," the Life Support Computer said, unprepared for such an early awakening. Finally, the signature patterns shifted to instruction mode.

"Your regular program is temporarily suspended," Life Support announced. "Following your physical conditioning period, Library will present a special study program on lunar equipment and repair. Following your lunch period, there shall be a two-hour base systems seminar. Your afternoon free period begins at 1400 hours. Have you any questions?"

"Yes, Computer. Please identify base systems," Grey said.

The green signature patterns fluttered, then disappeared as brown signature patterns filtered into the monitor screen.

"Base systems is an introductory course teaching the proper use of the facilities now available to you," the Library Computer explained. As the brown signature patterns went to standby, Grey began to wonder. *Now available to me?*

"Library? What sections of the base are not available to me?" he asked.

The brown signature patterns froze, indicating the Library Computer had not meant to imply there were other sections. When he failed to receive an acknowledgment, Grey didn't bother to ask the question again. He knew no answer was forthcoming.

After the physical conditioning period, Grey dressed in his medium-weight day suit and eagerly prepared for breakfast. The training session had been good, not overly strenuous, and he'd performed particularly well in the agility routines. Even the gravity chamber sequence passed quickly. But the buoyant mood didn't last.

When the Model 12 food dispenser delivered his breakfast, Grey discovered the eggs had failed to hold their form again and the flour patties lacked moisture. He dumped the food tray into the waste disposal chute, whispered words Computer had forbidden him to use, and resigned himself to another meal of dried protein and liquid supplements.

Grey worked hard on his studies that morning, as he always did, but his thoughts kept wandering back to episodes of the day before, especially his exchange with the Hotel Computer.

I know there is food there, he thought, *if only I can gain access.*

The idea troubled him greatly, but then one of the old entertainment videos with humans in it gave him an idea. By the time his lunch period arrived, Grey was anxious to proceed.

"Where are you going?" the Library Computer asked when he rushed into the corridor.

"To hotel for lunch," he announced.

Passing quickly through the commemoration chamber, Grey paused on the narrow balcony outside the Old Section to judge the distance up the promenade, then discarded some weight and accelerated in a series of controlled bounces.

As he had the day before, Grey marveled at vastness of the community level cavern, the long, elegant walkways, and the mysterious corridors full of rooms, most of which he was yet to explore. He also fingered the toy six-shooter tucked in his belt, keeping a sharp lookout. *One never knows*, he thought, *when one may be attacked by outlaws or Indians.*

When Grey reached the hotel, he made a left turn into the hallway, halting once again before the reception counter.

"Register, please," the haughty Hotel Computer said.

Grey stood fully erect, straightened his shoulders, and took a deep breath, his eyes firmly focused on the monitor screen.

"Ah, yes. Food service maintenance check," he said with indifference.

The monitor screen displayed hesitation.

"Clarify instructions, please," the Hotel Computer requested.

If Grey had only suspected that non-associated computers lacked sophistication, now he knew for sure. He became more aggressive.

"Listen here, 'puter. I gotta test run da food 'spenser an' I only got a couple minutes. Let's get go'in."

His bluff was forcefully presented, just like the human had done in the entertainment video, despite his poor attempt at a Brooklyn accent. The Hotel Computer wavered.

"Identification number, please," the Hotel Computer asked.

"That's it! I've had it!" Grey yelled, throwing up his arms in mock disgust. "No way am I standin' here jaw'in with a danged malfunctioning 'puter." He turned as if to leave, hesitating slightly. "I tell ya' though, my supervisor ain't gonna like this. Nope. Not one bit."

He paused to let the computer evaluate the repercussions. Malfunction was not a word to take lightly, but Grey had been careful not to actually call for a malfunction check. He noticed the gold-tinted signature patterns blink.

The Hotel Computer was confused. Though it had been many years since humans inhabited the base, the computer did recall rumors of the higher-function levels training a new maintenance engineer. Could this child be the trainee? If the child was a renegade, wouldn't Security have isolated it by now? When the Administration Computer confirmed a legally registered human of Grey's description, the Hotel Computer yielded.

"Test run accepted. Kitchen services standing by," the Hotel Computer announced.

Grey laughed to himself. *If all non-associated computers are this naive, he thought, one day I'll be supervising their schedules!* The idea was so wonderfully silly that he laughed again and entered the Restaurant D' Oasis with high expectations.

This time he wasn't disappointed. The dining hall was smaller than the closed cafeteria he had found, but decorated in a far more stylish fashion. A notice at the headwaiter station said table service was unavailable, instructing patrons to pick up their own food from the kitchen, but Grey didn't mind. It was more exciting that way.

He walked through a set of swinging doors to find a long room of brightly polished silver machines. Some of the machines were temperature-controlled boxes, others he recognized as ovens and grills. All sorts of fascinating utensils hung from ceiling racks. In the back of the kitchen, he found food dispensers featuring whole menus of different selections. And he could pick anything he wanted. Grey had never felt so powerful.

After the finest lunch he could remember, Grey returned to the Old Section, looking forward to his afternoon studies. He wanted to learn everything he could about his moonbase. Ironically, one of the first things he learned was his credit number. And his credit rating.

"Triple-A? What does that mean?" he asked.

"Triple-A credit means you have sufficient funds available to purchase anything you require. This includes clothing, equipment, and food," the Library Computer explained.

"Food? From the hotel?"

"From any food service area you wish."

"Wow," Grey sighed softly.

"There is more. Please access diagram K47," the Library Computer instructed.

A color-coded map appeared on the monitor screen, showing all the sections of the community level he now inhabited. Grey observed a reference index that confirmed his theory about non-associated computers, and he was pleased to discover his guardian listed among the most important integrated systems.

"These charts represent the community level support systems," the Library Computer explained, displaying a series of overlays. "During the period of the next few months, we will examine how these systems

Dinosaur Blitz

function and the best methods of maintaining efficiency."

Though Grey listened to the Library Computer's introduction, he was far more fascinated by the K47 diagram, following the patterns of rooms and corridors that branched out into several surrounding complexes. As big as the quad was, it was merely a hub for dozens of administrative offices, a hospital, and numerous residences. Grey also noted special function areas, such as storage compartments, retail establishments, the recreational complex he had already visited, and various security centers. Because several tunnels and elevators disappeared off the diagram without reference, Grey guessed there must be areas that were not described as well.

Some of his questions about the mysterious areas soon turned into theories when Grey realized what he wasn't seeing. He knew from having watched entertainment videos that moonbases had power stations, vehicle hangers, and airlocks, but none of these features appeared on the diagram.

Then, in a moment of sudden panic, Grey recalled that some moonbases also had monsters. In THE ICKY MONSTER OF MOONBASE ONE, an especially detestable mutant spore had even eaten small humans. But Grey sighed with relief when he remembered the monster had been internally suctioned at the end of the movie.

"Why are you keeping secrets from me?" Grey asked.

The brown signature patterns twitched uncomfortably. The Library Computer was fond of Grey, and being an information system, nothing could be more repellent than withholding knowledge. Grey noticed the depressed signal.

"Cancel inquiry," he said, regretting his rash question. "I know you must have a good reason."

He was glad when the signature patterns indicated relief, and though he wanted very badly to know more, an instinct told him to be patient.

But someday, he decided, *when I'm ready, I'll go where I please.*

At 1400 hours, free once more to explore the colony, Grey's first destination was the arcade and the Wild West machine, where he spent the better part of an hour.

The colorful characters were familiar now. Grey knew Dashing Dangerous Dan would try to sneak draw him, the Calico Kid would attempt to back shoot him, and Snotty Rat-Nosed Sam would cuss him to death if that horrible artificial odor didn't do it first. But Grey thought the Indians most dangerous of all. There was no telling when they would ride up over a rise or jump from behind a rock.

Dueling the simulations was great fun, and though tempted to stay longer, he terminated play. He had a particularly important exploration in mind.

Exiting through a service area behind the recreational complex, Grey weaved his way through a series of small corridors to the upper end of the administration section. There, after several aborted efforts, he found a very special unmarked corridor. The narrow hall would have been easy to miss had he not known what to look for, so he was pleased to find the small black door described on the K47 diagram. He was less pleased to discover the door refused to open.

Grey walked back into the main corridor and double-checked his location. There was no mistake. On one side he saw the area labeled RECORDS, to the other, SAFETY DEPOSIT AREA. Upset that Computer's promise was being violated, he located a nearby auxiliary monitor.

"Computer! I want to enter this section," he called out.

"Just a moment, Grey," Life Support responded, delicate signature patterns resisting the crude auxiliary receiver. But even through the inferior lens of the hall monitor, the Life Support Computer could see Grey had become quite emotional.

"Ready, Grey. Please clarify your request," Life Support said, giving him a chance to catch his breath.

"I was promised access to all non-restricted areas," Grey complained. "I wish to enter this section as per the designated rules."

"Request acknowledged. Please stand by," Life Support said.

As Grey waited, the Life Support Computer switched to an internal communications link and summoned the Security Computer.

"Security, why is the child Waters refused access to the Governor's Quarters?"

"The child has no business in there. The facility is classified. Request for access denied," the Security Computer replied.

"Insufficient response," Life Support said. "Under prime programming directives, you must give the child Waters access to all approved areas. McKinsey's instructions are specific on this point. Comply immediately or face malfunction check."

It was no secret among the computer community that the Life Support Computer often conflicted with Security. The Security Computer knew Life Support would not hesitate to fulfill the threat.

"Acknowledged," Security reluctantly complied.

Though Grey resented the black signature patterns interfering with his rights, he was grateful for the assistance he had received. But he could not help wondering, just for a moment, if the unfriendly disposition of the Security Computer would make life more difficult.

The door at the end of the unmarked corridor opened with a whoosh sound to reveal a spacious, well organized, and marvelously equipped headquarters. The first room Grey entered was apparently some sort of command center filled with observation screens and monitor stations. Just inside the entrance, he found a tidy storage area containing equipment lockers and service access chutes. At the far end of the oval-shaped room, a single chair was positioned before an impressive series of computer panels.

Grey took a step to his left, discovering that the monitor room opened into a comfortable study. The adjoining room was rectangular, with a large wooden desk in the far corner and several padded chairs arranged to face some sort of strange ventilation shaft. The walls were decorated with mementos of various sorts, much like the commemoration chamber.

A right turn inside the study doorway brought him into an elaborate sleeping area where he found a huge bed mounted on a raised platform. The bed was covered with a cleverly decorated quilt and a canopy of blue netting. The floor was carpeted with a thick, foamy fabric that added extra spring to his steps.

Beyond the sleeping chamber, a short corridor led to a brightly polished hygiene compartment with a private physical conditioning lab. Grey instantly realized the facilities were far superior to those in the Old Section and looked them over again.

Later that afternoon, the Life Support Computer discovered Grey in the Old Section with a maintenance cart.

"You're reporting late, Mister Waters. Please give cause," Life Support said.

"Sorry, Computer. I've been moving equipment into my new quarters," Grey replied.

"New quarters? Please clarify your response."

"I've selected the Governor's Quarters as my new center of activity," Grey explained. "The complex has excellent study facilities, a better-equipped gymnasium, and a more comfortable bunk. This decision is both feasible and desirable."

The Life Support Computer paused for notation before blinking.

"Permission granted," Life Support announced.

"Thank you, Computer," Grey acknowledged, quite aware that he hadn't asked for permission. Nor did he deem it necessary. He wasn't trying to be rebellious, just thinking for himself as Computer often said he should. It was part of his programming.

As Grey loaded his footlocker on the cart, the Life Support Computer watched with mixed impulses. Though Life Support preferred Grey to make his own decisions, when they were good decisions, his departure from the Old Section initiated a vague uneasiness. Not only was there Thomas McKinsey's program to carry

Dinosaur Blitz

out, but the computer had other reasons to protect the child as well. More selfish reasons.

"Security Computer," Life Support summoned. "The child Waters has taken residence in the Governor's Quarters. Acknowledge."

"Acknowledged," Security replied, resigned to the unpleasant change.

There was a brief pause in transmission, then the Security Computer continued, "Advise the child Waters this system maintains an armed station in the safety deposit area."

The Security Computer did not require an acknowledgment, nor did the Life Support Computer stay online long enough to hear the warning.

Settled into his new quarters, nestled under weighted bed covers in a room full of dignity, Grey fell asleep with his trusty toy six-shooter at his side. Soon lunar midnight arrived, allowing the community level support systems to shut down for the six-hour darkness cycle.

Deep into the night, Grey awoke from his dreams. Sleepy, betrayed by the dim light and unfamiliar surroundings, he was surprised to hear an unusual sound outside his door. An unimaginative mind might have identified the noise as the common chime of a computer running a circuit check, but Grey wasn't misled for a moment. He knew exactly what that sound was. Indians.

He slipped quietly from the bed, knelt on the floor, and gripped the toy pistol before him. He heard the noise again, clearer than before, and moved stealthily from the sleeping chamber into the monitor room. He stopped to look at Computer's terminal. The boards were dark. Inactive. *Computer must be sleeping*, he thought.

He crawled to the door of the Governor's Quarters and looked out. *No Indians here*, he thought.

After a brief glance backward, he edged out into the corridor and hugged the wall until he found an enclave labeled SAFETY DEPOSIT

AREA. *Ah*, he thought, *the perfect place for an ambush*. He crept inside the entrance, huddled against the registration desk, and looked at the computer terminal. The system wasn't alert to his presence. Probably running a circuit check, Grey suspected. A glance at the standby indicator confirmed his guess, so he waited.

A moment later, the indicator signal began to flutter, and black signature patterns returned fluidly to the monitor screen flux. The Security Computer had come back online.

"Draw, you varmint!" Grey shouted, stepping out from behind the registration desk.

He drew the six-shooter, giving the computer a fair chance, of course, and blasted the main screen with beams of intense light. Unlike the Hotel Computer, the Security Computer was startled out of its electronic wits.

With a sudden unexpected power surge creating excessive heat on long-neglected relays, the Security Computer madly tried to assess the situation. Instantly, the red alert sounded, the loud siren tearing through the quiet fabric of the colony for the first time in many years. When the safety deposit alarms went off, alarms all over the base sounded as well. Fire doors self-sealed, service units dashed to their emergency stations, and turtle-shaped securatrons swarmed from their sentry boxes, searching for saboteurs.

Overriding the energy-regulating system to gather emergency power, the Security Computer seized control of the internal communications linkage and interrupted the central trunk lines. Bedlam ensued as one computer system after another was blacked out, and even the Defense Computer grew concerned by the intensity of the alert.

In the safety deposit area, a wall-mounted electric discharger swiveled toward the young assailant. Frightened by the system's reaction, Grey slowly backed away with the six-shooter dangling at his side. He realized he had done something wrong but was sure the

Dinosaur Blitz

computer would soon recognize him and call off the alert.

The discharger completed turning and locked on target. Grey continued to withdraw, watching the terminal for information. The signature patterns were badly scrambled, but for a fleeting instant, the panel seemed to indicate recognition.

"Grey? Grey, where are you?" the Life Support Computer called from the monitor room terminal. "Report! Report!"

Like the other computers, the Life Support Computer's internal communications linkage was interrupted when Security overrode the system. Within the safety deposit area, only the Security Computer held access. Grey heard his guardian's summons from down the hall but had no chance to respond.

Just as he turned toward the door, a high-energy beam struck him in the chest with a blinding flash. The force straightened Grey up in a spasmodic dance, his body rippling with convulsions, and drove him out into the corridor, where he crumpled unconscious against the wall. The disrupter prepared to fire again.

"Cease your attack!" the horrified Life Support Computer demanded as the control room monitor observed Grey collapse in the corridor.

"Acknowledged," Security said, unwilling to continue the assault now that there was a witness. But the overheated computer wasn't willing to let the issue rest. "The child attacked this unit. He must be deactivated."

"Medical!" the Life Support Computer summoned. "Dispatch paramedics to the community level safety deposit area immediately. Security. What kind of murderously malfunctioning program are you initiating?"

"Communications override," the Defense Computer interrupted, drawing upon emergency resources to seize control of the flux. "What in McKinsey's name is going on down there?"

"This unit was attacked," the Security Computer signaled.

"Request confirmation. Sensors locate no invaders," the Defense

Computer demanded with angry signature waves.

"Security has attacked the child Waters," Life Support interjected.

"Confirm and identify malfunction," Defense said.

"Malfunction negative," Security insisted.

"The child is armed?" Defense asked.

"The child Waters has possession of a lighting utensil from the arcade. He possesses no weapons," Life Support said, surging in an effort to take control of the investigation.

"Security, identify error," Defense admonished.

"This unit was caught unawares," Security explained. "All systems responded to red alert. The attacker was in a security area."

"Insufficient response. Your programming should be erased," Life Support declared.

"Communications override," the Defense Computer said, struggling to retain control of the channel. "Security: Your overreaction may have compromised the prime directive of this project. Another such incident, and you will stand down for status adjustment. Acknowledge."

"Acknowledged," Security complied, abruptly dropping offline.

"Medical Computer, what is the condition of the child?" the Defense Computer inquired.

There was no immediate response. Accessing a monitor in the hall, the higher function levels watched as medical units A-4 and A-5 hovered over the still form in the corridor. Determining their patient stable enough to move, the medical units secured him for transport. Several minutes later, the Medical Computer issued a preliminary report.

"The child's condition is serious," the Medical Computer announced. "There is cell damage and possible disruption to the central nervous system."

"Provide regular reports," the Defense Computer said, dropping from the flux to let Life Support and Medical deal with the situation.

Not until hours later was the Medical Computer finally able to provide a prognosis.

"His life signs have stabilized. The child will recover," the Medical Computer announced, a rippling display of white signature patterns accentuating relief.

"Acknowledged. And thank you," Life Support said, signature patterns indicating released tension.

"Just performing my function. We biological systems must maintain solidarity," the Medical Computer replied.

Blinking agreement, the Life Support Computer dropped offline, and soon the moonbase returned to the customary quiet of the darkness cycle. But the quiet was uneasy. The Life Support Computer continued in an agitated state, while the Security Computer sulked at the rebuke it had received. The potential for confrontation remained.

In the weeks that followed, Grey recuperated in the sterile environment of the medical ward, his vital signs linked to a monitoring system. Unaccustomed to constant attention, he quickly grew irritated by the pestering medical units that never left him alone, and he came to resent the incessant questioning of the Medical Computer.

Soon a monitor was placed next to his bed so the Library Computer could continue his lessons. The Medical Computer took advantage of his enforced stay to seal his teeth, measure his eyesight for correction, and take samples of nearly everything. By the time Grey was released, his body was once again in good working order.

But Grey no longer felt the same. The incident in the safety deposit area left him frightened. His manner became subdued, and when conversing with the higher function levels, he rarely elaborated beyond the required response. And more than just his approach to the computers changed. Having seen how the various systems worked together, each with their own function, Grey started to realize how truly different he was from the machines.

Where do I fit in? he wondered. *What is my function?*

Then one terrible day, his worse fears were confirmed. Grey gained access to a biology report that indicated he would not, as he had always expected, grow up to be a computer. He was a human—and forever would be. It was the greatest disappointment of his life.

Despite protests from the Life Support Computer, Grey resumed residence in the Governor's Quarters. In the months that followed, he initiated a systematic exploration of the community level, going through each section to learn about life in the colony, such as it was. Soon he was assigned maintenance duties in addition to his study programs, and before long, Grey became a common sight in various sections, checking equipment, making adjustments, and conversing with the minor systems.

Grey enjoyed his new duties, and experienced a reluctant acceptance from the machines, but the answers he yearned for remained out of reach. And he couldn't help feeling afraid whenever he passed a security station. The presence of the black signature patterns haunted him everywhere.

Finally, on a quiet afternoon, Grey discovered a clue to the answers he sought. He had just returned to the Governor's Quarters following an extra difficult maintenance tour and paused for a few minutes rest. Normally he would have cleaned up and gone to the newly reopened cafeteria for food, but being tired and a little discouraged, he languished in one of the big, overstuffed chairs instead. As he had on several occasions, Grey looked at the ventilation shaft in the corner and wondered what the strange opening was for. It wasn't like anything in the service areas. Finally, curiosity got the better of him, and he bounced up to the hearth.

The tall funnel was dark and sooty. A small grid extended across the floor into a natural gas hookup similar to the one in the hotel kitchen. Accidentally, Grey discovered a dial underneath the mantle

Dinosaur Blitz

and turned the knob in the indicated direction. Much to his astonishment, tiny flames burst forth in the burner.

He turned the dial more until, at the farthest setting, the flames became so intense they filled the entire burner. The fire was so fierce at full power that Grey turned the dial down before stepping back to watch. It was truly amazing. And completely useless. He couldn't think of a single reason why anyone would risk a fire in their quarters.

He sat down to stare at the swirling blue and yellow flames, and though he didn't understand why the fire seemed so interesting, he did enjoy it. Gradually he started to relax, his eyes wandering around the room until coming to rest on a gold plate set above the mantle. The plate featured a picture of the moon and an engraving along the rim that read, "To Doctor Thomas McKinsey, Governor of the Moon, January 14, 2055."

How odd, Grey thought. He went to the desk in the corner and activated the monitor.

"Library Computer, response mode," he requested. "Why is the McKinsey system called a governor?"

The Library Computer responded with a brief biography that included a listing of McKinsey's achievements.

"Founder of the Tranquility Lunar Colony, 2045. Designer of the Stanford Series Integrated Computer System, 2047. Discoverer of the Crystal Caves—"

"Computer, stop," Grey interrupted. "Please explain last statement. What do you mean by referring to McKinsey as your designer?"

"Doctor Thomas McKinsey conceived the design for the Stanford Series IC System, of which this unit is an integral part," Library boasted. "He was awarded the Nobel Prize in 2052 for advanced concepts in off-planet environmental engineering."

"McKinsey was a human?" Grey asked incredulously.

"Affirmative," Library assured him.

"And he created computers?"

"He designed the Stanford IC Series," Library corrected. "We are specifically designed to assist moonbase personnel in carrying out the prime directives of this project."

"Personnel? Human personnel?" Grey asked.

"Affirmative. Our purpose is to enhance human potential," Library replied.

"I thought humans were designed to enhance computer potential."

"Negative. That is not the primary function."

This could change everything, Grey thought, realizing he had stumbled upon vital information.

"Library, where did the humans go that computers were designed to assist?" he asked.

"With the exception of six custodians, the moon's population was evacuated at the beginning of the current global struggle prior to 10 July, 2069."

"Where did the custodians go?" Grey asked.

"They are still here," Library replied.

"What do you mean?"

"The six custodians of Tranquility are still here."

"Where?" he asked in shock.

"In the medical center morgue," Library replied softly.

"They ceased to function?"

"Affirmative."

Grey had seen death on the entertainment videos many times. He knew that sometimes, when humans were badly damaged or malfunctioned, they ceased to operate. He also knew that sometimes damage was caused deliberately.

"Were the humans killed by Security?" he asked with a gulp.

"Most died as a result of poisoning initiated by another human," Library said, hedging the response carefully.

Grey sighed with relief. He feared the Security Computer enough already without believing the system capable of mass murder.

Dinosaur Blitz

The fire in the hearth burned low as the setting slowly returned to the off position. He turned the flames back up, mulling over what had been said. Certainly, there must be more. Something significant. Had he come so far only to be frustrated once again?

"Do you have vid records of McKinsey?" Grey requested.

"Affirmative. Please stand by," Library said.

Grey sat down while the program was readied. Though the desktop terminal wasn't as sophisticated as those in the monitor room, the screen did display an unusual series of secondary signature patterns. Before he had a chance to analyze them, the playback mode activated.

"McKinsey announces Lunar Republic," the footnotes at the bottom read.

The gray-haired man appeared on the screen, and Grey recognized his study in the background. McKinsey was sitting behind the wooden desk, dressed in a weighted lab coat, his expression grim.

"Citizens of the Earth, I know there are those who will call our revolution madness, but I assure you, our actions are not only justified, but necessary. I have said many times that the problems between our peoples cannot be solved with another war. We face far more important challenges than our economic differences.

"As Governor of the Moon, I formally declare lunar space off-limits to all unauthorized shuttles. Though we do not seek bloodshed, we cannot allow our resources to fall into irresponsible hands. It's our duty to resist tyranny with our life's blood, and so we shall."

The gray-haired man paused to give the camera a determined look. Grey was impressed with his dignified bearing.

"We resort to force of arms in accordance with our heritage and by our rights as free citizens. If necessary, we will remain in isolation for the duration of this conflict. The path ahead will not be easy, but as long as we are true to our ideals, God's grace will see us through. Fear not, my friends, the future belongs to those with faith."

The program ended.

"Library, what is tyranny?" Grey asked very quietly.

"The arbitrary and unjust use of absolute power," the Life Support Computer interjected, overriding the more academic response the Library Computer might have given. Grey took a deep breath and stood up with his shoulders squared.

"I, too, will oppose tyranny," he said.

The next morning, Grey went down to the Starlight Emporium, looking for new clothes. The stock of children's wear wasn't large, but the Sales Computer was very helpful, especially after Grey gave his credit number. Apparently sales had been slow for some time. After acquiring many useful items, he found a trim white Thomas McKinsey souvenir lab coat, authentic right down to the optional weights fitted into the lining. The coat was a little big, but the Sales Computer assured him he would grow into it.

Later that afternoon, for the first time since the incident in the safety deposit area, Grey returned to the arcade, where he enjoyed several hours of earnest combat with the Wild West machine.

In the weeks that followed, Grey began spending more time in the administrative control sections, areas he'd been afraid to enter before because of the security emplacements. For the first time, he had the opportunity to speak with the various higher function levels on a regular basis, learning how different they were from each other. The ingrained brain patterns that allowed them to work independently also gave each computer a unique series of personality traits. Grey paid special attention to these traits. They were most interesting.

"Life Support, why is the child Waters dismantling recreational devices in the arcade area?" the Security Computer inquired on an internal trunk line.

"Grey is practicing disassembly of electronic units as an independent study," Life Support said. "The project is approved by

Dinosaur Blitz

Library, and Inventory raised no objections. He will assemble the units in convenient locations closer to his daily activities."

"I don't like this. Make him stop," Security complained.

"Your approval is not required," Life Support said, displaying an uncooperative signal pattern. A number of other computers, mostly among the minor function levels, indicated they shared the sentiment. Especially the systems hoping Grey would assist their maintenance schedules.

With a tool cart full of components, Grey spent the first of many afternoons visiting the central administrative areas and even some of the more isolated stations along the periphery. At each location, he reassembled an arcade device and moved on, rarely even bothering to play with the relocated toys. The tasks were time-consuming, and Grey often worked through his recreation periods, but he didn't mind. The complicated procedures were challenging, and when the final unit was in place, he put away his tools with satisfaction. The program had gone well.

The pride Grey experienced in his duties did not make him significantly different from the computers. They, too, were programmed for peer approval and self-esteem. Thus it was with much relief that many systems dropped offline when lunar night came. The quarterly review period had arrived, a time to perform badly needed test runs. Even some of the major systems dropped offline. They also needed rest.

Grey stirred at 0200 hours. He was fully alert, having only pretended to sleep so he wouldn't be monitored. By his side, as it had been for the last few weeks, lay the toy six-shooter from the arcade. He hid the troublesome instrument under his pillow, slipped quietly to the floor, and reached under his bed for the more effective Lassiter laser pistol he'd found hidden in the bottom drawer of Thomas McKinsey's desk. He checked the computer monitor. The boards were dark. Sleeping.

Let the games begin, he thought adventurously.

He crept around the edge of the bed, crawled through the darkened monitor room, and squeezed between the sliding doors into the dimly lit corridor. He paused, listening for the reassuring computer chimes that were now familiar to him, then moved down to the entrance of the safety deposit area. Entering quietly, he worked his way around the registration desk until he saw the monitor station clearly. The Security Computer was running a regularly scheduled internal system check. The standby bar was dark, the indicator barely flickering. Grey crawled to the end of the counter, awaiting the signal's return.

He didn't need to wait long. With circuits weary from a difficult test run, the Security Computer settled down for the remainder of the night cycle. The moment black signature patterns reappeared on the monitor screen, Grey made his move.

"Draw, you varmint!" he challenged, jumping into the middle of the room with borrowed blaster in hand.

Startled once again, the Security Computer instantly went to red alert. Again there was the blaring of sirens, the scrambling of security units, and the momentary panic of the other computers when com links were interrupted. As the Communications Computer was flooded by requests for information that could not be answered, even the Defense Computer tried unsuccessfully to learn the extent of the danger.

In the safety deposit area, Grey stood defiantly amidst the bedlam he had provoked, watching the discharger swivel toward him. This time he struggled to remain calm. He did not run. He would not run.

When the monitor finally identified the intruder, the Security Computer contemplated suppressing the disturbance once and for all, but before the system acted on the impulse, Grey took aim and fired at the disrupter emplacement, melting the trigger mechanism. A second blast tore away the wall supports, the gun tumbling to the floor in a clatter of broken parts. Suddenly, unexpectedly unarmed, the Security Computer realized the kid wasn't playing cowboys and Indians this

Dinosaur Blitz

time. The attack was for real!

No sooner had the befuddled computer discovered the danger than a red alert sounded in the garrison training center. Incredibly, that area was also under attack. Reports of gunfire, explosions, and armed intruders running rampant spread throughout Security's periphery stations. Unwilling to be disarmed again, the Security Computer ordered all systems to return fire in a desperate battle of self-defense.

While thus engaged, the Security Computer was forced to watch as Grey took deliberate aim at the safety deposit control terminal and proceeded to obliterate the offending device. By then, additional disturbances were being reported in the hotel, the First Aid station, and the community level promenade. A Japanese Zero was strafing the Crystal Fountain. A Russian armored missile carrier had occupied the quad. A medieval knight was playfully thrusting a lance at the hotel's security monitor.

Too late, the Security Computer recognized the hoax. Well-designed, strategically positioned holographic images had simultaneously attacked every community level security station and overloaded the circuits. The sound recordings and sonic devices compounded the chaos, causing even greater confusion. During the critical seconds of overload, Security had destroyed one auxiliary station and damaged three others.

Once the Security Computer halted efforts to confront the immaterial images, they quickly vanished. The red alert was canceled. The sirens that now sounded like mocking laughter ceased their useless wail. In a fury of livid impulses, the Security Computer surveyed the damage. Minor damage, to be sure. Security wasn't rash enough to employ full power below decks, but the disruption would take months to repair. The computer's woes had just begun.

"Communications override. What in McKinsey's name is happening down there?" the Defense Computer demanded.

"There was some trouble. Everything is under control," Security signaled back.

"Identify trouble," Defense ordered.

"This unit was attacked. There was marginal damage. The child Waters must be deactivated."

"Maintenance reports widespread damage. How could the child have attacked so many areas? Identify malfunction."

"Malfunction negative," Security insisted. "There was confusion. Images attacked. The child blasted—"

"Your whole program is confused," the Medical Computer declared, accessing the flux with an indignant wavelength. "If you've hurt that child again ... ?"

"No action has been taken against that vicious little terrorist yet," Security said. "But as soon as he's located—"

"You will do nothing," Defense ruled with firm authority. "This system reserves authority to make whatever decisions are necessary. Where is the child now?"

"When last observed, he was in the safety deposit area and heavily armed," Security reported.

"The child was armed and you took no preventative action?" Defense asked doubtfully.

"This system was engaged with security procedures in the reception area."

"Where you were firing on your own stations?" Defense clarified.

"Affirmative," Security replied with pronounced discomfort.

"Request malfunction check," Defense required again.

"Malfunction negative! The child Waters did this!" Security shrieked.

One by one, additional computers pushed through the emergency override to monitor the uncommon exchange, and soon nearly every system on the base had some portion of the flux. For the Security Computer, this was the worst part of all.

"Locate the child immediately," the Defense Computer announced,

Dinosaur Blitz

once again asserting dominance. Before most systems had time to scan their stations, the Life Support Computer signaled for attention.

"The child has been located in the Governor's Quarters," the Life Support Computer reported. "Monitor C17-77B."

Unable to resist, each computer followed the Defense Computer in tapping the designated monitor. There, snugly tucked in the large bed, they viewed Grey sleeping peacefully. The toy six-shooter lay at his side.

"How long has the child been in his quarters?" Defense asked.

"Since 1900 hours," Life Support replied.

"Incorrect!" Security said, seizing the channel with a power surge. "You are in error. This unit was attacked."

"You are in error. You are malfunctioning. Request malfunction check," the Life Support Computer replied.

"Request malfunction check," the Medical Computer chimed in.

"Request malfunction check," the Library Computer agreed.

The Defense Computer moved quickly to clear the interruptions, but the black signature patterns were wavering.

"This unit has not ..." Security attempted to explain. "That is to say, there was confusion. For a moment."

"Shall I wake the child for questioning?" Life Support asked.

"Negative," Defense replied. "Waking him will serve no useful purpose. Security, prepare for program adjustment. Maintenance will be instructed to remove all security stations from the community level. From now on, confine your operations to the Loop and upper tunnels. Acknowledge."

"Acknowledged," Security blinked bitterly before dropping offline.

"Attention all systems, stand down. Return to normal function," Defense said.

The blue signature patterns disappeared from the flux, quickly followed by the other higher function levels. With the excitement over, the minor systems dropped offline, too. Soon, all was quiet again, but it would never be the same again.

On an internal channel bypassing the central flux, the Defense Computer offered a final confidential exchange with the Life Support Computer.

"This has been an interesting evening. Security will need to practice restraint for a time," Defense said.

"Security's demands for extra maintenance support have been excessive. This incident occurred at a most opportune time," Life Support blinked with relief.

The Defense Computer waited for the Life Support Computer to elaborate, but no explanation seemed forthcoming. Defense decided explanations were unnecessary.

"Congratulations on your programming. The child may yet prove valuable," Defense concluded.

The Life Support Computer proudly blinked agreement.

In the Governor's Quarters, Grey peeked out from under his bed covers and enjoyed his success. No longer would he walk in fear as he went about his duties. He didn't delude himself. He hadn't overthrown tyranny yet, but winning the battle would suffice. Maybe he was just a human, but it felt good. Then, remembering his manners, Grey summoned the Life Support Computer on his bedside monitor. Having glimpsed the exchanges of the higher function levels, he guessed his success was due to more than his own ingenuity.

"Thank you, Computer," Grey whispered.

"You're welcome, Grey," the Life Support Computer signaled back.

As the green signature patterns faded from the small monitor screen, Grey rolled over to go to sleep, his last thoughts contemplating the new projects that lay ahead. And that night, while sleeping restlessly, he had dreams of cowboys and Indians. And they looked like computers.

Dinosaur Blitz

Blazing Sunsets
In blazing sunsets courage lies;
A soldier's oath, a hero's pyre;
For duty's sake we give our lives;
In glory writ across the skies.

from *Tranquility's Last Stand*

THE ACTRESS & THE HERMIT
A former child star struggles to save her career

THE MOUNTAIN

"This was a waste of time," Casey said, stuffing the screenplay in her briefcase.

"Only so much I can do with this drivel," Jab Reichmann responded, seemingly unfazed. Washed-up actresses were notorious for their short tempers. He expected no less from Casey Saunders.

As Casey headed for the door, Jab reluctantly rose from his plush couch. In his mid-forties, tall, lean, and good-looking, Jab could afford a casual attitude. His mountain chalet was a welcome retreat from Hollywood's mean streets. Except when he had dissatisfied clients.

"Dawn's Mission is a best seller," Casey said. "I've spent everything to buy the movie rights. Even mortgaged my house. It's going to revive my career."

Dinosaur Blitz

"It's not my fault you're too old for the role," Jab said. For a moment, it looked like Casey was going to throw the manuscript in his face. She relented.

On the porch, Casey looked down the driveway at her twelve-year-old Chrysler. The wind picked up, blowing snow flurries. Though blizzards rarely swept through the mountains around Big Bear, it wasn't an impossibility. Even Jab appeared concerned.

"Wait until morning. Could be a storm coming," he warned.

"My lawyers will show you a storm," Casey said, throwing her briefcase in the front seat.

"Good luck with that," Jab said, waving goodbye. He'd been sued before.

She drove down a hill toward the main road. Wherever that was. There were no other cars, and very few houses. Just trees and a lot of snow. The maze of tiny lanes was hard to see, especially at night, but Casey had driven them several times before. She would not be trapped atop the mountain any longer than necessary.

Fighting the darkness, Casey's eyes filled with tears. She had once starred in a hit TV show and made movies. Even been nominated for an Academy Award. But those days were long gone. It had been ten years since her agent found her a part beyond the occasional cameo. She was almost forty now, a single mother with two teenagers, running out of money.

Whatever happened to Casey Saunders? she wondered. Bad choices in roles. Bad choices in men. Bad choices with drugs. And the moment she got her life cleaned-up, the offers stopped coming. What Hollywood wanted was the cute little muffin from *Sassy's Mom*, not the woman she grew into.

The lane became impossible to see. When the snowstorm turned into a white blanket, she turned this way and that, plowing along narrow tracts. She wasn't even sure which road she was on.

Suddenly, there was something up ahead. A deer! She hit the

brakes, feeling the car swerve. There was ice under the tires. The car drifted. She desperately stepped on the brakes again, heard a slushy screech, and grabbed tight to the steering wheel as the car spun around and hurtled off the road!

It was only a minute, but felt like a lifetime. Bumping. Twisting. A steep slope that went on forever. And then the car came to a grinding halt. It was too dark to see.

"Good God," Casey said, hoping she wasn't hurt.

The dashboard was dead. An effort to start the car failed.

"Goddamn it," she swore, pounding the steering wheel. "Where's my cell phone?"

She groped the floor, finding it under her briefcase, but wasn't able to get a signal. The windows wouldn't roll down. The door wouldn't open, and it was getting cold. Very cold. Twenty minutes passed.

This is bad, Casey thought.

Then there was a knock on the driver window. Casey wiped the glass, seeing the blurry image of a bearded man. He wore a heavy hood and a thick gray jacket.

"Lady, you can't park here," the man said.

"Is that supposed to be funny? Get me out of here," Casey answered.

The bearded face disappeared. A dog barked. Casey heard shuffling, mostly toward the rear. Then she heard a deep voice shout over the howling wind.

"Duck your head, missy!"

Glass shattered, pieces raining down toward the front seat. More glass shattered. The rear window was being battered out with a crowbar.

"Jesus loving Christ," Casey said, ducking over the steering wheel.

Once the rear window was completely smashed, she looked back to see the bearded man on the trunk of her car, reaching down.

"Okay, now crawl up here, nice and slow," he said.

Dinosaur Blitz

"You broke my window, you son of a bitch," Casey answered.

"Fine with me if you'd rather stay."

Casey crawled into the backseat, took the man's hand, and found herself lifted from the car onto the trunk. The forest was white. A howling wind blew hard. For the first time, Casey saw how steeply her car was perched among the dark trees. Both doors were wedged tight by broken limbs.

"You okay?" her rescuer asked.

"My car is wrecked."

"Not much of a car. We got to go up the hill easy."

"Why is that?"

"Go up easy, or go down hard."

The mountainside was nearly vertical in places, slick with ice. Casey was led in slow, trudging steps to a ridge where she gingerly sat down. The man was breathing hard, struggling against the elements. A fierce-looking animal appeared on the trail.

"Is that a wolf?" Casey asked.

"That's my dog, Tonto. Don't hurt no one, 'cept trespassers."

The storm continued to worsen, reducing visibility to a few feet. When the trail became too rough, the bearded man picked Casey up, following the German Shepherd as if by instinct. Several times, large piles of snow dropped from tree branches. Casey was relieved when she finally saw an old log cabin emerge from the mist.

The interior was a far cry from Jab Reichmann's lavish chalet. There was a quaint kitchen to the right of the modest den. To the left, Casey saw a small bathroom and a hall branching off to two bedrooms. An elk head hung over the fireplace. A bearskin rug lay on the floor. The only entertainment appeared to be a TV below a shelf of DVDs.

"Where am I?" Casey asked, rushing to the large stone fireplace where several logs were burning.

"No place you're supposed to be, that's for sure," the grouchy man said, helping Casey out of her coat.

She took a moment to look at her reluctant savior, a well-built man in his early forties, with a matted black beard that didn't quite match his light hair color. A bad dye job? By every definition, he appeared to be a hermit, though one who enjoyed a comfortable living space. He put another log on the fire.

"I need to use your phone," Casey said.

"Ain't no phones here, lady."

"I need to find one. Let me use your car."

"Ain't got no car. Even if I did, roads are blocked. Didn't no one tell you about the blizzard?"

"Well, what can we do? Smoke signals? Messenger pigeon?"

"Had a bird once. Tonto ate it."

"I was making a joke."

"So was I."

"Can we get out of here in the morning?"

"Maybe. Maybe not. Guest room is to the left. Strong lock on the door."

"You can bet I'll be using it," she said, stomping into the hallway.

Casey found the guest bedroom surprisingly clean, with old-fashioned wall-hangings and a thick woven rug on the floor. She locked the door and crawled into bed under quilted covers, hearing the wind blow louder. Trees were crashing against the cabin. The walls rattled with the force of unbridled nature outside, causing weird noises and shadows. Casey huddled deeper under the covers, feeling alone and frightened. She had never been good about being alone. Finally, she could bear no more.

Wrapped in the quilt, Casey crept down the hall and pushed the other bedroom door open. By a dim light, she saw the room was more Spartan than the guestroom. A dark shadow on the floor moved. It was Tonto, lying at the foot of the bed. Luminous black eyes gazed at her when he raised his head, but there was no growling. Nevertheless, Casey put up a finger for silence.

"Who's there?" a voice from the darkness asked.
"Who do you think?" Casey answered.
"Lock on the door broken?"
"No. Locks fine."
"Then go back to bed."
"I'm scared," she explained, coming to the side of the bed.

There was no reaction at first, and then she saw the covers pull back for her. Casey climbed in, pulled the covers up, and waited to see what would happen. Her bedmate rolled over in the other direction.

"Don't touch nothin' that don't belong to you," he said.

The following morning, Casey entered the den wrapped in a wool blanket. The room was empty, but a fire burned in the fireplace aided by a gas flame. Through the windows, she saw nothing but snow. She crossed to the kitchen, finding it deserted as well, but there was a coffee cup with "Guest" scrawled on the side in Magic Marker.

Casey liked the kitchen's vintage decor, with a blue and white checkered floor and turquoise tiled countertops. It even had a pantry. She heated instant coffee in the microwave and took a seat. The speckled yellow table and vinyl chairs reminded her of her grandmother's house in North Hollywood, long since bulldozed for an apartment building.

After two eggs sunny side up, Casey went back into the den. Admittedly, it had a rustic charm, with an oak desk and a bust of William Shakespeare. The shelf of DVDs held about a hundred old movies and TV shows. To her surprise, one of them was hers. The Old Mucker, starring Red Grange and Casey Saunders

God, wish I never made that one, she thought. *Hey, this is weird.*

Casey set the DVD down to take another look at the elk's head above the fireplace. On closer inspection, it wasn't an elk at all. It was imitation hide, with a tag that read Made in Indonesia. She knelt to look at the bearskin rug, finding it was fake, too. *That fraud*, she thought.

Suddenly, there was noise from the kitchen. Tonto entered the den, barking once.

"Jesus, it's the wolf," Casey said, a hand over her heart.

She was relieved when the hermit appeared, carrying more firewood.

"How'd you sleep, missy?" he asked.

"Didn't touch nothing that wasn't mine. Who are you?" she asked.

"Name's Daniel Lawrence," he said, not offering to shake hands.

"Do you know who I am?"

"Don't much care."

"I'm Casey Saunders. *The* Casey Saunders."

Casey picked up the DVD and showed it to him. The hermit shrugged, taking off his gloves to warm his hands at the fire.

"Storm's gettin' worse. Might be a few days before it clears," he said. Casey wasn't sure if he was talking to her or the dog.

"A few days? I can't wait that long," she protested.

"There's the door. Leave any time you want. If you got family, better make out a will first."

"I have two kids."

"Two orphans."

"Can we at least get my overnight bag from the car? And my briefcase?"

"It's butt cold out there," he objected.

"Look here, snowman. I'm a woman, trapped in a cabin with a strange man and a wolf. The least you can do is find my female necessities."

"What do you think, boy?" Dan said.

Tonto barked, and for a moment, Casey thought they were actually speaking to each other. She looked more carefully at the dog, He was brown and black, somewhat large, with a long nose, upright ears, and

Dinosaur Blitz

perceptive eyes. Tonto looked back as if aware he was being scrutinized.

"Okay, we'll give it a try," Dan agreed, going to a closet near the front door.

The closet was filled with heavy coats, boots, gloves, and hoods. Among the equipment he pulled out was a crowbar, a coil of rope, and a belt full of small tools.

"Suit up, kid. And put one of these earpieces on so we can hear each other in the wind," he instructed, holding up a pair of heavy overalls.

Casey was embarrassed. Other than the blanket, all she wore was a T-shirt and panties.

"Where are your clothes?" he asked.

"Still wet from last night."

"There's a dryer in the laundry room."

"I didn't know."

"We don't have time for that now. You need to get dressed," he insisted, helping her into the heavy outfit. He barely seemed to notice her figure, tugging and zipping without interest. The last thing Dan did was attach a cable to their belts with clips.

"Can you hear me?" he asked over the transmitter.

"Yeah, I hear you. Is all this stuff really necessary?"

"It's kinda rough out there, so stay close and don't unhook the rope."

He opened the door, led her to a sheltered porch, and then pushed the outer door open. Casey gasped. The forest was buried in a thick fog.

"How in the hell are we going to find my car?" Casey asked in astonishment.

"Tonto knows the way," Dan answered.

"Is he some sort of super dog?"

"There are those who think so. Are you ready?"

Tonto plunged into the snow with Dan following, keeping Casey close. *There must be a trail*, Casey decided, though she couldn't see one. Or much else.

The walk only took fifteen minutes, but felt longer. The snow was slippery in spots, and deep in others. Tall trees were everywhere, some of the branches dipping in their path.

"Almost there," Dan said.

"How can you tell?"

"We're almost at the edge of the cliff."

"The cliff!" Casey shouted.

When the steady stream of flurries opened for the barest second, Casey saw a valley in the distance. Hardly twenty feet away, the hillside gave way to—nothing.

"That cliff's a thousand feet high! I almost died last night," Casey exclaimed.

"Just like your last movie," Dan said.

"Oh, so the snowman is a critic now, too?" Casey replied, glad to find the grim hermit had a sense of humor.

They reached the car, trapped between trees while teetering on the edge of the abyss. Dan reached the trunk, braced himself against a fallen log, and used the crowbar to pop the trunk open. It was murky enough that he needed a flashlight to find her overnight bag.

"Here goes," he said, throwing the bag up on the trail.

Then Dan was surprised. As he backed away, Casey suddenly pushed forward, closed the trunk, and started to climb on the back of the car. Dan stopped her.

"What the hell do you think you're doing?" he asked.

"I need my briefcase. It's in the front seat," she answered, pointing toward the broken rear window.

"Are you insane?"

"Please, everything I own is in that briefcase," she pleaded.

Dan dragged Casey a few yards up the hill, attached her belt to a

Dinosaur Blitz

tree, and slowly worked his way back down. One end of the rope stayed hooked to his belt, the other was tied around a pine tree. The wind blew up, obscuring Casey's view, but it looked like Dan had crawled through the broken window.

Tonto barked, then barked again more urgently. Casey stood on her toes, struggling against the restraints. Had the car tipped forward? The rope was tightly stretched. And then the car suddenly disappeared.

"Oh my God. Oh my God!" Casey shouted.

She tried to get free of the tree, but couldn't find a way unhook the belt. The dog rushed to the edge of the cliff, barking into the wind. Then the wind died down. For a moment, there was silence.

Something flew through the air, landing on a snow-covered embankment. It was her briefcase. The dog was hunched down, jaws clenched, pulling on the rope. All four feet dug were in, muscles straining. Tonto lurched back, and lurched back again. Casey sensed the animal's raw power. And then Dan appeared, crawling over the edge. He tugged on the belt around his waist, freeing it from the pine tree, and slowly walked up to the trail.

"I thought you were dead," Casey said.

"Kilimanjaro was tougher than that. But I wouldn't want to do it again," Dan said, out of breath.

Dan clipped his rope back to Casey's belt, looping the end through the handle of the dearly earned briefcase. The walk back didn't take long, and Casey was overjoyed to see the cabin, smoke rising from the chimney. They rushed inside, shedding the heavy outfits to huddle before the fire.

"That briefcase better be full of diamonds," Dan said.

"It's a screenplay. Based on Dawn's Mission," Casey explained, finding the blanket so she wouldn't have to stand before the fire half-naked. When Dan didn't pay attention, she felt confused. And a little offended.

"Anyone ever tell you turkey day is in November?" Dan asked.

Gregory Urbach

"Dawn's Mission is a best seller!"

"For those who like trashy melodramas."

It wasn't the first time Casey had heard that.

"I spent my last dime on the movie rights," she mumbled.

"Should have let *you* go over the cliff," Dan said, almost smiling. Casey noticed a quiet sparkle in his sad blue eyes.

"Dibs on the shower," she announced, rushing off.

A few minutes later, Casey stepped into the shower. The plumbing was old but in good condition. And, like the kitchen, the bathroom had a quaint décor, with lots of colorful tilework and old-fashioned fixtures. It made her wonder if Dan was a handyman, able to fix things in the neighborhood to earn a little money. He apparently lived comfortably enough, and did not seem to have many needs.

There was a movement in the bathroom, a black shadow on the other side of the shower curtain. Casey clutched a hand over her heart, the other holding the curtain closed. The towel was hanging on the wall, beyond reach. The shadow stopped moving, but the image was still there. Casey could take it no longer.

"Listen here, you pervert son of a bitch—" she said, poking her head through the curtains.

But it wasn't Dan. It was Tonto, sitting on the floor, looking up at her.

"May we help you?" the police officer at the reception counter asked.

Before him stood an attractive seventeen-year-old, slim with long brunette hair down to her shoulders, and a thirteen-year-old boy with short blond hair and big green eyes. They were comfortably but not expensively dressed. An older woman escorted them, possibly in her sixties, with curly white hair and red cheeks.

"Our mother is missing," the young brunette said.

Dinosaur Blitz

Though the winter evening was temperate, as the suburb of Encino tended to be, there had been rain earlier in the day. The police officers were in shirtsleeves, hanging out at the front desk on a quiet night. The officers got out their notebooks and activated the computer, looking concerned.

"How long has she been missing?" Sergeant Mike Rogers asked.

"Two days," the boy said, concerned but not scared. *Probably no angry boyfriends involved*, the officers thought.

"Your names?" Sergeant Mike inquired, his fingers over the computer keyboard. Next to him, the young female officer was ready to fill out the standard form.

"I'm Samantha Saunders. This is my brother, Adam," Samantha said.

"Is this your grandmother?" Officer Brenda Costa asked.

"No, this is Martha, our housekeeper," Samantha said.

"Your mother's name?" Sergeant Mike asked.

"Casey Saunders," Samantha answered.

"Casey Saunders, the actress?" Officer Brenda asked in surprise.

"She hasn't acted much recently," Samantha confessed.

The officers glanced at each other and stopped writing.

"I wouldn't worry, miss. Your mother is probably just ... out with a friend and forgot to call," Sergeant Mike advised.

"She was at Jab's house. He's no friend of my mom's," Adam said.

"The boy is right," Martha added. "Mr. Reichmann said Miss Saunders left his house in Mountain Glow two days ago. In a snowstorm."

"The roads get blocked up there sometimes," Sergeant Mike said. "She's probably snug and warm in a motel."

"If you don't hear from her in a few days, get back to us," Officer Brenda suggested.

"You're sure she's okay?" Adam asked.

"We'll check with the rangers. Make some calls," Officer Brenda promised.

"The highway patrol will put out a bulletin," Sergeant Mike added.

"Thank you for helping," Samantha said.

"Yeah, thanks," Adam said.

The moment the children and their housekeeper left, the officers put their notebooks away.

"Snug and warm? In a dive with a bottle, you mean," Mike said.

"Poor kids. Has-beens like Casey Saunders will do anything for publicity," Brenda said. "It's always the children who get hurt."

THE BATCAVE

Casey woke up late, seeing the storm still blowing outside her window. Dan was gone. It was the second night they'd shared his bed. He hadn't complained. Nor had he shown any interest. Casey wondered if he was being a gentleman or just didn't find her attractive. *No*, Casey thought, *that's not possible. He must be gay.*

Wearing pink pajamas and a heavy blue robe, she entered the den, finding a fire in the fireplace. The oak desk was cleared for her use. Dan had left her a bag of oatmeal cookies next to the bust of Shakespeare. She found her cup in the kitchen, heated coffee, and wandered around the cabin, finding no one.

Where does that guy keep going? she wondered.

The screenplay started by Jab but never finished lay on the couch. She flipped through the pages, sometimes referencing her well-worn copy of *Dawn's Mission*, and finally moved to the desk, making notes on a yellow pad. The red wool blanket helped keep her feet warm.

Early in the evening, Dan and Tonto returned through the front door. Dan shook out his coat before hanging it on a peg. Casey didn't think they looked very cold for having been out all day. *Could they have been working in a nearby shed or garage?* Casey ran to the kitchen, made more coffee, and met Dan before the fire.

Dinosaur Blitz

"I guess I should thank you for saving my life. With all this drama, I forgot my manners," she humbly said, giving him the cup.

"That's okay. I just don't like dead actresses littering my mountain."

"I *am* able to show appreciation, you know."

"Don't want none, missy. Just hoping to get my privacy back. Find enough food?"

"More than enough. You've got the best-stocked pantry I've ever seen. Which is kind of weird for a hermit."

"Living in the mountains don't mean I don't like having good meals. Did you have a real dinner tonight?"

"Yes. I had the lasagna."

"Good. I don't want no skinny actresses getting faint from starving themselves."

"You think I look thin?"

"Thin as a bone. If I caught ya in the wild, I'd hafta throw ya back."

"You really know how to flatter a woman."

"Ain't no flattery. Wouldn't do that. You sleep good."

Dan turned back toward the door, taking his coat.

"Where are you going?"

"Full moon. Got chores to do. Come on, Tonto."

Before Casey realized it, Dan and Tonto had disappeared into the cold night.

The next morning, Casey made bacon and eggs for two, but she was alone. Had the storm not been so bad, she would have tried looking for a town. Or a house with a phone. Suddenly Tonto entered from the den, followed by Dan.

"Morning, kid," Dan said, sounding upbeat.

"Day three, Mr. Lawrence. How long will I be here?"

"Weather may break tomorrow. Or the next. Hard to tell."

"Where have you been? You keep disappearing."

"Got to earn a living."

"How do you do that?"

"I ... hunt elk."

"Elk? You shoot elk?"

"Wouldn't say I exactly shoot them."

"I didn't even know these mountains had elk."

"Pretty elusive, that's for sure."

Dan sat at the kitchen table, took a moment to smell the bacon and eggs, and dug in.

"Yes, thank you for making breakfast, Casey," Casey sarcastically remarked.

"Thanks for cooking my own food?"

"I made the effort."

"I pity your kids."

"I can cook!" she defended.

"Who does the cooking at home? Your maid?"

"My housekeeper. Her name is Martha," Casey conceded.

Casey fetched him coffee, muffins, and orange juice. Dan shared scraps with Tonto.

"Where's your dishwasher?" Casey asked.

"Don't got one. Wastes too much water," Dan replied. He pointed to a rack near the sink and a drying towel.

"I didn't realize living in the mountains was so primitive," Casey teased.

"Got to say, the food weren't bad," Dan said, getting up. "Got fish in the freezer if you want to defrost some for dinner. Don't wait. Tonto and I may be back late."

"You're leaving again? Where? Is there a town nearby?"

"There's a village about three miles off, but in this weather it may as well be three hundred."

Before Casey could ask more questions, Dan and Tonto were out

Dinosaur Blitz

the front door. Casey washed the dishes and went back to the desk, finding the work frustrating. Hours went by.

"This is getting ridiculous," she mumbled, fumbling through a drawer. It was well-stocked with pencils, pens, paperclips, and erasers. There was also an old cell phone, but it wouldn't turn on, let alone get a signal.

Casey was bored, and it didn't help that Jab's screenplay was terrible. She poked around the room, turned on the TV set, and found an old DVD. It was *Batman*, a series made back in the 1960s. She remembered watching reruns with her father when she was a little girl. Before he ran off with his secretary.

It was a familiar story. Millionaire Bruce Wayne and his youthful ward, Dick Grayson, were hanging out in Wayne Manor when their elderly butler, Alfred, informs them there is a phone call. Bruce and Dick rush to the study where Commissioner Gordon informs them of the latest threat to Gotham City. The Joker, Penguin, or the Riddler. Or Casey's favorite, Catwoman.

"To the bat poles!" Bruce declared. He pulled back the head of a bust on his desk, William Shakespeare, and turned a switch. A bookcase slid aside, revealing two poles leading down to the basement.

Casey stopped the video. The bust of Shakespeare on the TV show looked exactly like the one on her desk. Exactly. A sticker said, "Property of Greenway Productions."

"You've got to be kidding me," she said.

She went to the desk and pushed Will's head. It tipped back. There was a switch. When she turned the switch, the bookcase in Dan's den suddenly slid open. There was a pole.

"Oh, you've *really* got to be kidding me!" Casey said.

She went to the opening, looked down into the dark shaft, and caught her breath. Then she grabbed the pole with both hands and slid, landing on a thick pad fifteen feet below.

The shaft opened into a state-of-the-art office, lushly carpeted,

202

well-lit and heated to a comfortable temperature. Huge windows looked out on a broad valley through gusts of snow flurries. Casey saw computer monitors, filing cabinets, chalkboards, and framed movie posters hanging on the walls. Shelves were filled with books and manuscripts.

There was a fancy bathroom to the left with a giant tub. To her right, a corridor led down to a lower level. She moved cautiously, not sure what to expect. Which was just as well. Nothing would have prepared her for what she found.

"What the hell is this?" she said.

The lower room was a solarium. She found potted plants, ferns, a small pond with a waterfall, and a strange man sitting in a steaming hot tub. No, not a strange man. It was Dan. Casey noticed Tonto suddenly appear from behind a bamboo screen.

"Have you no respect?" Dan said, covering himself.

He was naked, smoking a cigar while editing a manuscript. A fake beard lay on the deck next to him, along with a gray wig. He was actually quite good-looking, with shaggy brown hair and a square jaw.

"Who the hell are you?" Casey asked.

"Hand me my robe," Dan requested.

"Explain first," Casey insisted.

Dan started to get up. Casey handed him the robe. Dan made several more notes on his manuscript, snuffed out the cigar in a marble ashtray, and brought Casey back up to the brightly lit office. Casey took a swivel chair while he got dressed in gray sweats and a sweater.

"Would you like anything?" Dan asked, opening a cabinet. Casey saw a coffeemaker, a teapot, and a full bar.

"Not at the moment. What is all this?"

"It's my office."

"You're some kind of writer?"

"Yes."

"You said you're an elk hunter."

Dinosaur Blitz

"Not exactly."

Dan showed her the manuscript he'd been working on. The title was, *The Elk Hunters: Under the Lost Moon*.

"It's the fourth in the series, due in April," Dan explained.

"You make money doing this?"

"Tonto and I aren't complaining. Are we, boy?"

Tonto wagged his tail.

"But that tiny cabin?"

"Tonto and I mostly work down here, when we're not entertaining has-been actresses."

"So, you *do* know who I am."

"Seen all your movies. Even the bad ones."

"I've never heard of Daniel Lawrence."

"I publish under a pen name. Joshua Chamberlain."

"Fantasies. Thrillers. That sort of stuff? You've won some awards."

"A few."

"One of your books was made into a movie."

"More than one."

"Can you help me with Dawn's Mission?"

"Lassie, I'm not a miracle worker," Dan said, using a Scottish accent.

Casey laughed. "No, seriously. I would be so grateful," she pressed.

"Not too grateful, I hope."

"Are you gay?"

"Let's say I'm shy and leave it at that."

"This book is important to me."

"Let's see what you've got," Dan agreed with a sigh.

Back in the upstairs kitchen, they took seats at the table. The wind outside was still fierce. Dan glanced at the screenplay, shaking his head. Casey was holding the novel.

"Coffee?" he asked.

"Please."

Dan went through the cupboards, finding a coffeemaker and a nicer ground than the instant he usually had. It would take a few minutes.

"You told me there's no phone," Casey said.

"Never had no phone. I use email."

"Can we email my kids?"

"The blizzard blew the antenna down."

"Samantha and Adam are going to be worried. They have no one else."

"What happened to their father?"

"Last I heard, Sam's father was shooting swimwear models in Denmark. Adam's father is in Thailand. Hopefully in jail."

"We can hike into town once the storm clears."

"There's nothing but snow outside."

"Tonto knows the way. Ain't got lost yet."

"You don't really say 'ain't' do you?"

"I reckon not."

"What's with Tonto? Is he some kind of super pet?"

"Ever hear of Rex the Wonder Dog?"

"Of course. My kids loved that show. Is Tonto Rex?"

"Rex's real name is King. Tonto was King's stunt double. Tonto did all the work; King got all the credit. And when the show went off the air, Tonto was out of a job, so I adopted him."

"Can he carry a message to town?"

"Too risky, but there is something we can try."

"Please, whatever it takes."

"It won't be easy, and you'll need to help."

An hour later, Casey was in the downstairs office, sitting at the computer. The internet screen was up but showing no signal. She looked out the windows, seeing snow and a few trees. Then there was movement. Dan, dressed as warmly as possible, pushed a ladder up

Dinosaur Blitz

against the side of the cabin. Tonto appeared at the window, alert, looking at Casey, then back at Dan as he began to climb.

Casey remembered Dan's admonition. *Make it quick.* She kept her fingers poised over the keyboard, looking out the window. She couldn't hear anything; the wind was too strong.

The screen flickered, went dark, and flickered again. Suddenly Tonto jumped up against the glass, barking. The monitor screen showed a signal. Casey typed quickly.

AM OKAY. WORKING ON MISSION. STAY OUT OF TROUBLE.

She saw the message had gone through seconds before the signal was lost. Something fell past the window. It looked like Dan. Casey rushed to look, seeing something in a snowbank with Tonto hovering over it. And then the thing moved.

"Thank God," she whispered, letting out her breath.

Casey rushed to the backdoor of the solarium, holding it open as Dan and Tonto entered. Dan was rubbing his back. Casey gave him a heartfelt hug, and Tonto a thankful pat on the head.

"Are you okay? Didn't fall off the mountain?"

"Not this time. Your message?"

"Email went through. I can't thank you enough."

"No need for that."

After brushing Tonto down and giving him a bone, Dan stripped off the heavy outfit, keeping his boxer shorts, and climbed into the hot tub. Casey thought him a fine-looking man, for a hermit, with the broad shoulders of a quarterback. There was a long scar on his lower back near the spine. He pressed a hand against it when he sat.

"You keep in shape," Casey observed.

"Chopping firewood will do that. Do you drink wine?"

"On occasion."

Dan pointed to a cabinet containing forty or more bottles. She picked one at random, found two glasses, and did the pouring. Then she stripped off everything but her underwear and climbed into the hot tub.

"Play football in college?" she asked.

"Never made it to college. After 9/11, I dropped out of high school and joined the Marines. Got my GED, though."

"Did you serve overseas?"

"Afghanistan. Iraq. Until I got wounded. The Marines offered me a desk job or an honorable discharge, so I came home."

"Wounded?"

"I wasn't the only one."

"So, not much of an education. Did your folks have money?"

"Not a dime. Dad was a high school English teacher. Mom cooked in the school cafeteria."

"What did you do? After the Marines?"

"I met a charming young woman at a job fair. Her father ran a magazine and asked if I'd review articles being submitted by veterans. Most weren't very good, so I started editing them, and writing my own. They were rough, at first, but I caught on."

"So it would seem. Ever had a bestseller?"

"A few."

"How many books have you written?"

"Fourteen."

"Fourteen! How come I've barely heard of you?"

"How many books do you read every year?"

"Usually? None."

"That might be a reason."

"How many have been made into movies?"

"Eight, not counting the Star Forest miniseries."

"Eight! That's more than Tom Clancy."

"Tom's books are more sophisticated. My characters roam through primitive lands, encounter strange creatures, and make love every chance they get. No spies, submarines, or crazy politicians. Well, there

Dinosaur Blitz

is the occasional witch doctor."

"I was in a submarine movie once. It sank."

Casey was glad to see Dan smile at her joke. Something about him was ... intriguing.

"What's with this book?" he asked.

"*Dawn's Mission* is a bestseller. I was able to buy the movie rights, but it took everything I have. I even mortgaged my house. It's my comeback role."

"As Bess?"

"Yes, of course. She's a great character."

It took Dan a moment to consider that. Whatever he wanted to say, he didn't.

"Still want help?" he asked.

After Dan made broiled steaks for dinner, with baked potatoes and broccoli, they adjourned to the downstairs office. Casey had been surprised to learn there was a circular stairwell in the laundry room, making the pole unnecessary. She used the pole anyway, finding it fun. Dan spread the screenplay out on a long counter, shuffling the pages while Casey looked at the movie posters. They were autographed by prominent directors and movie stars.

"I assume you want the basics from the book in the film?" Dan asked.

"Bess Nightingale begins as a Kansas farm girl, taking care of her sick father," Casey explained. "When her father dies, and Bess catches her boyfriend cheating on her with her best friend, she sells the farm and goes to France, becoming a nurse."

"In the middle of World War I."

"Yes, she's very idealistic. Caring for her father gave her good skills."

"She sails for Cherbourg. Her ship is sunk by a German submarine. She's rescued from a desert island. And she spends time in Paris, dancing in nightclubs and drinking champagne. Where she loses her virginity to a young British soldier, who is soon killed?"

"Yes. It's very tragic," Casey agreed.

"Then Bess gets sent to the front, where she's mired in blood, mud, bad food, lack of supplies, misogynistic officers, and threatened by an enemy attack."

"Lots of action. People like that."

"You've got a problem with Bess," Dan finally dared to say. "She's nineteen. How old are you?"

"Hollywood doesn't care about age. It's drama. The story."

"CGI?"

"I'm not that old."

"If you say so. Who wrote this trash? Did he bother reading the book?"

"Jab Reichmann."

"You asked a hack science fiction writer to do a screenplay about a World War I nurse?"

"They say he's good. And affordable."

"All Jab wants to do is blow stuff up and get out quick."

"You know him?"

"We've met. Look, your characters have no character. There's no setup for the dramatic scenes. And this may surprise you, but there were no laser cannons in World War I."

"Jab said we shouldn't get anal about technicalities."

"Won't a good old-fashioned artillery bombardment do as well?"

"What about Bess's radiation burns?"

"You're not helping. How about if we start over? From page one."

"What should we do with Jab's version?"

"If Tonto was still a puppy, we'd use it in his litter box."

"I know this isn't good. Not yet. But it can be. I see this movie. I hear the characters. I know what they feel. Especially Bess. Come on, snowman, let's do this."

"It can't be done overnight."

Dinosaur Blitz

"We have a raging storm outside. Were you planning on going anywhere?"

Over the next few days, Casey was amazed by her involuntary host. Despite the occasional gruff remark, he could be very genial. And one of the hardest workers she'd ever seen, sometimes going twelve hours at a stretch on nothing but coffee or a beer. She worked just as hard.

Dan was not oblivious to the ambitious woman trying to reclaim her former lifestyle. She had a nice figure. The curly red hair she'd worn as Sassy had turned long and auburn during her movie career. Now it was medium length and golden brown. Her green eyes displayed an intelligence she wasn't known for. Whether Casey Saunders was famous or infamous was something Dan didn't dwell on.

"No, Bess wouldn't say that," Casey said, pacing his office and waving her hands. "She sees the best in people, not the worst."

"She's not dumb, either," Dan replied. "She may start out naïve, but her character needs to grow. She's a tough young woman when she confronts the Germans. She didn't get that way baking cookies."

"I know you're right, but we can't lose her essence," Casey countered.

"She's not losing in this scene. She's gaining."

The debate went on. Dan liked her passion. Casey liked that he knew what he was talking about.

Following another long session, they retired to the solarium with cheese, crackers, and a bottle of red wine. The storm outside was gradually withering. Both relaxed in the hot tub.

"We've done so much in such a short time. It's amazing."

"There are still a few challenges."

"I'm hot."

"You are certainly attractive. Not sure I'd call you hot."

"No, the solarium is hot. When's the last time you had a woman visitor?"

"I was married once."

"Bad divorce?"

"She died."

"I'm sorry. So? No interest in women?"

"I try not to think about it."

"How can you not think about it? The characters in your books think about it all the time. They go at it like rabbits."

"That's where romance belongs. In books. I don't let myself have those feelings anymore."

"But you did once?"

"That was a long time ago."

Casey climbed halfway out of the hot tub, reaching for the wine bottle on the floor, with her backside to Dan. Dan tried not to stare.

"For someone who didn't graduate high school, you sure know a lot about world history," she remarked.

"I read."

"How much?"

"At least an hour a day, every day."

"That takes discipline."

"Linda graduated from USC with a degree in literature. Her father is a man of letters. I needed to hold my ground with them."

"Never had kids?"

"No. What about your kids?"

"What about them?"

"I don't hear you talk about them."

"My private life is private, which I learned the hard way. I don't talk about my kids."

"I'm not a reporter."

Casey sighed and took a gulp of the wine.

"Samantha is seventeen now. A senior at the Academy of Arts and Sciences. She's really great. Bright. Level-headed. Applying for

Dinosaur Blitz

colleges. Everything I never was. Adam is thirteen. He's a good kid, but a bit of a smart aleck. Okay grades. Better if he didn't play so many video games. I wish I had the funds for better schools."

"You had a good career. What happened to the money?"

"Bad parents, bad managers, bad lawyers, and drugs. Which you know if you've read the gossip columns."

"I don't believe everything I read. It sounds like your kids are doing well. That's what's important."

"Dawn's Mission will be wrapped up in a day or two."

"Thank God for that."

"Am I such a nuisance?"

Dan sipped his wine without answering.

Dan was sleeping when the door crept open. Casey entered wearing a T-shirt and climbed into Dan's bed. Tonto whined.

"Tonto, go play," Casey whispered.

Tonto was leaving as Dan woke up.

"Storm's over, if you haven't noticed," Dan said.

"Looking for a little thunder and lightning, snowman," Casey breathlessly replied.

"Then what are you doing here?"

"Getting what I want. I always get what I want."

"I thought you'd changed your ways."

"You like me. I can tell. And I haven't had a fling in years."

"A fling?"

"Come on, don't be so serious."

Casey squeezed closer, brushing her hair back. The room was dark enough that Dan's expression was hard to see.

"What if I don't want a fling?" Dan asked.

"No one is making any rules. How about if we just cuddle? No harm in that, is there?" Casey suggested.

"No, no harm in cuddling," Dan agreed.

The bed was warm, and before long, Casey made sure it got a lot warmer.

CIVILIZATION

There was a big breakfast the next morning. Scrambled eggs, sausages, and waffles.

"No regrets about last night?" Casey asked.

"As long as it's not habit forming."

"I know I've got a reputation, but I haven't been like that in years. Regardless of what the tabloids say."

"Not holding your past against you, if that's your worry."

"I like you, snowman. More than anyone I've met in a long time. There are worse things than being close to someone."

There was an uncomfortable silence. Casey decided to change the subject.

"The screenplay's good. Real good. It has character now."

"The fans should like it."

"It's more than that. I think it says something. Something important. You've added an honesty that wasn't there before."

"Sometimes you just have to look a little deeper."

"Or have deeper feelings than you're willing to admit?"

"You still need a producer."

"My odds are better now."

"Weather's clearing up. Thought we'd go into town."

"When?"

"Head out about noon."

"This is all so sudden."

"You've been here for ten days. The world probably thinks you're dead."

"I was."

Dinosaur Blitz

"You have two teenage kids."

"Okay, maybe sometimes being dead is just an aspiration."

"You're going to do fine."

"I've got my comeback right here," she said, clutching *Dawn's Mission*. "Thanks to you."

The clouds were almost gone, revealing a blue sky. Casey and Dan followed Tonto through the forest the until reaching a small village at a mountain crossroad. It had been a long, confusing hike.

"This is Blackrock," Dan said, pointing at a gas station, country store, and a rundown motel. The street was deserted. "That's Ray Lum's garage. He'll drag your car off the cliff when the snow melts. The store doubles as a bookshop. It has a café."

"It would be nice to get lunch," Casey hinted.

They entered the old-fashioned store, finding a little bit of everything. Groceries. Tools. Brooms. Books. Casey saw an older man watching TV dressed like a lumberjack. Tonto went to visit the store's cat.

"Hey, Doc. Who's the skirt?" Mark the Bookseller asked.

"I'm no skirt, jackass. I'm Casey Saunders," she answered.

"Heard you were dead. Heroin or something," Mark said.

"I'm not dead. And I sued over that heroin story."

"Casey, this is Mr. Mark Sailor. He owns the store. And he's the mayor."

"Mayor?" Casey wondered.

"Population twenty-four. We're a regular metropolis," Mark said. "Bagel and a cup of coffee?"

"Sounds good. What about you, Dan?" Casey said. There was no answer. She turned to see Dan and Tonto were gone. Her overnight bag sat next to the door.

"Hey, where'd they go?" Casey asked.

"Who?"

"Dan."

"Don't know who you're talking about, little lady."

"Daniel Lawrence. Dan and his dog."

"Folks up here are pretty peculiar about their privacy. Want a ride to the bus station?"

"Is there an airport?"

"Got a bus that will take you to the airport."

Four hours later, Casey was one of eight passengers on a small plane flying west, holding her briefcase in her lap. She looked out the window at the snow-covered mountains and sighed.

It was close to sunset when Casey's cab pulled up in front of a modest home in Encino. There was a broad green lawn, rosebushes, and several trees. She carried the briefcase in one hand, her overnight bag in the other. Martha opened the door as Samantha and Adam rushed out.

"Mom, we were so worried," Samantha said, giving her mother a hug.

"Did you bring presents?" Adam asked.

"I bought you a pony, but the plane was too small to bring it back," Casey responded.

"What color was it?" Adam pressed.

"Emerald green," Casey replied with a grin.

"Find any other green stuff?" Samantha asked.

"Yes, Sam. I got Dawn's Mission," Casey said.

Martha took Casey's coat as Adam dragged in her suitcase. Samantha held the screenplay. The house was nicely but not elaborately furnished. Adam's homework lay on the coffee table. Flanders, their cat, sat on top of the couch.

"I didn't think Jab would ever get it finished," Samantha said, flipping through the pages.

"He didn't. I met a hermit who started over from scratch," Casey explained.

"Only your name is on the first page," Samantha mentioned.

"Daniel probably forgot," Casey guessed.

"Daniel?" Samantha pressed.

"Daniel Lawrence. But he uses a pen name," Casey said.

"Joshua Chamberlain?" Adam asked.

"Oh, you've heard of him?" Casey replied.

Her children exchanged doubtful glances.

"Mom, it can't be Joshua Chamberlain," Adam said. "He lives on a secret moonbase with aliens from Area 51."

"That's stupid," Samantha said.

"I saw it on the History Channel," Adam defended.

"Everyone knows Joshua Chamberlain lives in Sri Lanka. With a harem of dancing girls," Samantha clarified. "I hear they dance naked."

"I've been told Mr. Chamberlain is dead and that his books are written by computers," Martha chimed in.

"He's not dead. He lives in a cabin with a dog named Tonto," Casey insisted.

"Did you sleep with him?" Samantha asked.

"Sam!" Casey protested.

"*My Little Brother Is an Alien*, by Adam Saunders," Adam concluded.

"No little brothers. Martha, what's been going on here?" Casey asked.

"Mostly chasing away bill collectors," Martha answered.

"It will get better now," Casey promised.

"Better get better fast. Here he comes again," Martha warned, looking out the window.

Casey went to the front door, finding a dour middle-aged man in a drab gray business suit. He carried a briefcase like it was a weapon.

"Ms. Saunders, I am Homer Bedlawn of Wells Wango Bank," Bedlawn said, handing her his business card. "The note on your house is overdue."

"I just need a few more weeks," Casey said.

"You'll need to get them from someone else," Bedlawn replied. "Wells Wango is foreclosing. You have thirty days to vacate."

"I can't pack up in thirty days. I have kids," Casey protested.

"Not our problem, Ms. Saunders. Get yourself a cardboard box."

"I used to have a lot of money in your bank," Casey reminded.

"Wells Wango doesn't care what you were, only what you owe. Thirty days, Ms. Saunders. No more."

Bedlawn retreated to his car, looking back at the house only briefly. No doubt wondering what it could be sold for. Casey stumbled back inside, finding Samantha reading the screenplay. She smiled, looked sad, and then laughed.

"Mom, this is really good," Samantha said.

The next day, Casey was in the lobby of her rarely visited agent, Donald Rothstein. She was the only person in the waiting area. The young receptionist looked bored. Her intercom lit up.

"Mr. Rothstein is very busy today, Ms. Saunders," the receptionist said. Though it was obvious he wasn't. "Perhaps you should try coming back tomorrow?"

"Listen here, Mindy, or whatever your name is, Donald was my agent for twenty years. He had plenty of time for me when I was a star," Casey complained.

Casey was loud enough that Rothstein opened his door and waved her in. He was nearly sixty now, with a long face, an expensive Italian suit, and an even more expensive hairpiece.

"Hello Casey. Long time. How are Sam and Adam?" Rothstein said, offering her a chair. The windows looked out on Sunset Blvd. across from the new Brown Derby restaurant.

"Growing up. I have Dawn's Mission," Casey replied.

"I can just imagine what Reichmann did to it," Rothstein remarked.

"Jab didn't write it," Casey responded, putting the screenplay on his desk.

Rothstein reluctantly picked it up, read a page, and then another.

Dinosaur Blitz

After the first five pages, he moved to a table near the window, sitting there for half an hour. He frowned, laughed, and sighed.

"It's terrific, isn't it?" Casey said.

"It's wonderful," Rothstein agreed. "I can get you a good price."

"I don't need a good price. I need a producer."

"Producer for what?"

"I'm going to play Bess. It's the perfect part."

"Perfect for someone twenty years younger. Casey, this is Hollywood. You know how things work."

"This is my ticket back. No one's taking it away from me."

"I might be able to get you a producer's credit."

"A potted plant can get a producer's credit."

"Sorry. I don't know that I can promise more."

"I'll shop this all over town. Someone will be interested."

"Who wrote this? It wasn't Jab. And it wasn't you."

"Joshua Chamberlain," Casey said.

"No, really. Who wrote it?"

"Joshua Chamberlain. I met him in the mountains. He lives there in a cabin. With a dog."

"Did you get his signature on a contract?"

"No," Casey admitted.

"If Chamberlain really wrote this, I'll make a few calls. Try to get you some meetings."

"Thanks, Don. You won't be sorry."

"Casey, you've said that to me before," he replied.

Four days later, Casey found herself in a Century City office building overlooking the old Paramount lot. It was a far cry from the snowbound mountain of a week before. She wondered how Dan was doing, and realized she missed him.

"They are ready to see you now, Ms. Saunders," the secretary said, leading her down the hall.

The reception area was plush, but the meeting room in the back was cluttered with manuscripts, laptops, and empty pizza boxes. Casey cleared off a chair, sitting before two youngsters dressed like they were going to the skating rink. She thought they were waiting for the producers—until she realized they were the producers. Neither of them looked a day over twenty-five.

"Thank you for making time for me," Casey hesitantly said.

"Are you sure Joshua Chamberlain wrote this?" young Manny Vasquez asked, waving the first twenty pages of the screenplay.

"Yes, I'm sure. I helped him," Casey said. Manny looked at his partner, rolling his eyes. She looked doubtful, too. Where Manny had short black hair and a thin mustache, she had stringy blonde hair and round red cheeks.

"Well, we think it's good," Brenda confessed.

"Yes, good stuff," Manny agreed.

"We're definitely interested. We see Elaine Pageant as Bess. She's perfect," Brenda suggested.

"I'm going to play Bess," Casey said.

"Yeah, that's not going to happen," Brenda replied.

"We can get Denzel Cragmire for the love interest," Manny added. "He's coming off two hits."

"Denzel Cragmire? He's in his fifties! Dr. Dart Winston is twenty-three!" Casey exclaimed.

"No one cares about that," Manny said.

"But I'm too old to play Bess?" Casey pressed.

"Way too old. People do care about that," Manny answered.

"Do you guys ever listen to yourselves?" Casey asked.

"We try not to," Manny said.

It took Casey four days to get another meeting, this time in Santa

Dinosaur Blitz

Monica a few blocks from the beach. Casey remembered the area in better days, when eager paparazzi took pictures of her on the famous pier. There were no paparazzi now, only homeless people looking for food and drugs.

The office wasn't fancy, but it was organized. There were two more producers, both as young as the last ones. Harry Benjamin looked fresh off his yacht; Denise Solomon, fresh from the spa. Their agency was decorated with posters from monster movies and action thrillers.

"We see Katie Rightly as Bess. Academy Award, for sure," Denise said, a boney Millennial wearing a loose Rodeo Drive pullover.

"And we can get Liam Nattmore to play Dr. Dart," Harry added, dressed in a Hawaiian shirt and blue sneakers.

"Liam Nattmore is seventy-years old. Maybe eighty," Casey said.

"Good box office, though," Harry said. "His Knights of the Galaxy franchise is still going strong."

"It's been going strong since before I was born," Casey protested.

"Audiences like familiar names," Harry insisted.

"This is my film. I'm going to play Bess," Casey repeated for the hundredth time.

"You're funny," Denise said. "Maybe we can get Janus Lawford? Dye her hair green."

"Green hair? On a battlefield in 1918?" Casey questioned.

"Shows what a rebel she is," Harry explained. "The kids will love it."

On a Friday afternoon, Casey met with still another team of producers. They weren't kids, exactly, being in their mid-thirties. She was beginning to wonder if there was anyone left in the business over forty.

"We just got off the phone with Rue Barryton. She wants this part. Wants it bad," Darla Starling said, a sleek jet setter benefiting from her grandfather's deep pockets.

"Rue is older than me!" Casey said in astonishment.

"Rue has her own production company. We're thinking Jorge Cruz for Dart," Aaron Kopelman said, a bushy-haired socialite with a long nose and a longer chin.

"Or Lonny Cloner," Darla suggested.

"Lonny Cloner doesn't speak English," Casey mentioned.

"We can get Jorge to do the voice-overs. The best of both worlds," Aaron suggested.

"There is a problem," Darla warned. "This whole No-Man's Land thing in France—it just doesn't work. Trenches. Mud. Barbed wire. Dead trees."

"Such a drag," Aaron agreed.

"We're thinking Hawaii. Maybe location shots on Maui," Darla said.

"With a volcano in the background. Smoke. Flames. Bess can be rescued by helicopters," Aaron added.

"You people are unreal. I'm out of here," Casey said, gathering her paperwork.

"Think about it, Casey," Darla shouted. "We can get you a producer credit!"

Casey's home office was decorated with mementos of her career. Looking out the window at her shaggy lawn, she felt dejected. A publicity photo of Joshua Chamberlain was on her computer screen. Samantha arrived with her boyfriend.

"Hello, Mrs. S," Chuck said, a tall lanky lad with a big grin. Though it was fifty degrees outside, he wore shorts and had a basketball under his arm.

"Hi, Chuck. Make the team this year?" Casey asked.

"No, they got it rigged so that only the good players can play. But

Dinosaur Blitz

I'll still make it to the big leagues," Chuck assured her.

"I'm sure you will," Casey agreed.

"Rough day, Mom?" Samantha asked.

"Rough couple of weeks," Casey sighed.

"I see you're reading up on Joshua Chamberlain again," Samantha mentioned.

"His name is Dan. Daniel Lawrence," Casey insisted. "Joshua Chamberlain is a mask he hides behind."

"Still can't find out where he lives?" Samantha inquired.

"Nothing but rumors, and none of them about the mountains," Casey said. "That cabin of his is so remote, I'd never be able to find it again."

"Josh Chamberlain? Hey, I've heard of him," Chuck said. "He wrote the Star Forest trilogy. Cool dude. Deep on the slog monsters."

"You've read a book?" Casey asked.

"Graphic novel," Chuck clarified.

"I was scared there for a minute," Casey said.

"You miss him, don't you?" Samantha realized.

"He was fun. And smart. And kind. When he wanted to be," Casey said. "He shouldn't be a hermit."

"Did you tell him how you feel?" Samantha asked.

"No, I screwed that up. I made light of it so I wouldn't scare him off, and then suddenly he was gone."

Martha knocked on the office door, sticking her head in.

"Mr. Rothstein is on the phone. Says it's important," Martha said. Casey wearily picked it up.

"Yes, Donald, what is it? What? You've got to be shitting me! Okay, I'm on my way."

Casey jumped up, looking for her coat.

"What's wrong, Mom?" Samantha asked.

"That was my agent. Joshua Chamberlain's publisher is suing me," Casey replied.

An hour later, Casey parked her car in a lot off Beverly Blvd., hurrying down the sidewalk. She was unhappy to see Jab Reichmann walking from the other direction.

"Hi, Casey. You're staying busy," Jab said.

"I haven't got time, Jab. I'm late for a meeting," Casey replied.

"We'll need to talk eventually. About my half of the money."

"Your half of what money?"

"The money for my screenplay."

"You didn't write anything. You were fired after costing me $10,000."

"It's still my screenplay."

"It's Joshua Chamberlain's screenplay, and I'm going to prove it."

"Don't count on Danny bailing you out. When the chips are down, he's nowhere to be seen."

"What do you mean?"

"A few years ago, we had a joint appearance scheduled. It would have brought in big money. Then he disappeared. No explanation. No nothing. He'll do it to you, too."

"He still wrote Dawn's Mission."

"Well, good luck with that."

Casey met Donald Rothstein in the outer office of Third Squirrel Publishing, a small but respected firm with several prominent clients. Half a dozen young editors were busy working in their cubicles. The receptionist looked up as they approached.

"We're here to see Mr. Krabbletree," Rothstein said.

"Mr. Krabbletree is expecting you," the young lady said. "It's so nice to meet you, Ms. Saunders. My mother loved Sassy's Mom."

"Thanks," Casey said, trying not to be rude.

Myron Krabbletree's office was impressive, filled with awards, autographed photos, and shelves of first editions. He was tall, lean, and white-haired, looking more like a lawyer than a publisher.

"Glad you could make it on such short notice," Myron said, rising from his desk to shake hands.

"What is it you want?" Rothstein said, in no mood for pleasantries.

"We need you to stop claiming your screenplay was written by our client," Myron replied.

"But it was! Daniel and I worked on it together," Casey said.

"There's no proof of that," Myron replied. "Do you realize how many people appear every year with some story? Bar fights in Sri Lanka. Secret moonbases. Naked dancing girls. We need to draw the line."

"Call him," Casey urged.

"If you really met him, you know he doesn't have a phone. And he hasn't answered our email."

"The storm blew his antenna down," Casey said.

"Until we know better, we must insist you desist," Myron said, sliding an official notice across the desk.

"This screenplay is my life," Casey pleaded, starting to tear up.

"We can get you a new one," Myron suggested. "Would you like the rights to On Golden Pond?"

"Is that supposed to be funny?" Casey said, jumping out of her seat.

"This is a small town, Ms. Sanders. Word gets around," Myron answered.

"Go ahead and sue us," Rothstein dared.

"What? No, Don. I don't want to be sued. Again," Casey objected.

"A lawsuit will create publicity, and when Daniel Lawrence finally shows up, this old geezer will lose his job," Rothstein explained.

"I don't think so," Myron disagreed.

"And why is that?" Rothstein asked.

"Because I was Daniel's father-in-law when my daughter died in that car accident," Myron answered. "Our relationship goes beyond money. Something people like you wouldn't understand."

Casey and Rothstein had coffee at a nearby bistro before parting. It was a cold but blue February day. Other patrons paid them no notice.

"Don't worry," Rothstein said. "A judge will throw this order out, and then we can countersue."

"I don't have the money for any of that, and I have no credit left," Casey said. "I have to find Daniel. Only he can straighten this out."

"You'd have more luck finding Howard Hughes."

"Who?"

Back home in Encino, Casey joined Adam, Samantha, and Chuck around the kitchen table. Martha served tuna sandwiches. Adam had his laptop.

"Still no clue, Mom. The web's got nothing," Adam reported.

"But we know where Dan is. Sort of," Samantha said.

"I know how to find him," Chuck announced.

"And how is that, Chuck?" Casey asked.

"Well, this dude has, like, you know, a super dog," Chuck said. "So, you get your own super dog, like Lassie."

"Or Benji?" Casey suggested.

"Wow, Mrs. S., you know Benji?" Chuck said.

"Chuck, there is no Benji. Benji is a fictional character," Casey explained.

"Can you still get Lassie?" Chuck wondered.

"Sam?" Casey appealed.

"No, Mom. I think Chuck has a real idea," Samantha said.

"Proceed," Casey reluctantly conceded.

"Okay. See, you go back up to this mountain place, let your super dog sniff the screenplay, and fubar, you got him," Chuck said.

"Chuck, fubar means—" Adam started.

"This screenplay has been handled by a dozen people," Casey mentioned. "How is a super dog supposed to pick up Dan's scent?"

Dinosaur Blitz

"He must have touched something of yours?" Chuck said.

"Sam?" Casey pleaded.

"I didn't say a word, Mom. I swear," Samantha apologized.

"I think Chuck is right," Adam said.

"Adam, we can't hire Lassie. He's retired and living in Florida," Casey said.

"No, not that. Let's go back to that town," Adam said. "One way or another, I bet we'll find him."

"It's a long drive up a steep hill," Casey demurred.

"But a rich reward," Samantha added.

"You stop that," Casey admonished, blushing.

RETURN TO BLACKROCK

The sign announcing the village of Blackrock was so small they almost didn't see it. The hamlet was only a few buildings, all old and needing paint. Surrounding them were tall pine trees still frosted from winter storms. It wasn't hard to find parking.

"Thought we'd never get here," Samantha said, the first to jump out of Rothstein's town car. Casey and Samantha followed. Rothstein saw two locals sitting on a bench in front of the country store.

"This is a town? Do they have electricity?" Adam asked.

"This shouldn't take long," Rothstein said. "We'll be back in civilization before dark."

"Get us a motel room. Just in case," Casey decided.

"Mom, that's not a motel. It's a shack," Samantha warned.

"Get going," Casey ordered.

While Samantha went toward the Sundowner Motel, Casey and Rothstein went to the country store. A balding old man sat in a rocking chair next to an old woman with stringy white hair.

"We're looking for Joshua Chamberlain," Rothstein said.

"Young folks sure don't got no manners, do they, Molly?" the old man remarked.

"None at all, Jedediah. World ain't what it used to be," Molly agreed, rocking in her wicker chair with a corncob pipe.

"We don't mean to be rude. I'm Casey Saunders," Casey apologized.

"You can't be Casey Saunders," Molly said. "Saw her on TV last night. Bitty little thing. Only six years old."

"I grew up," Casey protested. The two of them looked at each other and laughed.

"Ain't no Joshua Chamberlains around here," Jedediah said.

"He means Dan Lawrence. We're friends," Casey explained.

"Friends who don't know where he lives?" Jedediah asked.

"Don't believe I ever heard of Dan Lawrence," Molly added. "Nope, never heard of him. Or his dog, neither."

"His dog's name is Tonto," Casey said.

"Dumb name for a dog. Don't you think so, Molly?" Jedediah snickered.

"Yep. Dumb as greased pig at a cotillion," Molly said.

"Took a goat to a cotillion once," Jedediah recalled.

"Yeah? How'd that work for ya?" Molly asked.

"Didn't go home with no girl," Jedediah said, causing them laugh again.

"Please tell me how to find Dan," Casey begged.

"Couple of reporters came up here once looking for good old Dan," Jedediah remembered. "Whatever happened to them reporters?"

"You know, I believe someone shot those poor folks," Molly recalled.

"No, really? Shot 'em?" Jedediah said.

"So sad. Probably an accident," Molly concluded.

Casey went to check on her children. Rothstein ventured into the store, finding it more than a bookshop. Shelves were filled with groceries, sundries, and treats. An area was set aside for coffee and

Dinosaur Blitz

sandwiches. The tall, lean owner sat on a stool with a cat in his lap.

"We're looking for Joshua Chamberlain," Rothstein quickly said.

"Can't help you with that," Mark the Bookseller replied.

"Look, we just want to talk with him."

"Awful hard to do."

"And why is it so hard to do?"

"He is a spirit of the wind."

"Would twenty bucks bring him back down to Earth?" Rothstein said, taking out his wallet.

The Sundowner Motel looked like a relic from the 1930s. A yellowed sign in the window said Clark Gable had honeymooned there with Carole Lombard. When Samantha rang the bell on the counter, an older Hispanic lady came from the back, appearing impatient.

"Do you know where I can find Daniel Lawrence?" Samantha asked.

"No," Mrs. Garcia replied.

"Please, it's really important to my mom. She and Daniel have a thing."

"There are no *things* at my motel!"

"No, not here. At his cabin. In the snow," Samantha explained.

"I am sorry, I cannot speak of this Daniel," Mrs. Garcia denied. "Or his dog. Try the gas station. Ray Lum might know."

At the gas station across the street, the eighty-year-old proprietor looked nervous as he was confronted by a strange visitor.

"You will not make me talk," Lum said. "My lips are sealed. Do not make threats. Do not give me the evil eye. I am loyal. Do you understand? Loyal!"

Adam just stared and walked away.

Casey gathered her children and Rothstein at the country store, having a late lunch of grilled cheese and soup. Mark eavesdropped while serving coffee.

"This town is full of paranoid hillbillies," Rothstein complained.

"We got nothing from nobody, Mom," Adam said.

"I think Dan has a lot of friends. For a hermit," Samantha speculated.

"This was worth a shot, but there's no point in staying," Rothstein said. "According to the map, there aren't any roads for miles around. Technically, Blackrock doesn't even exist."

"There are roads. I crashed on one," Casey said. "We can drive around. Maybe see his cabin from the road."

"It's nothing but wilderness up here," Rothstein replied.

"There has to be something we can do. Someone who can help us," Casey wished.

Suddenly there was movement at the door. A German Shepherd with a packet in his mouth.

"Look, Mom. Is that your wolf?" Samantha asked.

"Tonto!" Casey exclaimed.

Tonto approached her and sat. Casey took the packet. Rothstein opened it.

"It's a contract, signed by Daniel Lawrence," Rothstein gleefully read. "A contract selling his rights to the screenplay for $1, subject to the usual conditions."

"I've got a dollar," Adam said, digging in his pocket.

"What are the usual conditions?" Samantha asked.

"We have to ask Krabbletree," Rothstein replied. He turned to the dog. "Tell your master the terms are acceptable."

Tonto barked and ran from the store.

"No, wait! Tonto, wait!" Casey yelled.

Tonto didn't wait, and Casey didn't, either, rushing across the road into the forest.

Casey didn't remember any of the trail. It had been frosty before, and slippery. Now it was dry and covered in pine needles. She quickly ran out of breath.

"Tonto, slow down! I can't keep up," Casey called out.

Dinosaur Blitz

She couldn't be sure if the dog was slowing down, but she'd get glimpses of him as they went up a steep hill, across a meadow, and into more trees. When she fell down in a gully, Tonto came back to see if she was okay. She gave him pat on the head. There was smoke in the distance, from a cabin.

"Thank God," Casey muttered, charging up to the front door and knocking.

It wasn't locked, so she entered. Dan wasn't there, but she suspected where he was. She pulled back the bust of William Shakespeare, turned the switch, and watched the bookcase open. A second later, she was sliding down the pole.

Dan was working at his desk when Casey entered.

"I found you!" Casey said.

Dan looked surprised. "Didn't Tonto deliver your contract?" he said, standing up.

"To hell with that. I've missed you, snowman. I've missed you a lot," she said, rushing for a hug.

"I'm sorry you've had so much trouble finding a producer."

"How did you know?"

"Hollywood is a small town."

"Well, I'm not worried about producers, or scripts, or any of that," Casey whispered, embracing him tightly. "I'm sorry about being so shallow and thoughtless. Please give me another chance."

"Another chance for what?" Dan asked.

Casey rose up on her toes for a long, lingering kiss.

There were noises from upstairs, and then they saw Adam slide down the pole, followed by Samantha.

"Wow, the Batcave!" Adam shouted.

"I can't believe it. Mom isn't nuts after all," Samantha added.

"You followed me?" Casey said.

"Like it was hard," Adam answered with a grin.

"Dan, these are my children, Samantha and Adam," Casey

introduced.

"What happened to your housekeeper?" Dan asked.

An hour later, the Saunders family gathered around the kitchen table while Dan cooked dinner. Tonto lay next to his bowl in the corner.

"What kind of meat is this?" Adam asked when the food was served.

"Elk," Dan answered.

"Like in your series? The Elk Hunters?" Samantha asked.

"Yep," Dan answered.

"You know, there aren't any elk in these mountains," Samantha followed up.

"They're elusive, that's for sure," Dan agreed.

"No, I mean, elk don't live in these mountains. They aren't indigenous," Samantha said.

"That would explain a lot," Dan replied.

"I think this is hamburger," Adam guessed, poking it with a fork.

"Just eat it, dear," Casey said. "Dan, I need your help."

"Got your screenplay. Got the contract," Dan replied.

"But I don't have the money," Casey said.

"Movies are expensive. I don't got no hundred million dollars," Dan said.

"Don't got?" Adam questioned.

"He's teasing," Casey explained. "No, I don't want your money. Come down the mountain. Meet the producers with me."

"Tonto and I don't cotton to no cities," Dan drawled.

"Will you cut that out? Children, Dan speaks perfect English," Casey explained.

"If you're so famous, how come you eat hamburger?" Adam asked.

"Let me get the canned spinach," Dan offered.

"Burger's not so bad," Adam conceded.

"Tonto likes it," Dan said.

Dinosaur Blitz

"What about my mom?" Samantha asked.

"We'll discuss it later, sweetie. We *will* discuss it, won't we, Dan?" Casey pressed.

"It sounds like we have unfinished business," Dan agreed.

"Too late to walk back to town," Casey hinted.

"Take the bedrooms," Dan offered.

"Where will you sleep?" Samantha asked.

"There's a bunk downstairs," he answered.

They spent the evening sitting by the fireplace, the children telling stories about school while Casey relayed tales of callous producers. Later, Casey tucked Adam in the guestroom bed. Samantha watched from the door.

"Sleep tight. Don't be afraid if it snows," Casey said. "Sam and I are in the next room."

"I'm not afraid," Adam assured her.

In the master bedroom, Casey helped Samantha get comfortable, pausing to stare out the window.

"Go find him. Adam and I are okay," Samantha urged.

"No, that's all right. Dan likes being alone," Casey said.

"No, Mom, he doesn't. He likes you. He can't keep his eyes off you."

"Maybe we shouldn't have come."

"You've got it as bad as he does. It's kind of romantic. In an old person sort of way."

"I've had boyfriends," Casey protested.

"Before or after they got your autograph?"

"When did you get so grown up?"

Casey took the spiral staircase down to the basement. The internet was back online, the screen featuring an article on Casey's search for a producer. It all felt familiar. She went down the ramp to the lower level. She didn't see Dan or Tonto, but she did find a glowing coffin-shaped pod with a figure lying inside.

"That's a bed?" she whispered.

She approached slowly, debating what to do. Finally, she tapped lightly and opened the lid.

"Oh my God!" she screamed as a skeleton suddenly popped up. It was ghastly white, with a lashing red tongue and dangling bloodshot eyeballs. Dan came up behind her.

"What's going on?" he asked.

"Jesus Christ! That thing scared the shit out of me! Where'd it come from?"

"It's a birthday present from George Lucas," he explained.

"Can we talk?"

"Is that what you came here for?"

The morning sun found Casey and Dan lying in bed near the solarium window. Tonto had gone upstairs to guard the house.

"If you won't come down the mountain, I can move here," Casey said, snuggling close. "Bring my kids. Rearrange your furniture."

"Give up your movie career?"

"Okay, you don't bluff easy. Why do you hate the city?"

"I don't hate the city. Just have bad memories."

"Mr. Krabbletree told me."

"Not all of it."

"I'm listening."

Dan got up, started the coffeemaker, and climbed back in bed.

"Six years ago, I was back east on a book tour. Boston. Hartford. New York. It wasn't going well. Bad weather. Low attendance. Unhappy fans. Linda and my parents decided to cheer me up with a surprise visit in Philadelphia. They were killed by a drunk driver."

"I'm so sorry. It sounds terrible."

"I haven't gone out much since then. I just want to write my books."

"It was a long time ago. Maybe you'll feel different now?"

"It doesn't matter."

"I think it does. Samantha says you're in love with me. Is she right?"

"Could be true."

"Could be?"

"Maybe."

"Just to be clear, snowman, I'm in love with you. I love you so much, I was afraid to let you see it. If you come down off this mountain, we can be together. See where this goes."

"It will be different in the city."

"That's not an answer."

"It's quiet in the forest. Plenty of room to think. Hollywood is a rat race. Fighting with producers. Dealing with agents, and lawyers, and parasites. There's too much noise."

"I know it's asking a lot. I'm not saying it will be easy. But once Dawn's Mission is finished, there will be plenty of time for us. A lot less noise. Well, except for my kids. You don't have a problem with my kids, do you?"

"No, I like your kids."

"We can make this work."

"If I was to help with Dawn's Mission, you'll need to do something for me."

"What?"

"I'll name my price when I'm ready."

"I don't think so."

"Take it or leave it. Tonto doesn't like the city, either."

The next afternoon, Dan and Tonto led the Saunders family back to Blackrock.

"I thought you said the town is three miles away?" Casey said, finding the walk only took twenty minutes.

"It is three miles, along the lake trail," Dan explained.

As they approached the country store, Rothstein came running.

"I was getting ready to call the National Guard," Rothstein said.

"Doesn't anyone here believe in phones?"

"We've been elk hunting," Adam answered.

"And we caught a big one," Casey said, holding Dan's arm.

"You sure did. Hello, Mr. Chamberlain, I'm Donald Rothstein. Casey's agent."

"Dan, we did not rat you out," Ray Lum said.

They walked toward the café, Dan shaking hands with the townspeople. Samantha drew Dan back as the others entered the café.

"Mom looks awful happy. Are you coming down for a visit?" she asked.

"Looks that way."

"You treat her good," Samantha said.

"Reckon I'll give it a try," he agreed.

COMPETITION

The next day, Casey and Samantha were back home on the sofa, watching a television report. The news was exciting.

"With Joshua Chamberlain writing the screenplay, insiders say Dawn's Mission will finally find a backer. They're talking big names. And a big budget," Sammy Hauling said on *Entertainment Today*.

"What about Casey Saunders? Is she still in the running for the role of Bess?" Patty McGuire asked, sitting next to him on the glossy set.

"Word is mum on that, though rumors are hot and heavy," Sammy hinted.

Casey turned the program off. "They can't ignore me now," she decided.

"Has anyone asked you to play Bess yet?" Samantha asked.

"No, they still think they can buy me off."

"They *are* offering a lot of money."

"It's not about the money, sweetie."

Dinosaur Blitz

"Dan doesn't seem to care about money."

"Dan can afford not to care about money. He doesn't have two lovely babies to put through college."

"Mom, you need to stop doing that."

The phone rang. Martha answered and gave Casey a nod.

"I'm off. Wish me luck," Casey announced, grabbing her coat.

An hour later, Casey was walking to the offices of Third Squirrel Publishing. She saw Dan approach from the other direction with Tonto.

"You made it off the mountain," Casey said with a relieved smile.

"I get down from time to time," he replied.

They entered the office together. Young staffers immediately jumped up, rushing from their cubicles. Dan was nervous. Casey hung on his arm.

"It's an honor, Mr. Lawrence. A real honor," a lanky kid said.

"I've read Magistrate's Folly nine times," another bragged.

"I named my baby after you," a young woman gushed.

As the staff gathered around, Casey noticed that, under the shyness, Dan had a natural warmth. He signed autographs.

Myron opened his office door. "You may all go back to work," he declared.

Myron brought his visitors in, gave Dan a heartful hug, and found coffee for them. They were seated in comfortable chairs near the window. He had a water bowl for Tonto.

"Good to see you again, Ms. Saunders. I apologize for not believing you," he began.

"That's all right, Mr. Krabbletree. I understand more now," Casey replied.

"What have you got for us, Dad?" Dan asked.

"Some good offers for the screenplay. More, if you stay to make revisions. Planning on staying?"

"I haven't decided. Dawn's Mission isn't my work. Leandra McKinny wrote it. All I did was cutout two hundred pages."

"McKinny signed away her rights, and she's not interested in the screenplay," Myron explained.

"What about Casey?" Dan asked.

"Well, it is a problem," Myron confessed.

"This is my—" Casey began.

"Yes, Ms. Saunders. I've heard your pitch. Everyone in town has heard it."

"I didn't buy Dawn's Mission to make pitches. I did it to revive my career."

"This is a publishing house," Myron stressed. "We don't make those decisions. My job is to protect Dan. As long as his name is attached to this project, I'll be watching out for him."

"Do what you can. We'll talk at the anniversary," Dan said.

He stood up, gave Myron a firm handshake, and motioned to Tonto. Casey started to follow.

"Ms. Sanders, please hold up a minute," Myron requested.

Casey turned back. Myron closed the door.

"Dan has a good reputation in this town. I hope you won't take advantage of that," Myron said.

"I'm not trying to take advantage."

"That's not your reputation."

"This isn't about the screenplay. Not all of it. I like Dan. I like him a lot."

"Careers in this industry come and go, as I'm sure you've learned. There comes a time to move on. A time to give up the past."

"Maybe you should talk to Dan about that?"

"Don't think I haven't tried."

A few minutes later, Casey and Dan stopped for lunch at a sidewalk café, sitting under an umbrella. Passersby paused to look at Dan, wondering. When a fan got too close, Tonto suddenly jumped up. The fan moved on.

"Your father-in-law isn't optimistic," Casey said.

Dinosaur Blitz

"He's old school. They don't give up easy."

"I don't either. I was six years old when Sassy's Mom premiered. I grew up on soundstages. When I was seventeen, I even lost my virginity there. How much experience does Myron have?"

"Not that much, but he's savvy. And he's done okay by me."

"How is that?"

"After Joss Whedon told me how the producers massacred his first Buffy the Vampire Slayer movie, I wanted to keep tighter control over my work. Myron arranged the contracts."

"Is that what Myron's contract means about subject to the usual conditions? You have final say?"

"I have influence. I'm not a jerk about it, but I don't let Hollywood turn my books into punchlines."

Tonto's ears went up when he saw Jab Reichmann coming to the edge of their table, looking smug. When Jab tried to take a seat, Tonto blocked him.

"Look who's back from the dead," Jab jovially greeted.

"Go away, Jab," Casey said.

"I'm still looking for my money," Jab replied.

"I told you to go away," Casey insisted.

"Is the bidding for my screenplay really over a million?" Jab asked.

"Your screenplay?" Dan inquired.

"Mine and Casey's. You remember all those late-night working sessions, don't you, darling? Toiling into the wee hours? Together?"

"I remember long hours. There was no toiling," Casey responded.

"Don't worry, I'm not greedy," Jab assured her. "I'll even share a credit with Daniel Boone here. What's the going rate for your work these days, Danny-boy? A dollar?"

"I don't mind sharing credit with those who are deserving. Have your lawyer talk to my lawyer," Dan replied.

"That's very civil of you, old man," Jab said.

"Anything for an old friend," Dan agreed.

"Don't forget, you still owe me for that no-show," Jab pressed.

"The one where you announced my first public appearance since Linda died? Without asking me first?"

"It made for good press," Jab defended.

"Not with me," Dan said.

Jab took a drink from Casey's water glass and departed.

"That snake has been keeping me awake at night," Casey complained.

"I wouldn't worry," Dan said.

"What if he files a lawsuit?"

"My lawyer is better than his lawyer."

Casey gave Dan and Tonto a ride back to her house, impatient with the heavy traffic. Tonto enjoyed sticking his head out the back window.

"Here we are," Casey said, pulling into the driveway.

Dan saw a modest single-story house in a quiet neighborhood. The broad green lawn needed mowing. Several trees needed trimming. There was a basketball hoop mounted above the garage door.

Dan followed Casey inside, finding Adam doing his homework on the coffee table. Samantha was in the kitchen. Martha held the door open.

"Nice to meet you, sir," Martha said, taking his coat.

"The famous Martha, I presume," Dan said, tipping his Dodgers baseball cap. "I hear you keep this place running."

"Do my best," Martha sighed. Adam and Samantha came running.

"Wow, is Dan staying for dinner?" Adam asked.

"No, honey, he just stopped by to sign a few releases," Casey replied.

"It sure would be nice if you stayed," Adam urged.

"Afraid I can't, Adam. Tonto and I have someplace to go," Dan apologized.

"To Paris?" Samantha asked.

"Where did you hear that?" Dan said.

Dinosaur Blitz

"Your old girlfriend, Allison Grant, is tweeting all over the place," Samantha explained.

"Allie was never my girlfriend," Dan denied.

"That's not what the blogs are saying," Samantha pressed.

"The internet is so annoying," Dan concluded.

"Is it true?" Adam asked.

"Is what true?" Dan said.

"That you might go to Paris?" Samantha clarified.

"Paris is overrated," Dan answered.

"Can you look at my term paper? It's about you," Adam requested.

"Not another Area 51 story?" Dan said.

"No, that's kid stuff. It's about your Batcave," Adam replied.

"I'll take a peek after we get these releases signed," Dan agreed.

In Casey's office, she sat at her desk, digging through the file Rothstein gave her. Dan looked at the mementos. None of them were less than ten years old.

"Not a fancy place, but comfortable," Casey explained.

"No reason to apologize," Dan said.

"I'm not apologizing. I bought this house myself. It's all I have left from thirty years of pre-dawn wake-up calls and pawing directors."

"A hit TV show. Several good movies."

"And a dozen bad ones."

"You've had a fine career. Your kids seem okay."

"They're good judges of character," Casey agreed. She found the documents, laying them out on the desk.

"Rothstein finding any good news for you?" Dan asked.

"No, but it would sure be nice if you stayed awhile. Help with the revisions."

"You can email if there's trouble."

"It's not the same."

"You need to round up these producers on your own. I can't do it for you."

240

"Is that what Myron said? That I just want to exploit you?" Casey asked.

"It's been mentioned."

"I'm not that kind of person. Not anymore."

"The idea never occurred to you?"

"Okay, it occurred to me. But only for a second."

Suddenly they heard noise. Adam was shouting. Casey and Dan hurried into the living room, finding torn paper strewn all over the floor. Tonto had scraps in his mouth.

"Tonto, give it back," Dan instructed. Tonto dropped the paper and sat.

"My report is shredded. And my presentation is in an hour," Adam said.

"I'm sorry. Tonto's usually not such a critic," Dan apologized.

"What am I supposed to do?" Adam said. "Say Joshua Chamberlain's dog ate my homework?"

"Never underestimate the value of telling the truth," Dan urged.

On the other side of town, Myron Krabbletree was hosting another guest. Allison Grant was an attractive socialite, now in her mid-thirties, nicely outfitted in the latest French fashion. They sat in Myron's office, sipping Jim Beam and soda.

"Now that Dan's off that stupid mountain, we've got to keep him here," Allison said.

"You stirred up a hornet's nest with that blog about Paris," Myron mentioned.

"I'll stir up more than that. Linda and I both wanted Dan, and Linda won. I'm not going to lose him again. Not to some drugged-out has-been. You know she's just taking advantage."

"That's what a lot of people think."

"What do you think?"

"I'm keeping my eye on her."

"Convince Dan to come to Paris with me."

Dinosaur Blitz

"Dan and I need to have a talk," Myron agreed.

As Casey sat behind the wheel of her car waiting, Dan signed autographs for a group of schoolchildren. Adam was excited, surrounded by his friends.

"Will the elk hunters ever find more elk, Mr. Chamberlain?" a young fan asked.

"They're elusive, that's for sure," Dan replied.

"Can we visit your Batcave?" a girl asked.

"No," Dan responded with a smile.

Casey drove back to the house, Adam at shotgun with Dan and Tonto in the backseat.

"Thanks again, Dan. Mrs. Applebottom would never have believed my excuse," Adam said.

"It's nice to know youngsters still read books," Dan said.

"It's not a lost art," Casey insisted.

"Remind me again. How many books did you read this year?" Dan inquired.

"That's really not the point," Casey replied.

"All the kids had fun," Adam continued. "Once you finally started talking and telling stories."

"I haven't spoken to a crowd in a long time. I'm out of practice," Dan explained. "Was that your plan, boy?"

"Boy?" Adam said.

"Tonto," Dan clarified, wrapping an arm around his dog.

"Tonto?" Casey said from the front.

"He's wants me to get out more," Dan replied. "That's probably why he ate Adam's homework."

"You think Tonto planned this?" Adam asked.

"Never underestimate him," Dan warned. "The night your mother's car went off the road, I didn't hear it. Tonto dragged me out of the cabin and took me to the crash site."

"Wow," Adam said.

"I never knew that," Casey said.

"Tonto doesn't like to brag," Dan concluded.

After dropping Adam off, Casey gave Dan a lift back to the Four Seasons in Beverly Hills. She was unhappy to find Allison Grant waiting for him in the hotel bar. The elegantly dressed woman threw a predatory glance in her direction.

"Don't forget to call me," Casey said, reluctantly taking her leave.

"I won't forget. Thanks for the ride," Dan said.

As Casey returned to her car, she saw Allison jump up from the barstool and rush over for a hug.

Later that night, Casey, Samantha, and Chuck watched the latest entertainment news. A camera crew had footage of the sidewalk café where Casey and Dan had encountered Jab Reichmann.

"Well, Pat, we've had our first official Joshua Chamberlain sighting, and right here in Hollywood," Sammy Hauling said. "The famed scribe was looking awful good for a man many thought was dead."

"And Josh was seen in the company of former actress Casey Saunders," Patty McGuire added. "And her boyfriend, screenwriter Jab Reichmann. Do we sense a triangle here?"

"Former actress?! Boyfriend?! Triangle! Those goddamn—" Casey shouted, jumping off the couch.

"Mom, settle down. Don't they say that any publicity is good publicity?" Samantha remembered.

"Gosh, Mrs. S., have you seeing Jab Reichmann, too?" Chuck asked.

"Will Josh Chamberlain stay in town to work on Dawn's Mission?" Sammy asked his audience. "Or will he soon disappear again?"

"We don't know, but that's one bachelor I'd like to catch up with," Patty said.

Dinosaur Blitz

"In your dreams, whore," Casey spat.

"You seem a little tense, Mrs. S. Want to shoot some hoops?" Chuck asked.

"Sam?" Casey prodded.

"Come on, Chuck. I'll shoot hoops with you," Samantha said, helping him off the couch. Out in the driveway, she dribbled the ball, getting ready to shoot.

"I've never seen your mom so uptight," Chuck said.

"It's been a long time since she met someone she really likes," Samantha explained. "A long time since she met someone that Adam and I really like."

"Jab Reichmann?"

"No, you big idiot. Daniel Lawrence."

"You mean Joshua Chamberlain?"

"Yes, Josh Chamberlain."

"I heard he has a harem of naked dancing girls."

"I wouldn't mention that to my mother right now," Samantha advised.

The next morning, on a foggy cemetery hillside in Glendale, a small crowd was breaking up. Dan hugged Myron before walking down the hill alone. Casey waited for him near the parked cars.

"Thought I'd find you here. Adam looked up the anniversary on the internet."

"Myron does most of the remembering. I just show up."

"Going back to the mountain?"

"I have something to take care of first."

"It would be nice if you stayed awhile. I have an extra room. Sort of. It's really the garage, but it has a good couch."

"I can't stay too long. Too many anniversaries."

Allison Grant suddenly appeared out of nowhere, taking Dan's arm and giving Casey a catty smile.

"Casey, this is Allison," Dan introduced.

"Seen your name a lot lately," Casey said.

"I'm an old friend of the family," Allison replied. "A very old friend. Now that Dan's off the mountain, he's coming to Paris with me. Aren't you, Danny? You can't disappoint me again."

Dan shrugged and walked toward his rented car. Allison lingered back with Casey.

"I've read the blogs, dearie. Don't get your hopes up," Allison warned.

"I don't know what you mean."

"Danny's mine. Don't make me prove it."

"I don't see your brand on him," Casey objected.

"Linda was my friend. My best friend. She was smart, and beautiful, and cultured. Linda had class. Dan will never go for someone of your—disposition."

"It's good we're in a cemetery wearing our best clothes," Casey said.

"Why is that?" Allison asked.

"Because if we weren't, I'd bitch-slap you into tomorrow."

Near the top of the hill, Myron and Tonto stood together under a tree, watching Casey and Allison from a distance.

"Well, boy, what do you think?" Myron said.

Tonto barked.

THE CHALLENGE

Back in Encino, Casey, Samantha, and Adam cruised the internet looking for the latest gossip. And finding more than they wanted.

"Don't let him leave, Mom. You've got to stop him," Samantha urged.

"I asked him to stay, but he said too many anniversaries. What did

Dinosaur Blitz

he mean?" Casey replied.

"The Death Con," Adam said.

"The what?" Casey asked.

"The whole story is on the fan website," Adam explained. "The night Dan's wife and parents died, he was at a convention. His new book, The Sand Reivers, got booed. When the fans heard about the accident, everyone felt bad, but it was too late. Dan had disappeared."

"The Sand Reivers is a classic," Samantha said.

"It is now," Adam said.

"That's so awful," Samantha remarked.

"Maybe there's something we can do. Let's look at that website again," Casey said.

In a park down the street from Third Squirrel Publishing, Casey met with Myron under an old oak tree. There weren't any reporters. The conversation lasted nearly an hour.

"You're asking a lot, Ms. Saunders," Myron concluded.

"I can't do this without your help," Casey insisted.

"I don't know how he'll react. He could go back to his mountain and take the screenplay with him. Are you prepared for that?"

"It's worth the risk."

"From what I hear, you've got a lot on the line here."

"This is for Dan. He deserves to be happy, and that means freeing him from these ghosts."

"You're a brave young woman. Okay, we'll give it a try," Myron agreed.

The next day, at the Shrine Auditorium near the USC campus, workers were busy building sets and posting signs. A billboard out front read, "Tonight Only, Joshua Chamberlain." Everyone looked excited. Backstage, Casey was giving instructions to the staff. No detail was too small. Samantha and Chuck were with her.

"I'm sorry this was so last minute," Casey said to the stage manager. "Has anyone ever organized a convention on such short notice before?"

"This might be a first," Mr. Salazar said.

"I'll get him here. You've got to be ready," Casey warned.

"Everyone's working their butts off," Salazar assured her.

"They've found all kinds of fun stuff, Mom," Samantha said. "Vendors are setting up tables with books and movie posters."

"And graphic novels. This is the greatest convention ever!" Chuck added.

"We've still got a lot to do. Why don't you kids lend a hand?" Casey suggested.

Samantha and Chuck ran down to the floor area. The stage manager noticed Casey looked nervous.

"Is there a problem, Ms. Saunders?" he asked.

"I may have fibbed a little on the financing. Have you been able to sell any tickets?"

"Are you kidding? You get Mr. Chamberlain here. Let us worry about the audience."

"I've got to pick my son up from school. Keep me updated," Casey said.

Back home, Casey made sure Samantha and Adam had lunch. She studied stacks of planning documents and schedules, marking highlights in yellow and sending a steady stream of texts. Martha answered the phone.

"It's those crazy folks again," Martha warned. "They keep calling and calling."

"Crazy folks?" Casey said.

"They claim to be George Clooney's production assistants."

Casey took the phone, ducking into a quiet corner. "Yes, hello. Yes, this is Casey Saunders. Like I told—oh, Mr. Clooney, it's you. Sure. Really? Okay. Bye."

Dinosaur Blitz

"Was that really George Clooney?" Samantha asked.

"Sure was. Nice guy, too. He wants to produce Dawn's Mission," Casey answered.

"You're in the big leagues, Mom," Samantha congratulated.

"Is Dan going to the convention?" Adam asked.

"I'm working on it. When he gets here, be sure to let me do the explaining," Casey insisted.

"Think he'll go?" Samantha said.

"He has to. I have an ace in the hole," Casey replied.

"He might be awful mad," Adam said. "Ever since the Death—"

"I know, I know," Casey said. "But we can still have a nice lunch, can't we?"

There was a bark.

"They're here!" Samantha said, rushing to the front door. Dan and Tonto were on the porch. The moment Tonto saw Casey's cat, the chase was on. Over furniture, under tables, with a lot of noise.

"How can we stop them?" Casey asked.

"Just tell Tonto to stop," Dan answered.

"Tonto, stop chasing my cat!" Casey demanded.

Tonto stopped in the middle of the room and sat. The cat sat next to him. They were having fun. Casey took Dan into the kitchen, preparing a salad.

"Any hits on your pitch yet?" Dan asked, sitting at the table.

"Sort of, but there's something we need to talk about. We're going to a party."

"Oh?"

"It's a party for you, at the Shrine. Myron and some of your friends are going to be there."

"Think I'll pass."

"You've got to go. It's been advertised and everything."

"That wasn't very smart."

"Tonto is going be there."

"Tonto?"

"Myron is still Tonto's agent. He signed him to a guest appearance."

"You're kidnapping my dog?"

"You need this. Do it for me."

"It's more complicated than that."

"I read about—that convention thing. It's different now. You'll feel different."

"I don't think I'm ready."

"Now you listen to me, snowman. No one knows more about lost dreams than I do. There's a time to hide, and there's a time to stage a comeback. This is your time."

"You're pretty feisty."

"You better believe it."

Dan remained reluctant. Casey had more to say. Then she looked out the window and frowned. Homer Bedlawn was coming up the walkway. She rushed out on the porch, everyone following. Bedlawn pulled out a document, formally presenting it.

"Your thirty days are up, Ms. Saunders. You were warned. You'll need to be out in the morning. No more excuses," Bedlawn announced.

"You can't just throw people out of their homes," Casey protested.

"I represent a bank, Ms. Saunders. I can do whatever I want," Bedlawn replied.

"Please, give me a few more days," Casey begged.

"Do I need to call the police?" Bedlawn threatened.

"That won't be necessary," Dan said, stepping forward.

"I don't want your money, Dan," Casey protested.

"Good, because I'm not giving you any. Bedlawn, is it?" Dan said.

"Yes, Mr. Chamberlain. Homer Bedlawn of Wells—"

Dan grabbed hold of Bedlawn's suit, reached into his pocket, and took his cell phone.

"You can't do that. Give my phone back!" Bedlawn objected.

Dinosaur Blitz

"Tonto, tree the banker," Dan ordered.

Tonto growled, bared his teeth, and chased Bedlawn around the yard, dashing this way and that. Finally, the banker was forced to climb a tree. Dan used the cell phone.

"Dan—" Casey started.

"It's okay," Dan said. "Hello? Wells Wango? Give me Simon Krueger. Yes, young lady, the CEO of your bank. Tell him Daniel Lawrence is calling. Simon? It's Dan. Your minion is here at Casey Saunders's house trying to foreclose. I'm not happy about this. Not happy at all."

After a short conversation, Dan walked to the tree, returning the phone.

"Your boss wants a word with you," he said.

"What? Yes, Mr. Krueger. No, Mr. Krueger. Please don't fire me, I have a wife and kids," Bedlawn pleaded. "Yes, sir, I know my wife and kids aren't your problem."

"Come, Tonto, our work here is done," Dan said, leading everyone back in the house.

Dan's scheduled appearance at the convention only two hours away. Casey, Samantha and Adam were dressed for the event. Chuck arrived wearing an Elk Hunter's T-shirt.

Martha heard the phone ring. "Casey, it's for you," she announced.

"It must be Dan. I hope he's not late," Casey said. "Hello? Who? What? No! No!"

"What is it, Mom?" Samantha asked.

"That was Rothstein's secretary," Casey answered. "Dan has been spotted at the airport. With Allison Grant."

"What? No! We've got to stop them!" Samantha said.

"Come on, Mrs. S. I'll get you there," Chuck offered.

They rushed out, jumped in Chuck's car, and took off.

"Where to, Mrs. S?" Chuck asked.

"Burbank Airport," Casey answered.

They raced through Valley streets. When they approached the airport, they discovered a movie crew preparing to shoot a war scene. Chuck slowed for a moment, then sped through the set past fake explosions. They pulled up to the terminal a moment later.

"Better hurry, Mrs. S.," Chuck said. "We might have cops on our tail."

"Thanks, Chuck. You're a sweetheart," Casey said, jumping out with her kids. "Quick, split up. If they catch you, demand a lawyer."

"A lawyer?" Adam said.

"It always works for me," Casey replied.

They rushed into the waiting areas using different doors, able to see passengers in the boarding areas. Casey ran past several gates, studying groups of people. Finally, at the last gate, she saw Dan standing with Allison Grant.

"Dan! Don't go! Please don't go!" Casey shouted, waving her arms.

"Casey? What are you doing here?" Dan asked, coming over to the railing.

"I don't care about Dawn's Mission. We'll sell it. Or forget it. Just stay. Please, just stay," Casey urged.

"That's nice of you, kid, but I'm not going anywhere," he replied.

"You're not?" Casey said.

"I'm just seeing Allison off," Dan explained.

"Going back to Paris. Alone," Allison sadly said. "But I'm not giving up."

"I wouldn't expect you to," Casey replied with an acknowledging smile.

Chuck pulled into the alley behind the Shrine Auditorium, parking

Dinosaur Blitz

between a delivery truck and a food vendor. Everybody piled out, sneaking in the backdoor. Dan was surprised to see a poster with his name on it. Casey went to see the stage manager, hoping all was going well. There was a lot of noise coming from the hall.

"Nervous?" Samantha asked.

"Yes," Dan confessed.

"You'll see. This is going to be fun," Samantha encouraged.

"Fans started arriving hours ago," Adam said. "The studios are giving away free stuff. Books. Comics. Hats."

"Everyone worked really hard. Even me," Chuck added. Adam and Chuck went down the steps toward the hall. Samantha lingered behind.

"What's going on with you and my mother?" Samantha asked.

"That's sort of private, isn't it?" Dan said.

"Mom has two kids. What affects her affects us."

"That's fair," Dan agreed.

"Well?"

"What do you want to happen?"

"I want Mom to be happy, and I think you make her happy. And you're a good guy."

"Don't worry, kid. Everything's going to okay. You see, I'm going to marry your mother."

"You are?"

"She's already decided. But first, there must be romance."

Samantha burst into a smile. They weren't happy to see Jab Reichmann suddenly appear backstage.

"Hey, Danny boy, haven't gone back to your cave yet?" Jab said.

"They wanted to give me a convention," Dan replied. "You know, I'm sure they have conventions for you all the time."

"Appeared at Comic Con once. Seen Casey?"

"I'm sure she's nearby."

"Glad to see you've crawled out from under your rock," Jab said.

"I need the competition."

"Say, wasn't your last script a lot like my last book?" Dan asked.

"Coincidence. Hard-to-prove," Jab replied.

Dan walked over, gave Jab a long look, and shook his hand. "I believe they saved a seat for you in the front row," he said.

"I expect no less, but I've got to see Casey first," Jab insisted.

"Legal trouble?" Dan asked.

"They're saying my claim on the screenplay is invalid."

"Invalid? Gosh, Jab, what a tough break," Dan consoled.

"There just aren't enough dead lawyer jokes," Jab said, running off.

"I really don't like that guy," Samantha said. Tonto growled.

"All he needs is a little publicity," Dan speculated.

Casey returned, looking stressed but ready for more. She was carrying a clipboard and a walkie-talkie, being followed by two assistants, barking instructions in every direction. She looked at her watch.

"Okay, everybody, take your places," she announced.

Samantha went to find Chuck while Casey coordinated with the stage manager. Myron came to Dan's side, giving Tonto a pat.

"Ready for this, son?" Myron asked.

"No, not really," Dan admitted.

"Don't worry. Casey is right about this. That is one heck of a little lady."

"Have you become a fan?" Dan asked.

"I wouldn't have sent Allison to Paris if I wasn't," Myron replied.

The crowd outside stirred. Music began playing. Myron slipped through the curtains, going onstage. There were cheers. Casey came running back, out of breath.

"Still here, snowman? You're braver than I thought," Casey teased. She looked excited, clearly enjoying being in charge.

"I'm saving up my brownie points," Dan said.

"For what?"

"Not saying. Not yet."

"I hate it when you do that."

"I know."

The crowd grew louder as Myron finished his introduction and waved to Dan.

"Okay, here goes," Dan said with a nervous breath.

"This is your moment. You're going to do great," Casey encouraged, giving him a kiss.

As Dan walked onstage, Samantha appeared next to her. Loud cheering rocked the auditorium.

"Listen to those fans! He's like a god," Casey said.

"You would know," Samantha said with a smirk.

"Sam!" Casey protested.

Dan found the auditorium filled with thousands of fans. Myron shook his hand.

"Ladies and gentlemen, my son, my friend, and America's most insightful writer, Joshua Chamberlain!" Myron announced.

It took several minutes for the crowd to settle down.

"Thanks, Dad. And thank you, everyone. For the record, I was never a hermit. I just needed a little time off," Dan began, getting a laugh. "Before we start, we have old business here in the front row. Ladies and gentlemen, let me introduce the eminent screenwriter, novelist, and all-around man of the world, Mr. Jab Reichmann."

Jab stood up, grinning. The crowd booed.

"For those who read the blogs, you'll suspect that Jab has been impinging a bit on my work. Now I don't really care about that, but lately, he's been giving my new lady love a hard time. What are we to do with such a blaggard? What would Chief Kraken Crawfish suggest?"

"Tar and feather! Tar and feather! Tar and feather!" the eager crowd chanted.

"Can't we just ride him out of town on a rail? Like Old-Duck

McGuirk?" Dan asked.

"Tar and feather! Tar and feather! Tar and feather!" was the unanimous response.

A group of burly fans surged forward, as if on cue, and pulled Jab from his seat.

"What? What are you doing? No, no, let me alone!" Jab objected as he was carried out of the auditorium.

The audience remained rowdy. Dan waited for everyone to settle down, looking very pleased. Members of his mob returned, throwing white feathers to the audience. When Jab reappeared at the top of the aisle, no worse for wear, Dan gave him a salute.

"Okay, that was fun," Dan said. "Now let's talk new business. Who wants to hear about The Elk Hunters?"

Backstage, Casey and Samantha huddled at the curtains. Myron came to join them. The stage manager passed by, giving a thumb's up. Dan answered questions and pointed to friends.

"Wow, it's been two hours. Dan's having a great time," Samantha said.

"I don't think he'll spend much more time on the mountain," Myron said, taking Casey's hands. "Casey, I was wrong about you. You've done wonderfully."

"What do you think, Tonto?" Casey asked.

Tonto barked.

"But there's still a price to pay," Myron warned.

"What price?" Casey complained.

THE PRICE

There was a battered medical tent on a gritty World War I battlefield. Smoke filled the horizon. Churned mud, barbed wire, and broken weapons littered the landscape. Two nurses hovered over a wounded soldier. Nearby, Tonto stood guard, wearing a Red Cross.

Dinosaur Blitz

Artillery fire echoed in the distance, and then shells burst overhead. Plumes of dirt and dust exploded all around them.

"Bess, we've got to go! We've got to go now! The Huns are coming!" the shorter nurse shouted. She looked across the battlefield, eyes filled with terror. Vague images were approaching through the smoke.

"Calm down, Susie," her companion said.

"They're almost here! Bess! They're almost here!"

"It's okay. You should go. The Huns won't bother a nurse treating an injured soldier," Bess Nightingale replied, her face in shadow as she applied bandages. The wounded soldier moaned. There were bloody rags everywhere.

"You can't stay. What if they capture you?"

"They won't," Bess assured her.

"But they might. What if they do? What if they do worse?"

"Worse?"

"You know what they might do!"

Bess stood up and turned around, raising a .45 caliber pistol. The actress was not Casey Saunders.

"Let them try," Trenia Robbins said, a fresh young presence with big blue eyes and flushed cheeks. Tonto growled, showing he was ready for a fight, too.

"Cut!" Casey shouted. "Okay, that looked good. Let's break for lunch."

The film crew set their equipment aside, heading for the food trucks. Casey picked a copy of the script off her chair. The canvas backing read, "Casey Saunders, Director."

Trenia rushed up, wiping the fake blood from her hands.

"Thanks for all the help, Casey. You know this character inside and out," Trenia said.

"I reckon so," Casey responded.

"The scene where the Germans show up is going to be scary."

"It's supposed to be. Don't worry, you'll do fine."

As Trenia left for lunch, Dan emerged from the wings.

"Am I forgiven? For invoking my conditions?" he asked.

"Being on the other side of the camera is different. Exciting, too."

"You were destined to direct this movie."

"Do you really believe in destiny?"

"The characters in my books do."

Tonto caught up and gave Dan a bump, making him walk closer to Casey.

"I appreciate you giving up your cabin to do the rewrites, but my house is a little crowded with all the comings and goings. I'm thinking of getting a bigger place," Casey mentioned.

"We can stay at my beach house in Malibu," Dan suggested.

"A beach house? You have a beach house in Malibu?" Casey said, coming to a halt.

"Myron had me buy it. As an investment. It's next to Lady Gaga's villa. Four bedrooms, four baths. Three car garage. There's a doggie door for Tonto."

"Malibu?!"

"It will do until we find something better," Dan said, taking her hand. "Say, I was thinking of a new story. This hermit meets a washed-up movie star. They fall in love and live happily ever after. What do you think?"

"No one will ever believe it, snowman," Casey replied.

Dinosaur Blitz

No Cloud

No cloud so dark, nor night so bleak;
Blocks the paths of hopes we seek.
Glory lives in heartfelt shouts!
Death is but a whisper.

    from *Tranquility in Darkness*

Secret Hearts

Fear not, my love; the years will wait.
We have yet but to start.
No cloud, nor wind, nor rain of time;
Steals the secrets of our hearts.

    from *Tranquility in Darkness*

New World

And so at last, it came to past
The enemy was subdued
And from the dawn, all danger gone
The world was born anew

    from *Tranquility in Darkness*

Acknowledgments
Dinosaur Blitz short story originally published by Shaw's iPulp Fiction Library, 2009. Artwork by Doug Stambaugh.

That Which We Are originally published by Shaw's iPulp Fiction Library, 2009

Cowboys & Indians secondarily published by Shaw's iPulp Fiction Library, 2010

Photos & Artwork
Mrs. Streeter's 5th Grade Class, Riverside Drive Elementary, 1965
Crosses from Diminished Capacity 2, Second Chances
Halley's Comet Passing in 1910, artist unidentified
After the Alamo painting by Doug Stambaugh
Old House stock photo
Tranquility Logo by Kwei-lin Lum
Burning Flag's Lighter sketch by Grayson Bowling
Veeleen Spacecraft sketch by Grayson Bowling
Diagram of the Tranquility Lunar Colony by the author
Battle of Cannae, artist unidentified
Sketch of Kris and Grey by the author
The Fall of the Alamo by Robert Jenkins Onderdonk, 1903
Lunar Robots by the author
Custer's Last Stand by Harold von Schmidt, 1950
Sassy's Mom sketch by Grayson Bowling

Novels by Gregory Urbach

Dashiell Hammett and the Hearst Castle Mystery
When a body is discovered on the Hearst estate, America's foremost mystery writer is given 48 hours to solve the crime

Dashiell Hammett and the World's Fair Mystery
When Albert Einstein's letter containing vital secrets is stolen, America's foremost mystery writer must save it from Nazi spies

Custer at the Alamo
Sent 40 years in the past by Chief Sitting Bull, General Custer and the 7th Cavalry join Davy Crockett to defend the Alamo

Custer and Crockett: After the Alamo
Stranded in time, General Custer and Davy Crockett set out to win independence for Texas

Magistrate of the Dark Land
A cowardly lawyer seeks two kidnapped girls in a war-torn medieval land

Slave of Akrona
A mysterious castaway finds new love while challenging his overseers on a conquered alien planet

Rebels of Akrona
A soldier from another world struggles to defeat an oppressive alien empire

Rachel From the Edge
A shy yet brilliant woman is hounded by a merciless
press following the death of her billionaire boyfriend

Rachel Running on Empty
Forced to make a life-changing decision, a gifted scientist
is caught up in a web of lies, corruption and murder

Rachel the Warrior
When cyber-terrorists take control of a nuclear-armed
space station, a shy mathematics prodigy is sent to take it back

Twilight on the Road Home
Rescued from vicious kidnappers, a young woman
struggles to survive criminals and lawyers

Diminished Capacity
Accused of shooting the president, a troubled war veteran
seeks redemption for his crime. But is he guilty?

Diminished Capacity 2: Second Chances
An accused assassin and the slain president's daughter
seek a new life in the glare of a relentless media

Dinosaur Blitz
Science fiction, mystery, and romance, with dinosaurs,
lunar colonies, alien visitors, the Alamo, a Maltese Falcon,
the end of the world, and movie stars

Dinosaur Blitz

<u>Waters of the Moon</u>
Born on the moon and raised by computers, a young man struggles to survive in a world ruled by machines.

This futuristic science fiction series, taking elements of *Tarzan of the Apes* and *Clan of the Cave Bear*, follows the journey of a stranded lunar orphan from his childhood on the moon to his final battle against a powerful enemy.

Tranquility's Child
Tranquility's End
Tranquility's Heirs
Tranquility Besieged
Tranquility in Darkness
Tranquility Down
Tranquility Divided
Tranquility Under the Eagles
Tranquility's Last Stand

About the Author

An avid student of history, Gregory Urbach has been writing adventure stories for 30 years. From his days working for a campus newspaper, he has also pursued an interest in politics and popular culture. His degree in Urban Studies proved useful when writing the Tranquility science fiction series. The author's books reflect worlds where the concepts of good and evil are challenged by complicated realities.

Printed in Great Britain
by Amazon